YOU CAN FOLLOW ME

JO BRENNER

HIGH RISE PUBLISHING

Editing provided by Jennifer Prokop of Jen Reads Romance LLC. Proofreading provided by Suella Reads.

Cover design provided by Ever After Cover Design.

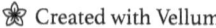 Created with Vellum

For all the horny little lovesick messes like me.

AUTHOR'S NOTE ONE

THIS BOOK ENDS ON A CLIFFHANGER.
THIS BOOK ENDS ON A CLIFFHANGER.
THIS BOOK ENDS ON A CLIFFHANGER.
Good. You have been warned. Please proceed.

AUTHOR'S NOTE TWO

When I started writing *You Can Follow Me*, I was in a pretty bad space, mentally. We were about six months into the pandemic and I was so lonely I ached with it. So I read, and read, and read—mainly dark romance. And while it may seem counterintuitive, the dark scenarios in those books are what helped me find my way back to the light.

Kara, Conor, Micah, and Luke came to me in a fever dream. They've lived with me for a long time, and, in a number of ways, have kept me going over the past couple of years. My hope is that their romance—as twisted, complicated, and difficult as it may be at times—gives you the same kind of delicious joy as it gives me.

That said, all I want to do is to entertain, and the last thing I want to do is cause anyone pain. Like most dark romance, there are elements to this story that some readers may find uncomfortable, triggering, or just not for them. I'd rather you skip the book and read something that does bring you excitement and joy, because that's what reading's supposed to do. You can visit my website for content notes.

Otherwise, I hope you enjoy. And maybe, just maybe, if you're also struggling right now, following Kara, Conor, Micah and Luke's journey to love and happily ever after will help you feel a little less alone.

1

The second Kara opened the door to the bar, testosterone hit her like an alpha male freight train.

I want to be on an alpha male freight train. She tried not to let the thought show on her face.

She was there for one reason, and one reason only. Kara had purposefully booked a hotel on Coronado Island because she knew the Naval base was here, she had googled Navy SEAL bars, and she had dropped off her luggage and headed out immediately to fulfill her fantasy.

She was thirty. She was still single. She was horny as fuck. And she was going to fuck a SEAL tonight.

She hadn't expected to be so intimidated by the pheromones in the bar. Hell, she hadn't expected there to be obvious pheromones, period. Breathing it in, Kara squared her shoulders, lifted her chin, and ignored the pragmatic, slightly worried voice in her head that said, *get the hell out of here, Kara, before you end up sucking off more than you can swallow.* She ignored the male laughter coming from somewhere behind her, and hopped on a stool at the bar.

A woman with short blue hair and tattoos covering her arms turned and saw her. The bartender looked Kara over, clearly made a judgement, and called down the bar to a shaggy-haired, lanky dude who was stacking glasses, "We've got another one."

"Another what?" Kara asked, wiggling her hips so she could drag her tight black dress back over her thighs.

The woman laughed. "This is a SEAL bar, but then you knew that already, didn't you?" She didn't wait for Kara to respond. "Warning—things here can get intense. So if you're looking for a hero and a romance, try Wally's—it's got your usual Navy guys there."

"Fuck that. Can I get a Corona with three slices of lime?"

The woman grinned. "I like you. What's your name?"

"Kara."

"Sally. You here for a while, or just passing through?"

"Just until Monday."

"Two days. Woman like you, you should be able to accomplish what you came here to do in that time."

Kara hoped so. She felt eyes on her, but when she turned to look, no one was looking back.

Sally passed Kara her Corona, watching with one eyebrow raised as Kara floated one lime slice after another.

"So. Why SEALs?" Sally asked.

Kara took a swig of her Corona. The lime overpowered the bland beer, just the way she liked. She shrugged.

"Why not?"

"Hmm." But before the bartender could push, another patron waved her over, leaving Kara to her thoughts.

She wasn't a hundred percent sure when the "fuck a Navy SEAL" idea first came to her. Ever since she'd started having sex, she'd made her way through various male subcultures, archetypes, and job titles. There was the teenage dirty hipster musician phase, the college rumpled academic phase (god, those philosophy grad students were tedious), the post-college rodeo cowboy rebellion phase (somehow, even the young ones had bald spots they hid with their Stetsons, and boy, was that a letdown), the fireman phase (apparently being a hero made you lazy as fuck in bed), and a very short-lived i-banker phase (until she decided that, as nice as it was for someone else to pay for dinner and drinks, listening to them bitch about the stock market wasn't and wouldn't ever be worth it). And, of course, the academia redux—and look how well *that* had gone.

So why military guys? And SEALs, specifically? No one among her family and friends had joined the military. Had she imprinted on the romance novels she read—the ones she'd hid from the highbrow authors and literary hopefuls that made up her undergrad and grad school life? Had she always unconsciously yearned for the impossible hero who'd keep her safe? Or was there something else that made her body go tight and hot when she saw a man in uniform?

She wasn't looking for someone to sweep her off her feet and carry her into the sunset. She had twice-married, twice-divorced parents and a mother who warned her that "love is a media-created fantasy for the uneducated, sweetie," when she'd first discovered her daughter reading Harlequins and then promptly replaced them with *American Psycho*, *Fight Club*, the King James Bible, and other books about horrible men. She had a group of friends with relationship horror stories and the inexplicable emotionally masochistic natures that meant they kept trying. Maybe pre-New York Kara wanted romance, but post-New York Kara wanted casual, expectation-free fucking.

Whatever she was looking for, she hadn't found.

Yet.

When she'd loaded up her hatchback and fled New York for wider, more open spaces, stopping in various small towns and medium-sized cities for a few days to a few weeks, she hadn't formally decided to add various military dudes to her proverbial little black book. It just turned out that, when she sat in local bars and swiped through matches, she inevitably swiped right on the guys standing in a uniform. (Not the white savior ones standing in a desert surrounded by brown children; she had *some* limits.) And sometimes they'd swipe right back, and sometimes they'd come meet her at whatever bar, and they'd play pool (she'd lose) or darts (she'd win) and a few beers and some flirting led to more drinks and some sort of action or other.

It was fun.

It was empty.

It was "expanding her horizons."

Sex was sex was sex, apparently.

It was enough.

She wanted more.

Maybe a SEAL was that more, the epitome of testosterone and alpha male inclinations she wanted in bed, even if she didn't quite want to admit it to herself. And not just that. As objectifying and squicky as it was to choose partners based on the toughness of their careers, a SEAL would be the ultimate challenge, wouldn't it? Proof that she could do, get, and handle anyone? And that she finally didn't give a fuck what anyone else thought of her? If everyone back in New York thought she was a soulless slut, why not enjoy it?

Whatever.

She could overanalyze her motivations and choices all night. It wasn't going to get her what she wanted, which was to fuck the epitome of military prowess.

Feeling weighed down by the testosterone, Kara swallowed and turned.

She counted three guys—a brunette, a blonde, and a redhead, like the male version of the witches of Eastwick—gathered around a table covered in beer cans. Mostly Bud, some Coors and Miller scattered throughout. They were flirting with two beautiful, model-thin women. Part of Kara automatically wanted to leave; with her frizzy-curly red hair and not-at-all-svelte body, there was no way she could compete.

No. She'd worked hard to get over her insecurities when it came to putting herself out there. New York Kara, who never spoke up in grad seminars and didn't defend herself against the rumors and accusations, was dead and buried. She'd promised herself she'd do what she wanted from now on. She'd always *try*. She'd put it all out there—why else was she wearing this unnecessarily fancy little black dress when she'd rather be in frayed shorts and a tee? And if she struck out tonight, she struck out.

She wasn't going to let herself strike out.

She turned back to Sally and the other bartender—the guy was named Jake—and chatted for a while, pretending to ignore the action happening behind her.

And then the jukebox powered on, and Zac Brown Band's "Chicken Fried" filled the bar.

It wasn't that she didn't like the song, but it didn't fit her mood, and if she didn't change things up, it was going to be a night of pop country hits and god knew what else.

Hopping back off the bar stool, she strode to the old jukebox—an obvious relic from the nineties—trying to seem normal and not like she was about to faint.

They were all hot, body-wise. Not inhumanly beautiful

like magazine cover models, but that made things easier. Made them more real. Made this more real.

Maybe that wasn't easier.

Before she could chicken out, she pulled a credit card out of her purse and started perusing the options.

Sure enough, the next song cued up was "Sweet Caroline." She shook her head and flipped through albums.

Someone stood behind her, not touching, but close. She didn't look, but she could smell him, and god he smelled good. Spicy and warm.

Fucking pheromones. Amazing.

"You know, you don't automatically get music privileges," he said, voice deep and smooth. It wove around her like silk, made her want to stretch and let her hair out of her high ponytail.

Instead, she said, "You know, you aren't supposed to play 'Sweet Caroline' until the bar's closing."

"Is that right? Where'd you learn that, college? Grad school?"

Well, that landed on target. But he seemed amused, not contemptuous.

She raised her shoulders and dropped them, aware that her shrug exposed even more thigh. *Good.*

"Yup."

"Where?"

"Berkeley, then Columbia."

"Smart girl." He sounded impressed, not surprised. "So, what song are you choosing that's going to disrupt our bar?"

"Still deciding."

"Tell you what. You can choose two songs, as long as I get two vetos."

"Hmmm," she pretended to consider. "How about three songs and one veto?"

He laughed, and the sound sent vibrations down her back. She was tempted to turn around and see him, but the anticipation was more fun.

"You drive a hard bargain. Okay, smart girl, let's see what you've got."

He brushed her back with his chest before moving to her side. She could see broad shoulders and ripped muscles out the corner of her eye.

Taking a deep breath, she turned to look.

Fuck. There went her "not cover model gorgeous" theory.

Dark brown hair, short and tight to his scalp. Deep brown eyes framed by an unfair number of eyelashes. His face was more rugged than sculpted, except his lips, which had obviously been designed by some long-dead Italian artist.

That perfect mouth smiled. She could feel him looking her over, and if she wasn't imagining things, his eyes darkened further.

He was in her space, but not crowding it. Heat and energy and so much sex appeal pulsed off him, she had to resist grabbing his ass and hauling him to her.

Taking a deep breath, she pointed to the first song. "'Add It Up' by the Violent Femmes?"

"Good choice." He pressed in the letter number combo. "What's next?"

She flipped more, then landed on something and laughed. He'd hate it.

"'Harder to Breathe' by Maroon Five."

"Veto."

"You sure you want to use your veto this early?"

He glanced back at the duo behind him. "Unless you want to piss these guys off, I'd skip it."

She inhaled sharply, speaking before she could stop

herself. "Maybe I want to see what you all will do when you're pushed."

"Don't like to be pushed, daring girl. We like to do the pushing."

Kara felt her cheeks go warm at the implication.

"Do you like to be pushed?" he asked, seeming serious.

Her thighs clenched. She flipped her ponytail. "Maybe."

"Hmm." The sound was almost a growl as he studied her face.

Her cheeks had gone from warm to blistering hot. Before she stumbled across a sexual landmine, she changed the subject.

"How about Marcy Playground?"

He watched her for a moment, as if he were considering digging deeper into his question, but must have decided to let it go, because he asked, "Which song?"

She'd show him daring. Kara winked. "Which song do you think?"

He raised his eyebrows, like he thought she was just playing games, but when she didn't relent, his gaze turned admiring.

Although he didn't speak, she knew that when he added the song to her queue, the brush of his hand against hers was intentional. And *holy shit.* Kara had never really considered hands brushing to be particularly exciting or noteworthy or illicit, but just the faint hint of calluses on his fingers from the light touch singed her, like she'd stuck her own into an electric socket. Heat spread everywhere. Her whole face was on fire. She felt disoriented, almost dizzy. If she was prone to flights of fancy, she'd think that the floor had rotated beneath her feet.

Fortunately, she wasn't. But damn, this guy was potent.

"What's next?"

"Huh?"

He chuckled. The sound was like velvet against her skin.

"What song's next, distracted girl?"

Oh, she hadn't planned that far ahead.

"Maybe I want it to be a surprise."

He leaned down, his lips brushing her ear. "Tell me."

Shivers wracked her. He was a one-man weather machine, wasn't he?

"Why don't you make me?" she countered.

His eyes darkened, but all he did was "hmm" again. Another sexual landmine, and even though Kara had placed it between them, she wasn't sure she wanted to set it off. She glanced away and flipped through the options to give herself time. His eyes were on her. Like kismet, she saw the perfect album. She'd never known a bar to carry Metric in the juke-box, but by some miracle, this one did.

Instead of telling him, she keyed in the combination.

He looked at the code, then the song, then back at Kara.

She tilted her head, shrugging. "You already used your veto."

He shrugged, his shirt riding up, exposing a line of tan, tight skin. He was intentionally mimicking her, wasn't he?

"Risky, but I guess we'll see how it goes."

She laughed, but he didn't, just continued to watch her. And once again, even though Kara wasn't prone to flights of fancy, she could feel herself drowning in his dark eyes.

"Conor," one of his friends called. "Leave the woman alone and get your ass back over here. We want to hear the story about Vegas again."

Disappointment flooded her, but she didn't show it to him.

Oh well.

"Nice to meet you, Conor."

She turned to go.

"Wait."

He grabbed her wrist and tugged her back to him. It was a forward-as-hell move from a stranger and should've pissed her off. Instead, her thighs clenched—again. It was something about the presumption, the pushiness of the move, the dominance, the implied ownership. So subtle but it felt *good.* The thigh clench shouldn't have been obvious, but something must've given her away, because he blinked and his lips curved. The moment stretched between them, his big hand still holding her wrist, gentle but unyielding.

Reluctantly, she pulled free. He released her immediately.

"You know my name. I don't get yours?" he asked.

She could use a stupid line like, *come find me and find out*, but she was done with silly games.

"Kara."

"Kara." His lips formed the word, drawing out the two syllables. She swallowed. His eyes grew darker. "What brings you to Coronado? You aren't from here."

She shrugged, looking away. Sex was one thing, baring her secrets was off the table.

After a moment, he nodded, seeming disappointed. "I hope you chose well, Kara."

"Or what?"

He grinned but said nothing and left her where she stood.

Ugh. She walked back to the bar and pretended she couldn't feel him still watching her, thrilled and scared and disappointed and *wanting* so immediately and so much it shocked her.

"Well?" Sally raised an eyebrow.

Kara shrugged. "Struck out."

"Huh." Sally passed her another Corona and a glass full of lime wedges. "I wouldn't be too sure of that."

The first two songs played, and she no longer felt his eyes on her back. She glanced over, and he was immersed in conversation with his two friends. The blond was built like a heavy-weight wrestler, the redhead was tall and tan, towering over the other two, even seated. Before Conor could catch her, she glanced away.

What-the-fuck-ever.

She was about to give up and go back to her hotel— maybe tomorrow night would be better, maybe she'd aimed too high—when the third song clicked on.

"Gold Guns Girls" by Metric was dirty and sexy and angry and loud. And it seemed like no one but Sally had heard it before.

"Well, that's definitely a choice," commented Sally. "Looks like someone's noticed."

Kara turned her head. Conor was staring across the bar at her, not smiling, not anything, face unreadable. That fanciful nonsense feeling, the one where the floor spun underneath her barstool, hit her again. She was suddenly terrified, and she wasn't sure why. She didn't know why it seemed like something monumental was about to happen.

Smart girl.

Daring girl.

Distracted girl.

Kara snorted. More like overly-imaginative girl. Because it felt like she could either walk out now and go on with her life, totally normal and fine, or she could stay—but if she did, she was taking a fork in the road and would never be able to double back. She'd only felt this way once before— when Christopher Johnathan kissed her in his office, surrounded by piles of his own books, right before she'd decided to kiss him back. *That* was a fork in the road she wished she'd never taken. Based off that, she should leave. A smart girl would leave.

But as she began to reach into her wallet to pay for her drinks, Conor rose from his chair, licking his lips.

She wasn't going anywhere.

He made his way over to her. He lacked that cowboy swagger she'd gotten used to and then grown to hate a few months ago, but made up for it with purposeful steps and a gaze that narrowed on her like a missile.

"Good luck," Sally said to her as he reached them.

To Conor: "What can I get you?"

"Not drinking," Conor said, but his eyes were on Kara. He eyed her Corona.

"Imported? Fancy."

Kara rolled her eyes. "Oh, you have no idea how fancy I can get."

"I think I have a pretty good idea."

Sure he did.

"Shoot."

He stroked his chin, fake pondering.

"Let's see—from that dress, I'm guessing first dates mean a wine bar and a shared charcuterie plate. You're a tourist and are shockingly fascinated by everything, so I'd bet vacations are usually to ski towns or trekking through Asia. From the way you talk, you're either a writer, an artist, or a teacher. You're from LA or New York, and even though you tell yourself you hate 'the city,' you'll never leave. From the way you avoid questions, my hunch is you're running from something. From the way you flirted with me, I hope you're single. And based on your music choices, I'd say it's not because you can't find someone, but because you did, and he burned you—bad."

"You found me on Facebook, didn't you?" Kara asked, only half kidding. He'd read her mind, her interests, her desires, even part of her backstory—and she didn't like it.

She *didn't*.

"Anyway, you were close, but wrong," she said. "I used to live in LA *and* New York; right now I live nowhere."

At that, something flashed in Conor's eyes, only to disappear.

"So, passing through?"

Kara nodded. "Just passing through."

"For how long?"

She shrugged, her timeline suddenly becoming flexible.

That same look —a squinting of the eyes, a tightening of the jaw—slid over his face, there, then gone.

"Let's go get fro-yo," he said, abruptly changing the subject.

Kara laughed. "Do people still eat fro-yo?"

He copied her shrug, and she stared transfixed at his shoulders for a second. They were just so...shouldery.

"No idea. I've never had it, but I figure you can introduce me," he said.

Sally leaned over. "Conor, it's 11 p.m. Nowhere on Coronado is open, much less serving frozen yogurt."

But Conor wrapped his huge hands around Kara's waist, and, before she could say anything, lifted her off the bar stool and set her on her feet.

"Hey," she started, but he released her and held out his hand.

"Come on, sweet girl. Let's go get dessert and you can tell me all about Berkeley and Columbia and being a wanderer, and I can tell you about how I grew up on an organic dairy farm in upstate New York and have to deal with an older sister who thinks the reason *I'm* still single is because I'm a Scorpio."

She took his hand.

They never got fro-yo, of course. Instead, they walked back to her hotel in the dark, barely talking. He didn't release her hand, but he didn't look at her, either.

When she got to her hotel room, she began to unlock the door. He stopped her.

"Kara," he said, his voice sounding strained. "We don't have to do this. *You* don't have to do this. We can grab an Uber out of Coronado and go get something to eat. Get to know each other. Take this slow."

Rage, white hot and surprising, shot through her. How *dare* he.

She glared. "Have to? I don't do anything I don't want to do."

He nodded, relief and anticipation written across his face.

"I'm holding you to that."

Before she could get angrier, he swiped the key card from her and grabbed both of her wrists with one hand, pushing them above her head and crowding her against the door. He paused for a moment—*was he checking her reaction to the manhandling? Why was she getting off on this?*—but she just pushed her hips against his, already feeling frantic. His mouth descended on hers, hot and hard. They both groaned from the contact, and then he was coaxing—no, coercing— her lips open with his, and for a few dizzy, breathless moments, the floor began to spin again and she forgot her own name.

He pulled away and spoke against her mouth. "If I do anything you don't want, say veto."

And with that, still holding her wrists with one hand, he unlocked the door and pulled her into the room.

He didn't even flip on the light. Clothes were removed, by him, by her, she had no idea. Then they were on the bed and his hands were everywhere, and so were hers. He didn't so much kiss her as eat at her mouth; she got her lips and teeth on his neck. There was some wrestling—a lot of wrestling— that ended up with her facedown on the bed, him holding her wrists behind her back. His teeth nipped her ear.

"Kara, struggle like the good girl I know you are," he said, and a secret part of her—that apparently liked this kind of shit—woke up and gasped. And so she struggled, writhing underneath him, trying to buck him off. He laughed, deep and low, like a caress, and then he did caress her, working his free hand under her hips and rolling his fingers around her clit, making her buck again.

"Fuck, so wet," he muttered, and then he lifted himself off her.

"Conor?" she asked, worried. Had she done something wrong?

His voice was strained when he asked, "Is that for me, Kara? Or is that for living out your SEAL fantasy?"

She twisted her neck to look at him. She couldn't see much of his face, but this was obviously important. And maybe *that* was why she wanted to hide behind the SEAL fantasy excuse. The last time she thought the reason she picked a man mattered, the last time she had thought she mattered, look how it turned out. And yet here she was, with a man who she had spent only a few hours with, if that, and he seemed to know her better than Chris had. Conor not only knew what she wanted more than any man had ever bothered to learn, he seemed like he cared.

And fuck, if that wasn't terrifying, she didn't know what was.

So yeah, she wanted to lie. To say it had nothing to do with him, to maintain distance, to get back some of the control he'd taken. It was scary, feeling seen, but also *exhilarating.* And fanciful Kara was back, because the minute he'd brushed her fingers with his in the bar, it had felt like...

...fate.

She didn't want to lie. As absurd as it sounded, she thought she might hurt him. And she hated the idea of hurting him.

"You," she admitted, which earned her a gentle kiss on her bare shoulder, a bite where he'd kissed her, and circles from his fingers where she needed them most.

"Thank you, sweet girl," he said, playing with her clit until she shook from it.

Right when she was about to start begging, he pulled her back against his chest, tore open a condom wrapper and rolled a condom onto his cock, lifted her hips, and pushed inside her.

Kara *exploded.*

"Jesus, did you just come all over my cock?" he asked, almost in disbelief, and she felt embarrassed, except then he pulled out, flipped her over, and said, "Do it again."

She lost track after that, both of time and of how many orgasms he gave her. He ate her and she sucked him off, he slapped her ass and she scratched his back, and they fucked for so long and so hard she almost passed out.

Hours later (days? weeks? months?) they collapsed, gasping. She tried to roll to the side but he dragged her back, pulling her on top of him, wrapping his arms around her. Kara usually hated feeling trapped, but this was a trap she didn't want to escape.

"Kara," he said.

"Hmm?" She hadn't expected to cuddle, but she might as well enjoy it for as long as it lasted.

He sighed.

"You smell like my parents' farm."

She laughed so hard she snorted.

"Did you just snort?"

No, she refused to be embarrassed about that. She pushed on his chest until he loosened his arms. Kara straddled his waist, noting that, even soft, his cock was still huge.

Show-er and grower, she thought, snorting again.

"That's adorable," he teased.

"Did you just compare me to horse manure?"

"No." He squeezed her hip. "Your hair, it smells like bee balm."

"I have never met a single man who knows that."

He released her back, wrapping a finger in one of her curls and tugging. "It grows everywhere on the farm. My mom loves it."

Kara relaxed. "As long as you're comparing me to a flower, I guess that's okay."

"It's a weed, actually."

She smacked his chest. "Dick."

He smacked her ass in retaliation, before pulling her back down to lie on his sweaty chest. "I thought I hated the smell for so long. Turns out I was wrong."

"You mean you don't hate it as much? Glad to help," she teased.

"No," he said, voice quiet. "I think I could grow addicted to it."

Her heart stopped.

"Conor..."

He interrupted her, which was good, because she didn't even know what she was going to say.

"Why, sweet girl? You could've had your choice of any man in that bar. Why choose me?" His voice, still quiet, had a tinge of uncertainty. "Or was it because I was lucky enough to get to you first?"

It was the same question he'd asked earlier, except now she was coming off the orgasm high instead of climbing toward it.

"Because," she said, equally quiet. "You called me smart girl."

And I haven't felt smart in a very, very long time, she was careful not to say.

He squeezed her again, kissing her hair, like he'd heard her anyway. "Did someone make you feel not smart? Because I'll kill the asshole."

There was an idea.

She shook her head, both at him and at that thought. Chris needed to stay in New York. He didn't get to intrude on this... whatever this was.

"Thank you," was all she said, but the thank you was for so much.

They fell silent, Kara listening to Conor's slowing heartbeat as he stroked her back.

"What were you going to say before?"

"I don't remember."

"Okay, shy girl," he said, cricking his neck to kiss her hair again before settling back on the pillow. "Maybe you'll remember in the morning."

He fell quiet again, but the quiet felt like a shared, magical thing between them, a cord pulling them closer together.

There she was, being fanciful again.

As Conor's breathing slowed, his arms relaxing around her, she berated herself. Sex was one thing. Pillow-talk and imagining a connection where there wasn't one would only get her in trouble.

She rolled off him. Cuddling like this was the issue. It made her yearn for things she didn't *really* want, even though oxytocin said otherwise. The one time she'd thought she did, everything had blown up in her face. That's why she was here, wasn't it? And besides, it would be stupid to get attached. She was leaving in two days. All he'd done was compliment her on the scent of her shampoo. Not really the stuff of great love stories.

She curled up on her side away from him, trying to ignore the way the cold seeped into the negative space where his body had been.

But at some point in the night, whether it was him or her or both, she ended up spooned against his chest, his arms wrapped tight around her waist. And in the morning, as he worked a hand between her thighs, and worked her into a half-awake state of lust before working his hard, thick cock inside her, setting up a slow rhythm, as he kissed her neck and whispered, "Good morning, beautiful girl," she forgot why it was so bad to be fanciful.

Afterward, she lay in bed in a satisfied heap while he dressed.

"Shit, I can't find my phone," he said. "Can you call it?"

He gave her the number and she called, only for it to ring in his jeans pocket.

She rolled her eyes. "Smooth."

"Hey, I had to get your number somehow." He finished pulling his clothes on, before coming to the bed and kissing her.

"Come out with me tonight," he said.

"For what? To talk? More sex?" she asked.

"Why not both?"

Why not? Why not spend some more time with him? She was leaving, wasn't she? So there was no real risk. Her body tightened at the idea of more Conor-administered orgasms. Her chest tightened at all the other ways he could praise her through the modified nicknames. Even with the professor, she'd never felt like this.

"Come on, brave girl. I know the best burger place in California."

And there it was.

"Well, I can't turn down a trip to In-N-Out," she teased.

He came back to the bed, kissing her, a closed-mouth kiss sparking spirals of promise and dread.

"I can do better than In-N-Out, fancy girl."

"Prove it."

oly motherfucking shit.

Conor stretched on the beach after his run. At 10 a.m., the sun was already high in the clear blue sky, waves lapping at the sand. Even though his body was fully functional, his mind was like a malfunctioning computer, just a blank screen with an error message: *She fucked you good and hard, man. Even if you were the one doing the fucking.*

When Conor had first spotted the cute, curvy redhead at Joe's Bar, looking like a fish out of water in her tiny, tight-ass black dress, heels, and look of determination, he'd been hit by the urge to fuck her. Not out of the ordinary; Conor was hit by the urge to fuck a lot of people. But as soon as he got a look at her face, heard that low, husky voice, and experienced Kara's enticing mix of insecurity and sass, the sensation in his gut increased from urge to urgency.

But he hadn't expected *that.* The way she teased him, inviting him to match her sass with his domination. The way she got off at his commands, while giving as good as she got, but simultaneously submitting...the way she fucking dared him to push her harder, fuck her harder, with only a tease and a smile. *Damn.*

And it was more than sex. She hadn't meant to, but she'd shown him little hints of some deep, underlying pain riding quietly alongside the bravado. Conor didn't get off on insecure, needy women. But Kara hadn't been needy, just a little bit vulnerable and a whole lot interesting.

Smart as fuck? Check.

Adventurous? Check.

Sweet as hell despite the tough shell she tried to present? Check, check, check.

Conor hadn't known this about himself, but that last part was apparently checkmate for him. He took a deep breath, releasing it, digging his toes in the sand to stay grounded. It wasn't working. Because Kara wanted *him.* Yeah, he wasn't a complete idiot. She'd come to the bar wanting to get laid by a SEAL. But his internal bullshit reader knew she hadn't been lying when she had said it was him she wanted, not the fantasy. His body had known, by the way she'd settled into him in sleep. His cock had known, by the way she'd pulsed around him, so hot and wet and tight.

Jesus fuck. He ran a hand over his mouth. Just the thought of her pussy made his cock hard and his mouth dry.

In the distance, some of his SEAL team members surfed. Others lay on the beach with their families. Conor couldn't bring himself to join them. He had too much energy to burn. He rubbed his chest, which ached sweetly when he thought of Kara, curled up on him, a soft purring heap of sexy curves and quiet attitude. Fuck, were these feelings?

He grinned wryly. Yeah, these were feelings. Conor was man enough to admit this was a first.

Before he could tell himself to play it cool, he texted her.

Did you get any more sleep?

The dots of her response showed up. He waited impatiently.

I masturbated instead.

Jesus. He adjusted himself.

Do you even know who this is?

The dots appeared and disappeared a few times.

I hope it's the man who fucked the brains out of my head last night. Otherwise—sorry, random stranger.

Conor laughed.

I don't think we're strangers anymore. We still on for that burger tonight?

The dots seemed unsure this time. Conor held his breath as he waited, feeling like a fool.

Only if you take me somewhere I can get Animal Fries. Which In-N-Out?

He released his breath.

I'll come get you. 7 pm, gorgeous girl.

She sent back a string of emojis of animals interspersed with french fries.

Conor was about to put away his phone when another text came in from one of his teammates, asking how the hot redhead was. Usually he'd respond with something like *I'd ask but her mouth is full*, but something stopped him. Partly out of this need to respect Kara and this thing, whatever it was, but mostly? He wanted to keep her to himself.

Popping his phone back in his pocket, he dropped to the sand for push-ups. He needed to burn that energy, especially when he remembered she was only *passing through*. Could he get her to stay for a little longer? Did he even want her to?

The ache in his chest reminded him that yeah, he definitely wanted her to.

Fuck.

Kara was already waiting outside her hotel when he pulled up. She had her eyes closed, headphones in, moving her head to some song that either mattered more to her than keeping an eye out for his arrival, or she was psyching herself up to see him again. Conor didn't like either option.

He *did* like what she was wearing. Instead of a tight little dress, she was in teeny tiny, frayed jean shorts and a low-cut white tank. Lacy white bra straps peeked out beneath the tank top, setting off her tan.

He parked his truck and hopped out. Her eyes opened when he was a few feet away, and she rewarded him with a surprisingly shy smile.

"I'm early," he told her.

"I like that in a man."

He walked around the truck and opened the passenger door for her. She rolled her eyes.

"I don't think I've ever met someone so chivalrous," she said.

He shrugged. "I don't do it for every woman."

"Bullshit."

He considered, reaching for her waist and boosting her up into the car. "Okay, I do do it for every woman, but I never drive women around in my truck unless they're related to me."

Kara didn't say anything, just craned her neck back to search his eyes. Was she running her own bullshit scanner?

Conor squared his shoulders, annoyed she would doubt him, but when she leaned forward to pull his face to hers

and brush her mouth against his, the annoyance disappeared. He couldn't help himself; he deepened the kiss,
coaxing her mouth open. Their tongues played. His blood
heated.

Finally, Kara pulled back, murmuring, "We could take
this back to my hotel room."

Conor leaned back in and bit her lower lip. When he
released her, he said, "Nope. Promised you Animal Fries,
and I always keep my promises."

One side of her mouth tilted up in a smile. "I like to hear
that."

Damn it. That ache was back in his chest. It didn't help
that he could smell bee balm again. He buckled her in,
something about the small act filling him with unfamiliar
contentment. And based on the way her smile grew, she
liked it, too. Closing her door, Conor strode around to the
driver's side, not sure if he'd ever been this excited for fast
food.

After picking up burgers and her required Animal Fries,
Conor drove them to the beach. They sat on his truck bed
side by side, eating and staring out as the sun set over the
ocean.

They ate in silence. Kara had been quiet in the car,
and she was quiet now, but she wasn't lost in thought.
Every so often she glanced over at him and smiled, and
each time it was like a beautiful little stab wound in his
heart.

Conor only felt this comfortable with two of his teammates, and they weren't just his closest friends, they also

were the only people he trusted to have his back, no matter what.

And here was this stunning woman, who screamed out her orgasms so loud he worried the hotel would complain, but shared the quiet with him like it was solely theirs.

She also ate like a slob.

"You're a mess."

Kara stopped mid-bite of her burger, glaring at him.

"Are you judging my burger eating style?"

"Just stating a fact. You've got sauce all over your face."

She stuck her tongue out at him, the only clean part about her. But he remembered how dirty that tongue had gotten last night, when she'd licked and sucked his cock and swallowed him down.

Fuck, how could she be so sexy and so cute at the same time?

"At least I eat a burger the way it's supposed to be eaten. Burgers are messy, thus, messy eating."

He laughed. "Thus?"

"*You* eat a burger militantly, like you're planning a battle against it. I've never seen someone eat a burger as precisely as I'm guessing you make your bed."

He raised an eyebrow. "Are you accusing me of being anal retentive?"

Kara shrugged one bare shoulder, momentarily distracting Conor with an array of freckles. He hadn't gotten a chance to map them with his tongue, but he'd rectify that tonight.

Maybe he'd get a chance to rectify it multiple times, over multiple nights. He couldn't identify exactly why she made him feel this way—insatiable to touch her, to fuck her, to even hold her—but he could guess. That mix of vulnerability and mystery he'd spotted before, the juxtaposition of

wanderlust and longing to belong somewhere in her eyes...
she wasn't clingy, and Conor was confronted for the first
time in his life with the desire to cling. Conor, who was in
control of everything in his life, including his emotions, felt
his control slipping. And maybe that was okay, as long as
she slipped with him.

What the fuck was up with him?

She interrupted his train of thought—a good thing,
because he was starting to spiral.

"You know, maybe you should get a little messy, too. It's
only fair." There was a threat of mischief in her eyes.

"Whatever you're planning, don't do it," he warned, but
his breath sped up.

"It's my duty," she deadpanned, crawling over to him.

"Kara—" he warned again.

She planted a wet, sloppy kiss on his mouth, getting
burger sauce and mayo all over his lips and chin.

Conor should've been repulsed, but he had been craving
her mouth since he'd put her in his car, so he deepened the
kiss, absorbing the taste of hot sauce and mayo and her, so
sweet it canceled out the rest.

Kara pulled back, grinning wickedly at him. "Delicious,
right?"

"Right," Conor said, feeling his control slip more.

And when she nibbled her way down his chin, it slipped
even further from his grasp. And when she sucked on his
neck, he lost his grip on it entirely. Possessed with the need
to overwhelm her in the way her mouth on his neck overwhelmed him, he grabbed her, pushing her down and
rolling over her, not even caring that his knees were digging
into the edge of the open truck bed.

"You pushed me on top of my Animal Fries," she
complained, and sure enough he saw cheese oozing out

from under her shorts. He rose into a plank on one hand above her so she had room to maneuver her hands.

"Even more of a mess," he chided. "Better take them off."

"We're in public," she argued, brown-gold eyes huge.

"Be a good girl and take your shorts off, Kara," he repeated, still balancing on one hand so he could pull down his own shorts with the other and fist his cock.

Those big eyes clouded with desire as she did what she was told. She'd barely wriggled her shorts and panties down to her knees before he was rubbing his cock over her slit, confirming she was wet enough to take him. He thrust inside her, marveling again at the tight fit of her pussy. It had been tight the night before, too, but now, with her legs trapped together by her shorts, the clasp of her made it even more difficult for him to work his way inside. He had fucked plenty of people over the years, and maybe it was bullshit to think this way, but no one's pussy had ever fit him so perfectly.

So caught up in the feel of her surrounding him, Conor didn't realize he'd said it out loud. But Kara was shaking her head no while saying, "Yes, like we were made to fit, fuck fuck fuck," and the admission and the way her pussy rippled around him filled him with triumph. He thrust into her, again and again, working in and out of her perfect fucking pussy and working *her*, determined to make her orgasm.

"You good with that, baby girl? You can admit that your pussy stretches around me like she was made to please my cock? This little pussy is meant to come for me, and only for me."

He rolled his hips, feeling her tighten almost impossibly more, her eyes shutting. From the pleasure? Or to block out his claim?

Fuck that.

He changed his angle, knowing he hit her g-spot when a strangled cry broke from her.

"This little pussy is going to come for her owner, isn't she? Going to squeeze the hell out of my cock like it's her fucking duty."

It was his words that took her over, because Kara screamed as she orgasmed, milking his cock. His guts clenched, his balls boiled, and then he was coming in her *hard*, not just giving up his seed, but his very fucking heart and soul.

He collapsed on top of her, distantly realizing he forgot a condom. And—shockingly, disturbingly—not caring.

"Conor?" she asked, her body stiff, probably from the same realization.

"I get tested regularly," he said immediately. "You're safe, sweet girl."

She relaxed under him. "I have an IUD."

Was that disappointment in his chest?

Conor rolled off her, fear thudding in his heart. What was this woman doing to him? His mind warred. He wanted her to stay, he wanted her to get the hell out of here before she changed him irreversibly. He had lost his sense of equilibrium; he had never felt as centered as he did with her beside him.

Wheels rolled over gravel as a car pulled in next to them.

Shit.

He sat up. Kara was already pulling up her panties and shorts, buttoning the latter closed. Conor stuffed his still half-hard cock into his shorts, promising himself he'd be back inside her soon enough. He hopped off the truck and helped her down.

Perfect timing. An older man stepped out.

"Nice night to watch the sunset," he said as he rounded his car and approached them.

Conor wrapped an arm around Kara. "Too bad you missed it."

The old man smiled knowingly. "Used to take my wife here. Proposed to her here. She's been gone for five years now, but I still come here to watch the waves and talk to her. This is a magical spot, kids. But you seem to have figured that out."

With that and a wave, he ambled down to the beach.

Conor turned Kara into his arms.

"Conor," she started, and he knew it was going to be some negation of the man's words and the magic he knew they were both feeling. He wasn't going to let her ruin it.

"Come home with me," he urged.

She sighed. "Let's go back to my hotel room. I already paid, it's my last night here, and I still haven't used that bathtub."

Last night here.

Conor, back in control, put the words out of his mind.

"Then we better use that bathtub."

She laughed into his chest. "I don't know if we'll both fit."

"Oh, we'll fit," he promised.

They did fit. Just barely, with his back against the tub and her back to his chest. But it was the perfect position for him to play with her pussy, sucking on her neck and working her swollen clit gently and her pussy hard, until she was a writhing mess in his arms, crying for him to stop as he made her come again, and again, and again, still not satisfied when the water had gone cold and she was limp and boneless against him.

"Stop, Conor, please. It's too much!"

It would never be too much.

The realization hit him like a rock. By this point, he should be itching to leave.

He'd figure it out later. More important things to worry about, like wringing another gorgeous orgasm out of her, watching her surrender to him and the way he made her feel. It was the only way he felt like they were on even ground.

"Are you vetoing? Because I'm not stopping until I'm good and ready, unless you use your veto."

She fell silent, and he slowly, gently, stroked his fingers over and into her, and when he bit her neck, marking her as his, she orgasmed again. Finally, he relented, satisfied, moving her out of the way so he could get out of the tub before lifting her out and carrying her back to the bedroom, not even caring that their wet bodies were soaking the sheets, too focused on her red, swollen pussy, presented to him like a gift.

"I know it hurts, but you're going to let me fuck you, aren't you, generous girl? Going to let me come inside you again, nothing between us?"

The room was too dark to read her eyes.

"That takes a lot of trust," she told him.

"So trust me," he countered, desperate to feel her bare again. "You did before."

"I was in a lust haze before."

"And you aren't now? Kara." He gripped her shoulders. "I would never hurt you. I told you. I never break promises."

He meant it with everything in him. The idea of hurting

her made him feel sick, and Conor never felt sick anymore —not even when he killed someone. God, this woman. She made him feel. So fucking much.

"That's why I need you to promise, Conor."

Oh, vulnerable girl, he thought, but didn't say. If she knew he could see how scared she was, how fragile, she'd run.

Kara nodded, and Conor rolled onto his back, lifting her on top of him and lowering her slowly, so slowly, onto his cock. She slid down, down, down, her breath coming in short gasps as her pussy swallowed him.

"Ride me, cowgirl," he said.

"God Conor, you're so..." her voice was tight. Was he hurting her? But then she pushed even lower, until she was pressed against him and he'd hit the back of her.

Fuck, fuck, fuck, he chanted in his head.

"What, big?" he teased, trying to hold onto at least a shred of control.

"Yes, but also...." She lowered her hands to his chest, using the new position to grind against him. "So. Corny."

Conor's heart squeezed, tighter than the grip Kara had on his cock.

"What else am I?" he asked.

She rocked her hips again, her breath quickening. "Pushy."

"Yeah," he agreed, thrusting up into her, hitting a spot deep inside her that made her clench even tighter around him as she keened. "But you like that."

When she recovered her breath, she started to lift and lower her hips, his cock sliding out of her before taking him again.

She lifted until he almost slipped out of her, hovering over him.

"Demanding."

Grabbing her hips, he pulled her back down onto him as he thrust up again, keeping the movement slow and smooth.

"You like that, too."

She wiggled on top of him, but he kept her planted where she was.

"Controlling."

He released her hips, placing his hands under his head to keep himself from grabbing her again.

"Do you want to be in control, powerful girl?"

Her eyes glinted and glistened at the new version of his nickname for her.

"How are you this kind?"

His heart, pounding from the feel of her, temporarily stopped.

Carefully, he asked, "Are you not...used to kindness? From men?"

She leaned down to kiss him.

"Not real kindness."

And his heart sped back up. "So you know this is real," he affirmed.

In answer, she kissed him again, settling something inside him. And then she rose and lowered, rose and lowered, faster and faster, pushing them both higher and higher. Conor had to inhale deeply to keep his orgasm in check.

"You think I'm powerful?" she asked.

He thought back to the way she kept daring him, how she was on her own, going somewhere, searching for something, taking risks while still seeming grounded. Lost, but centered.

"I think," he growled, aware of how hard his cock was getting, how sloppy wet she was, "That you're brave, and daring, and reckless. And that you're scared of how much power you could have."

Over me, he didn't say.

She was rocking her hips now, writhing all over his cock, but even though her body was going wild, her eyes were focused on him. He gripped tight to the headboard to keep from grabbing her.

"I wish I had power. I didn't before when..." she trailed off.

"Magnificent girl," he told her. "You have power. If you didn't, I wouldn't feel this challenged."

Something about his words made her melt on top of him, her pussy clenching tight. But she couldn't seem to get there.

"Conor," she whimpered.

"Poor girl," he crooned at her. "Did you get off too many times?"

"Please..." she begged.

Begging him. Needing him. Sure, it was during sex, but Conor's chest swelled knowing he could give her this.

"I've got you, baby girl," he reassured her, pulling his hands from behind his head and sitting up, pulling her to him, sharing sweat as he bounced her into her final orgasm, and when her pussy gripped him perfectly, because they were the perfect fit, Conor finally let go of his control, vision going dark as he came inside her and made a gorgeous mess of them both.

As they both calmed, he kept them connected, tucking her head into his chest, relief cooling him when she didn't pull away.

After a little while, she murmured, "I should go get cleaned up."

"But I like you messy."

She laughed, not coy or teasing but real. "I thought you hated mess."

"I don't mind *this* kind of mess."

"Well, I don't love being full of your come."

"Fuck that's sexy. Say that again."

She laughed again. "Conor, a UTI is seriously *un*sexy."

Conor reluctantly released her, watching her ass as she walked into the bathroom, marveling at the sex they'd just had. Each time was different, each time blew his mind, each time made him want more.

His earlier thought returned, bringing worry with it. He felt like he couldn't get enough, but she was still planning on leaving. And he had no idea why, what she was doing out here, what she was running from, even though it was obvious she was running from something. What put that sad, faraway look in her eyes. *Why* she was reckless enough to go to a bar by herself and bring a stranger back to her hotel room without even texting anyone as a backup plan.

As much as Conor wanted to spend the rest of the night buried so deep inside her she'd never forget the feel of him, they also needed to talk. He was obsessed with getting the answers to those questions, even if it meant he'd have to open up about shit, too.

He was ready for her when she came back and crawled back on the bed, pulling her against him and stroking her side.

"So," he started.

"So," she mimicked.

"Let's play a game."

"Is it a sexy game?"

"It might be," he said. "Each person gets to ask three questions. Each person gets one..."

"Veto?" she raised an eyebrow. "I guess that's our safe word now."

Conor smiled, glad they were on the same page.

"Let's call it two truths and a veto."

She glanced away from him, like she was debating. Her innate curiosity won out against her desire to keep her cards tucked away where he couldn't see them.

"I'm first though."

"Sure." He began to play tic tac toe along the dip in her hip.

"Why'd you join the military? And why the SEALS?"

"That's two questions," he told her.

"They're basically the same question," she argued.

He shook his head but let her win. "My dad was in the Navy. Not a SEAL, a medic. Before he died—cancer—" he qualified for her, touched when she took his hand in hers and squeezed, "he told me the two things he was most proud of was doing his duty for his country, and raising me and my sister, Samantha. And I guess," Conor's throat worked—*Jesus, were those tears?* "I always felt like he was watching me somehow, and I wanted to make sure he was proud. And," he shrugged, "I wanted to get my college degree, and my mom didn't have the kind of money to send me, and I didn't want to take out a million loans. Would rather have Uncle Sam be indebted to me than the other way around."

Kara lifted his hand in her tiny, delicate one, pressing her lips to his wrist. Sparks shot off in Conor, and his chest ached, the way it always seemed to around this woman.

"I want to ask another question, but I don't want to waste it. But I'm curious..."

"What I got my degree in?" Conor laughed, a little bashful. "Music theory."

Kara dropped his hand. "That is...not what I expected."

"Yeah, well," he shrugged, still embarrassed. "My friends give me shit for having an 'artsy soul.'"

"I like your artsy soul. What do you play?" she hastened to add, "I'm not wasting my next question on that."

Conor laughed. "Guitar."

Kara grinned. "Dreams of being Led Zeppelin?"

Conor shook his head, looking forward to surprising her, even if it made him feel oddly vulnerable to admit to it.

"Leonard Cohen."

Kara kissed him. "I think that's the sexiest thing I've ever heard." She considered something, then added. "Although if you don't know what Hallelujah is really about, I take back what I just said."

"Sexier than when I tell you how tight your perfect little pussy squeezes me?"

She rolled her eyes, but he could tell she was blushing in the dim light from the bathroom and the moon.

He relented. "It's about sad sex."

And what happens when a man falls in love with a woman who doesn't love him back. He kept the sobering thought to himself. It was irrelevant anyway. Conor didn't love her, he didn't love anyone other than his mom and sister.

"It's about sad *Jewish* sex. The theme of my people." She attempted a laugh, but it was like she sensed what he was thinking, because her eyes looked distant.

"Maybe I'll play it for you some time," he offered, testing her.

Kara pulled back, barely an inch, but he felt her absence like it was a mile.

"Your turn," she said lightly.

Frustrated that she'd rather air her secrets than make trivial almost-plans for the future, Conor played hardball.

"Why are you on this road trip? What are you running from?"

Kara's shoulders went stiff. "That's two questions."

"Hey, I gave you two related questions before. It's your turn."

She sighed. "I was living in New York. Grad school for creative writing. Something happened. Well, that's not right. I did something, a lot of somethings. They were pretty shitty and I regret them, but I got caught up and wasn't making wise decisions, and like what usually happens when you make shitty choices, there are shitty consequences. I sort of... ruined my reputation, and my whole life there. So I dropped out of school, bought a used car, and decided to drive around for a while. See America."

Conor kept his thoughts from showing on his face, not wanting her to see how he was both grateful she'd opened up to him, and frustrated she wouldn't tell him more.

Careful to phrase it as a statement instead of a question, he said, "So you're trying to find yourself."

She shook her head. "No, I know who I am. I don't necessarily love who I am, but I know myself. I'm trying to change. But I'm not trying to find myself, I'm trying to find a place that I can call home now. A place where I belong." She laughed, the sound quiet and sad like the opening strains of the song they'd just been discussing. "I'm not sure if I belong anywhere, to be honest, but I like the open road. I like feeling free."

"It's less scary with other people when the stakes are lower, and you can leave anytime," he said, trying to keep the accusation as gentle as possible.

"Maybe. Maybe I just don't know how to stay anymore. Maybe I'm not capable of it. Maybe I don't want to be."

Conor resisted the urge to flip her on her back and show her how well he could *make* her stay.

"Your turn," he told her.

"How do you do what you do? And still keep..."

Ouch. Going for the jugular, wasn't she?

"...keep my humanity?" he tried to keep his voice light.

"Keep yourself sane," she corrected.

"They teach you how to compartmentalize. And you learn fast. That part of my life—the part that can hold a sniper rifle in my hands, take aim, and shoot to kill, it's separate from the rest of me. Goes into a box when the mission is completed. And it helps, that even though I'm committing murder—because I know it's government-sanctioned murder, no matter how some people might try to soften it— what I do is for the collective good. The people I kill, Kara, they do terrible things. And I'm not an idiot. There are people I'm supposed to protect who also do terrible things, but at least I'm saving the world from some of them."

She started to say something, but he held up his hand, needing to get this out—even though he never said these words to anyone. "A lot of guys who do this... they turn to alcohol, or they become violent and addicted to throwing their fists, or they stick their dicks in pussy after pussy so they can forget what it's like to kill someone, even for a little while. I'm lucky, because I have friends who keep me from falling down that hole, and vice versa. But I think I'm looking for something bright in my life, because sometimes it feels pretty fucking dark."

Kara was silent for a moment, then she started kissing his neck, his naked chest, his stomach. His body clenched in response, but he stilled her with one hand.

"It's my turn again."

"We can finish playing later," she told him. "I want to..."

"Avoid more probing questions?" he asked wryly.

"No, for once," she said, surprisingly honest. "What you said... I can't imagine that. How you keep yourself whole. But it makes me want to try and give you a little bit of that brightness, if I can."

And then she was making her way down his body, her lips on his skin, and she was taking his already thickening cock in her mouth, licking and sucking, and Conor, once again, released his control over his emotions but took control over her body instead, wrapping a fist in her hair and directing her movements, whispering to her to take him deep, until he felt the crown of his cock touch the back of her throat. She swallowed around him, and he was groaning *yes, baby girl, greedy girl, sweet girl, perfect girl, yes, take all of me,* and he was coming, and coming, and coming. And as he orgasmed, his hand still gripping her hair in his fist, he wasn't sure if he could ever let her go.

For a while, there were no questions, no vetoes, just filthy sweet whispers in each other's ears, as they made a perfect mess together. And the fragile bond that had begun to form between them grew stronger.

Conor was asleep on his stomach, one arm thrown wide, the other holding her hip, possessive even in sleep. Kara checked her phone. It was 2:03 a.m. She had planned to be on the road by eight, but that seemed unlikely.

She started to move, and Conor opened one eye. It was almost scary how alert he became so quickly, but then he'd probably learned it on the job, hadn't he?

A job where he could die at any moment. The thought sobered her quickly.

"It's still my turn for another question," he reminded her.

Kara lay back down, dreading where this was going next. But a deal was a deal, and if he was going to keep his promises, the least she could do was not renege on their game.

Even though it was still up in the air if he was going to keep his promise.

I'll never hurt you, he'd said, and she hadn't bothered to point out that he couldn't see into the future, and everyone hurt everyone, eventually. It wasn't just that he would cause her pain, if she stuck around long enough to give him a chance. Kara knew deep in her bones that if she stayed, eventually she would be the one to hurt him. That's what she did, hurt people. It was why she was committed to never staying anywhere. Conor was right. No real stakes if lasting relationships weren't formed.

"Go for it," she said, hiding her dread.

"You're traveling the country. Alone. Getting drunk by yourself, taking strangers back to your hotel room. Fuck, we even had sex without a condom—although that was both our faults. Still, I need to know: Why are you so reckless with your life? Are you punishing yourself?"

The question punched her in the throat. She tried to roll away.

"Veto," she said desperately. "Veto, veto, veto."

Conor didn't release her, stroking her hip, trying to calm her like a caged, rabid animal.

"Okay. Okay. But I get one more question. And you're out of vetoes," he warned.

She could demand he leave. Leave herself if he refused

to go. But she tried to calm her breathing, avoid the black hole that threatened to swallow her. Technically it was no worse a question than his first, but before he'd let her side-step the details. The answer was something she never talked about or even thought about, too overwhelmed by the guilt and shame she felt whenever she thought of what she'd done with the professor. It took two to destroy someone else's marriage, but she was half accountable. Chris still had his literary and academic careers, but he lost his wife and family, and she could remember that ravaged look on his wife Molly's face when she showed up at Kara's apartment, demanding to know if Kara was fucking her husband.

Kara shut down her emotions after that. Tried to retreat into emptiness for a while. The only time she really felt anything anymore was when she took risks. Most of them included flirting with and then fucking strange men, knowing they could hurt her, knowing they could do worse. But they also included staying in sketchy motels and driving late at night. Maybe she was punishing herself in a way. Maybe she was just trying to stave off the pain. Thinking about it didn't help.

Conor pulled her into his chest, wrapping his arms tight around her. She held herself stiff against him. He didn't speak for a bit, like he was considering questions and discarding them. When he sighed into her ear, tingles traveled through Kara's body, and she relaxed into his hold.

"Have you ever been in love?"

Kara stiffened again. "That's a pretty intense question to ask someone you've only been on one date with."

Conor laughed. "I got you Animal Fries, that counts as ten dates. Besides, you already used your veto," he reminded her.

"Conor..." she tried again, but she wasn't sure what to say.

"Secretive girl, my cock has been inside you too many times to count. Bare. I think we can share this much. It's a low stakes question, anyway."

It wasn't.

She already felt so vulnerable. But what could it hurt to answer? She was leaving.

"I thought so, once. I excused the stupid shit I was doing because it was for love. All's fair, right?" She closed her eyes against the blossoming tears, happy he was behind her so he couldn't see her crying. "But I was wrong. It wasn't love, it was some...starstruck, power-struck spell, some need for male approval from an authority figure, some belief that I was above it all. Love that's an excuse to hurt people... it isn't love. It's selfishness."

And as an inherently selfish person, Kara wasn't sure if she was even capable of the real thing, but she didn't share that part. It was irrelevant.

Conor lifted a hand from her waist to brush his fingers across her cheek, catching some of her tears that had escaped. How did it feel like he knew so much about her, in so little time? Why was she telling him so much?

"Your turn to answer," she said, desperate to take the attention off her and put it on him, to put them on even footing.

"The game is two truths and a veto, remember?"

"Conor." Could he tell how much she needed this from him?

"Yeah. Fair." He paused like he was thinking, stroking her hip in a pattern like he was spelling out a word. "For a while, I didn't think I was capable," he said, echoing her own thoughts. "I love my mom and sister, I loved my dad, I'd do anything to protect my teammates and trust them implicitly, but with what I do for a living, well, I didn't think there was enough left of my soul to love someone, romantically. But recently? I don't know." He paused again, and for the first time sounded unsure of himself. "Maybe I was wrong. Maybe I didn't know what I needed."

That feeling from the first night, of the ground spinning around underneath her, returned. She wanted so badly to ask what brought the change on, but part of her knew. And it scared her *shitless*. What he was hinting at was something she couldn't have, couldn't match, didn't *want*.

Liar, that voice told her. It had been quiet for a while. *You want it, you're just a coward.*

But Kara knew better than to listen to that voice. It had gotten her in trouble once; it wouldn't again.

She could feel the letters Conor was tracing more distinctly now. It was a game she'd always been good at—the professor had loved to trace multisyllabic words on her naked back and make her guess them. But the word was simpler now—the name of the man who held her.

It should've scared Kara more. Not only the outright claim, but the similarity to the man who had destroyed her life, the man whose life she'd destroyed. But Conor stopped, switching to stroke her hair instead, humming under his breath, and Kara settled, trying to set her fears at bay.

Just for the night, she told herself as he hummed. *Just for the night.* She didn't recognize the song at first, but then it came to her—he was humming the chorus to "Wolves Without Teeth."

"We have the same taste in music," she murmured to him.

"Except for Maroon 5," he noted.

"You just don't see the appeal of Adam Levine."

He was quiet for a moment, then said, "You'd be surprised."

Huh.

Kara filed the knowledge away, liking that he trusted her enough to share that with her.

As they began to fall back asleep, she murmured, "If I weren't so reckless, if I played it safe, we wouldn't be in this bed together. And I think even if I never knew what I missed, I'd still regret it. I'd know, somehow."

He squeezed her hip. "I promise," he was saying, but she was already drifting off when he responded, so she never heard what he was promising.

He woke her again, twice in the night. The first time he held her down, shoving deep inside her, again and again as he whispered filthy things in her ear, asking her if she liked it when he made her do things she didn't want to, telling her that he knew she did, *your pussy grips me so tight when I don't let you move, doesn't it, dirty girl? I'm going to make you do so many things, and you aren't going to want to admit it, but you're going to* love *all of them.* And when he made her orgasm so hard she screamed herself hoarse, a part of her wondered if she could love more than just the sex between them.

The second time, he fucked her slow and gentle, face-to-face, but his grip on the back of her neck and the look in his eyes was just as dominant and controlling as always. When she tried to look away from him, he held her still, telling her *no, you stay where I put you*, and she was too tired to fight him. He whispered, *I promise, sweet girl*, in her ear as he came, and she didn't know what he was promising. And as she came, this time with him, like some terrifying magic, she felt like he'd broken her apart and remade her and she didn't know into what, and that was the the most frightening part of all.

When Kara woke, the sun was high in the sky. Conor was still wrapped around her. They were curved together like quotation marks. And his cock was hard against her ass.

Even though she'd slept well in his arms—better than she had in months—she couldn't shake off the dread. She needed to get on the road. She needed to get away from the promise and threat of him. The way he looked at her, touched her, read her so easily, let her in and demanded she do the same... Kara had absolutely no control. He'd taken all of it. As if the second their hands touched in the bar, he'd stolen it.

She needed to leave.

She tried to slip out of his arms. He tightened them around her.

"Where are you going?"

"I need to check out." She tried for lightness. "Or they'll charge me extra."

"Okay." He released her and stretched. "Let's shower, check out, and we can go back to my place."

"I can't." She was already crawling off the bed. "I need to get on the road."

He sat up, his hand playing over his naked chest. His eyes narrowed. "Appointment somewhere?"

"Next stop on my journey." She shrugged. "You know how it goes."

He rolled off the bed, prowling toward her, cock proud and beckoning. "I thought you were a wanderer. Where do you have to be?"

She shook her head. "Conor, it was a good weekend—"

"Great weekend. Amazing weekend. Super weekend.

Fucking fantastic weekend," he interjected. "The kind of weekend that changes—"

"—A nice fall fling," she said.

"Everything," he finished. Then froze, having heard her. "Fling?" he asked, voice almost scary in how quiet it was.

"Fling." She repeated, refusing to back down. "And I think it's better if we leave it that way."

He loomed over her, his face hard, something working behind his eyes.

"You're scared," he stated.

She nodded. "Terrified."

He looked surprised, like he hadn't expected that from her. His eyes softened, and he settled a big hand on the back of her neck. "I'm scared too, captivating girl. Let's be scared together."

She pulled away. "No, you don't understand. I'm terrified because I know how this ends, and I'd rather not go down that path again."

Conor stepped back. "Wow, whoever he was, he really did a number on you, didn't he?"

If Kara had hackles, they would've risen. "That's none of your business."

His next words were like ice picks, stabbing into her skin.

"Again, I've come in your pussy so many times over the past night, I think you owe me a little explanation for why you're being so cold. Or do you need me to fuck you again to get you hot? Is that what it takes?"

"Veto," she spat at him. "Veto, veto, veto."

Conor shook his head like he was disgusted with her. "Have it your way."

Turning away, he grabbed his clothes, giving her his

back. His tattoo of an eagle carrying the words *Semper Fortis* in its mouth glared at her.

"Conor—"

He pulled on his shorts and shirt, shoving his feet into his sneakers without bothering to tie them.

"Keep yourself safe, Kara," he said, muttering something else as he stormed out the door, slamming it behind him.

Kara stood there, unsure she'd heard his last words right.

Or I promise I will.

The dread grew, but she shook it off, telling herself she was ready to leave the sun and sand behind her and get back on the road, where she *felt* safest.

Even if she wasn't.

She sent him a text a year later.

Hey, it's Kara. I don't know if you even remember me, but I'm sorry for the way we left things. I'm back in San Diego this week —can we get a drink?

Conor never replied.

3

_____

Almost two years later...

"**E**xplain why you decided not to go out with him again." Lola demanded.

Kara sighed, sipping her wine. How the hell did she explain to her best friend that even though her date had seemed great on paper, even better when they texted before they met up for drinks, when they met, there was no spark? Worse, she felt almost repulsed, sick to her stomach with guilt. It was ridiculous, because who was making her feel guilty? Kara had been single for years, and the closest she'd come to even caring about someone romantically... no, she wasn't going there. The past was better left in the past, where it couldn't hurt her or send her into a regret spiral.

"Hey, spacey." Lola clapped her hands to get Kara's attention back. "You haven't answered my question."

"I wasn't interested. I don't know, Lo." Kara buried her face in her hands. "I'm just not in a place to date right now."

"Bullshit." Lola wasn't impressed with her answer. "That's not even close to true. You've been doing great for almost a year now. You're in therapy, you have a decent job at that advertising agency, you even settled down and rented a whole apartment instead of subletting. You've been talking about getting a basset hound. About starting to write again. We have plans to go volunteer at the farmer's market in Logan Square every Saturday! There's no more reason for the commitment phobia, Kara. You're healing. You need to let the past go. *All* of it."

Kara laughed, a little rueful, a lot bitter. "I don't think someone like me ever heals."

"Why? You didn't do something evil. You slept with our thesis advisor."

Kara raised an eyebrow.

"Okay, so you slept with him a lot. Like, a lot a lot. And maybe," Lola put her fingers together to signify a small amount, "you did an itty bitty bit of homewrecking and destruction. You were in your late twenties. We all do stupid shit in our late twenties. Lord knows I did."

Kara put a hand on her friend's. "Want to talk about it?"

Lola shook her head. "Nope, not distracting me. This is about you. It's been three months of you going on first dates and only first dates. You've basically left a sea of rejected, dejected Chicago men in your wake. The only reason I can think of is that you're still thinking about *them*."

Kara tried to deny it, but her throat closed up. She put her head in her hands.

Lola groaned, imitating her. "Kara, you had a few hot flings on your epic road trip. You have to move on."

"But what if I made a mistake? Sometimes I have dreams about beds made with hospital corners."

Lola laughed. "The military guy, right?" She shrugged. "Maybe you did, maybe you didn't. No regrets, remember?"

No regrets.

Kara had so many regrets, she'd lost count.

"Just one second date," Lola coaxed. "What about that veterinarian? You've always wanted a dog, he has like, six. And he was cute and seemed sweet. He brought you tulips."

A nice touch, even though her favorite flower was as far from a tulip as you could get.

Kara sighed, knowing it wouldn't go anywhere, but not wanting to let her friend down. Lola was the only one who had stuck by her after the fallout in New York. Kara had lived on her couch for months while she looked for a job, and Lola had never once complained. And maybe her friend was right—she was never going to move on past Conor, Micah, and Luke if she didn't try to meet someone else. She hadn't had sex in over a year. It was time.

"I'll go out again with the vet."

Lola clapped with delight before signaling the waiter.

"This calls for prosecco."

Kara shook her head, laughing. "Champagne tastes."

"Sparkling wine tastes," her friend corrected. "And like you can talk, Miss Charcuterie."

Charcuterie. Kara remembered Conor correctly guessing her preferred date meal, before shoving the memory—and all the feelings it dredged up—away.

Picking up her phone, she pulled up the dating app, messaging the veterinarian back. She hadn't responded to his last message, requesting dinner.

Let's do it, she replied. Even though her heart wasn't in it.

Definitely. The reply was immediate.

She put her phone back down, accepting the prosecco glass their waiter handed her. As she clinked flutes with Lola, she thought she felt someone watching. Jerking around, she scanned the street.

No one was there.

But that sense of foreboding stuck with her through the rest of dinner and followed her home.

When Kara got home, she stood at her front door, that same bad feeling overwhelming her. A voice whispered to her not to unlock it. But that was silly. She had no reason to be worried about her own apartment.

It had to be something else. Like that ever-present, aching loneliness. These days, it followed her like her shadow. God, when was the last time she touched someone, really? The last time someone touched her? When was the last time she'd felt anything? It was a good thing she was going out with the veterinarian. Even though retreating into her head was *so much easier* than confronting the dread in the pit of her stomach.

She dismissed the foreboding, unlocking her door and entering her apartment. She hung her keys on the hook and switched on the light.

And froze.

Was someone breathing?

She listened more carefully.

No. It was silent. Her mental state was making her shaky.

Still. Even though moonlight filled her apartment, she walked around, flipping on the rest of the light switches and bathing her space in artificial gold light, chasing the shadows away.

It would be *really* nice if there was someone—expected and welcome of course—waiting for her when she got home. Just here, hanging on the couch, ready with a hug or a kiss or just a "how was your day, honey?"

She definitely needed a dog.

It was good she was going out with that veterinarian again. She just needed to psych herself up for it.

Sticking her leftovers in the fridge, she entered the bathroom, stripping as she went. God, she needed to wash the day away. Dinner with Lola had been nice, but it hadn't staved off the feeling that this—a stable but boring and stressful job, a small, boring and bland apartment, a potentially stable if boring and bland boyfriend (Kara winced at that; it was exceedingly unkind of her), and the omnipresent, clinging loneliness—was all her life would ever be.

Feeling too maudlin to care, she didn't even bother switching the bathroom light on—the moon was full and bright and bathed the room in silver light, and that was all she needed to be able to see. She turned on the shower, twisted the knob to scalding. Stepped in and slid the glass door closed.

Kara considered masturbating as a distraction. It didn't really work these days—something always kept her from getting off. But she wanted to try. If she couldn't orgasm on her own, how was she supposed to orgasm with someone else?

She hadn't had sex successfully in over a year. She'd tried, but the guy had been so nervous and she'd been so distracted she'd faked an orgasm when he fingered her before making an excuse and ditching him. He'd been pissed when she didn't return the favor, and never called her again. She hadn't cared.

She'd had a lot of decent sex over the years; some even objectively good. But great sex? There'd only been three men, in three different cities, all in the same year. The men had been remarkably different, except for one thing in common. Just thinking about it made her thighs clench.

They'd all figured out she wanted to be controlled. They *made* her, even though she wanted it. Convoluted as fuck, but it wasn't just—or even—about "liking it rough." It was a control thing, a power thing, a... who the fuck knew thing. Kara had always known she was sexually submissive, and although at first she'd felt ashamed, by now she was fine with it. There was nothing shameful about it. But what she hadn't known—or admitted to herself—was that she wanted *all* the power taken from her. She wanted to say *no* knowing she'd be forced to make it a *yes*. She wanted to fight back—and lose. But the three men—first Conor, then Micah, and finally Luke—had fucked her into acknowledging she wanted consensual nonconsent in her sex. It wasn't something she would ever apologize for, but it wasn't something she could ever talk about, much less tell a man she was getting to know. For a moment, she imagined trying to share that with the veterinarian, and almost laughed. At best, he'd try earnestly and fail, thinking a pair of furry handcuffs and some lighthearted spanking would scratch her itch. And worst, he'd be disgusted and never talk to her again.

Kara tried to accept reality: She'd never have that again. Giving up control was terrifying, and yet she'd trusted three near-to-complete strangers to know where her limits were, respect them, keep her safe. At least physically. She'd trusted Conor, Micah, and Luke with her body, but she didn't trust anyone with her heart. Not after Chris. That was the problem.

Sighing, she moved her fingers down her body and touched herself, picturing those three times the world had tilted. There'd been dominant Conor, who first made sure she was comfortable and then ramped up the pushiness to full on forceful. The way his control had unleashed her passion had been a revelation. And when he told her to *struggle like the good girl I know you are*, something had sparked in her, a flame she'd never been able to extinguish, and never wanted to.

She gasped. *There*. That felt good.

And Luke. Redheaded, tan, and tall as fuck, with a cock to match, he'd towered over her when they'd met in Denver. She'd had a panic attack on a climbing wall, and he'd climbed up after and rescued her, talking her down from the panic and encouraging her to finish climbing. And a week later—during an argument on a sunset hike—he'd dragged Kara into a cave, picked her up, and fucked her against the cold rock wall.

He was one of the rare guys she'd actually dated. They hooked up for a month; his excitement about sex, and her, was addictive. So was how adventurous he got—hogtying her with climbing rope and making her come until it hurt, shoving his cock so deep in her throat she choked and not letting her up for air until she almost blacked out, spanking her harder than she'd ever imagined she'd be able to tolerate, much less get off on. He was sadistic in his tastes, although he tempered them for her. And afterward, he was always gentle, generous. Caring.

Kara had thought she'd made it clear to him that she only wanted a casual fling, but when he started prying into her personal life and making things emotional, she'd scrammed.

It was for the best.

Frustration built as she moved her fingers faster—it felt good, but not good enough. Was she now going to be one of those women who couldn't orgasm? *Relax*, she told herself, and pasted a memory in her head. It was blurry, softened by the oh, three or four French 75s she'd imbibed the night she met Micah.

Micah. God, *Micah*. She'd met him after Conor but before Luke, and she'd never forget him. Only a few inches taller than her, but so muscular and broad it was almost scary. Dirty blonde and a scar above his eyebrow, and the bluest eyes she'd ever seen.

They'd been at the same restaurant on Christmas Eve. They'd bonded as two lonely Jews, although she never learned why he was in town. After convincing him to eat the charbroiled oysters and "best biscuits in New Orleans, even though they're definitely not kosher," she'd taken him to Frenchmen Street and they'd danced for hours in club after club, before heading back to her Airbnb. He'd been confident and challenging, and for one night, she forgot how depressed she was. He got in her head, twisting her around until he didn't even have to make her do what he wanted, she just did it herself. Where Conor had ordered and Luke had overpowered, Micah had manipulated. It had hurt when she'd woken the next morning to find herself alone.

And fuck her, but she had loved the way all three of them touched her.

Moving her fingers in gentle circles around her clit—she was so close—she imagined them now, Conor holding her down and telling her to struggle, Luke shoving his cock deep in her throat without mercy, and Micah's low, scratchy voice, the way he'd said—

"Don't you dare come."

Kara whipped her head around, covering her body with her hands.

A man stood in shadow, the lower right side of his rugged face bathed in the silver light from the moon. She could barely make out his features, just that he was tall and broad and his voice, flat and hard, moved over her body, lighting it up in an abrasive caress.

She'd been right. Something had been off when she got home. She should've trusted her gut. Kara opened her mouth to scream, but she couldn't get the sound out; her fear had rendered her silent.

Inhale, Kara. Exhale, slowly. Don't have a panic attack. Her phone was on the vanity, all she had to do was reach over and press the emergency function.

Her heartbeat slowed, and she swallowed, finding her voice. Sort of.

"Who are you?" she choked. "What the hell are you doing in my home?"

He didn't respond at first. Feeling his eyes on her bare, exposed skin, she hunched over to hide herself from him.

"Get out of the shower, Kara."

Oh god, he knew her name. How did he know her name?

Don't worry about the whos and the hows and the whys right now. Focus on getting away.

She looked at him, not looking at her phone, not wanting to give away her plan.

"Okay."

As she stepped out of the shower, she reached for her phone—

—and he grabbed her, dislodging the phone from her hand, where it clattered to the floor. Kara ducked, scrambling for it, and he dragged her back up to standing, pulling her tight against his chest.

Everything about him was hard, from his chest to his cock, pressing through his jeans against her bare ass. She struggled against him, hands wild, pinching, hitting any part of him she could find. He stood solid and still. Didn't even flinch.

Fuuuuuuuuuck!

"The phone was an obvious choice," he informed her quietly. "If you think someone's really about to harm you, scream."

"What are you here to do, if not harm me?"

He didn't answer, so she took his advice and opened her mouth to shriek for help. In response, he clamped a hand around her mouth.

"I don't want to hurt you, Kara. Doesn't mean I won't. You don't want to push me—not this time."

Push him? This time? The words rang like a memory, muffled by her panic.

"No screaming, got it?"

She nodded and he released his hand from her mouth.

"Please," she begged, voice breaking. "Please let me go."

"Hands at your sides."

It didn't matter who he was, how he knew her name, or what the hell he was here for. Steal from her, torture her, rape her, kill her, *fuck*, none of it was good. Everything inside her was screaming *run.*

As if he read her mind, he wrapped his right hand around her throat, squeezing, not enough to harm her but enough to get his point across.

Be smart. The man was bigger than her, stronger than her. Reluctantly, Kara complied with his demand. He released her throat, wrapping his arms around her waist instead. She looked in the mirror, their eyes catching. The taunting heat in his gaze made her thighs clench again, which was such a shocking, upsetting reaction, Kara had to squeeze her eyes shut for a moment. When she opened them, he was still watching her.

This couldn't be happening.

"Do. Not. Move."

She opened her mouth again to—

"Do. Not. Scream. You will not like the outcome, Kara. I promise."

She closed her mouth, and stood shivering as he released her, grabbing a towel and drying her off, his movements careful. The contrast between his harsh words and almost tender care shook her even more than the situation did. Why was he being so gentle with her?

"What do you want from me? Why are you here?"

He still didn't answer, just finished rubbing her dry before nudging her forward, still naked. She stumbled, wet feet sliding across the tile.

"Walk," he threatened softly, "or I'll carry you."

She walked. Her mind raced, rapidly sorting through exit strategies only to discard them, telling herself repeatedly that screaming or fighting without a clear plan would only get her hurt and she'd lose any chance she had of surprising him. If she could even surprise him. He'd caught on quick to the phone idea, anticipated when she was about to struggle or scream. He was one step ahead of her, which meant she had to get two steps ahead of him. It was the only way she was going to get out of this alive.

In her now dark living room stood an imposing figure. He wasn't as tall as the threatening man behind her, but even in the dark she could tell he was muscular and broad. The power emanating from the men surrounding her sucked all the air out of the room.

The man behind her leaned over and flipped on the light.

And Kara went from fear to relief to confusion and back to fear. So fast it gave her emotional whiplash.

"Micah?" she whispered in disbelief. After he'd snuck out on her that night in New Orleans, she assumed she'd never see him again.

Micah was a few inches taller than her, but it was his broadness, his scar, that had intimidated her and made her knees weak when they'd met. She recognized the Star of David necklace around his neck, but the tattoo peeking out from under his left sleeve was new. He'd told her that he didn't have tattoos because, much as he liked them, he wanted to be buried in a Jewish cemetery.

"Been a while, baby," he said, voice gruff and eyes unreadable as he scanned her body.

"Tell me what the fuck is going on," Kara demanded, forgetting for a moment that she was naked, about the frightening man behind her.

The moment didn't last. The man behind her nipped her neck with his teeth.

"Demanding girl," he chided, "you don't get to give the orders. Now or ever."

Only one person in her life had ever talked to her like that. *Good girl, clever girl.* She thought he was nothing more than a part of her past, an almost figment of her horny imagination, a ghost that haunted her. Had tried so hard to forget, to move on. So what the hell was he doing here, in her apartment, acting like a woman's worst nightmare? And why was Micah in her apartment, cool and collected, like he had a right to be here when he most certainly didn't?

"Who the hell are you?" she asked the man behind her, already knowing the answer.

He chuckled. The last time she'd heard that chuckle, he'd been so deep she'd felt his laugh from inside. So many times, she'd regretted leaving. Had asked herself why she'd let what happened in New York dig so deep into her head she'd run at the first sign of intimacy. Had beaten herself up for being too fucked up to recognize a good thing when it stood in her hotel room door, asking her to stay.

But god, she'd never forgotten him, on top of her, beneath her, behind her, trapping her wrists in his hands, and his smooth, deep, dark voice, telling her to use her veto.

"You know who I am, memorable girl," he said, and the confirmation stole the last remaining air from the room.

The floor spun, the walls moved, the panic attack that had been looming hit—and hit hard. And even though Kara had told herself not to do anything stupid, to focus on her survival, she couldn't help it. Lifting one bare foot, she kicked his knee and raced down the hall toward the kitchen, hearing a satisfying groan behind her.

His feet pounded behind her—it wasn't a particularly long hallway—catching her just as she crossed the threshold. Kara felt herself go weightless as he wrapped his arms around her from behind and lifted her in the air, carrying her back into the living room as she kicked him, punched him, clawed at his arms, her breath going tight and shallow as she tried desperately to free herself, to escape. Anything other than having to confront this new reality: That two men she'd formerly fucked and dreamed about constantly had turned into nightmares.

This was it. This was how she died.

Fuck that, the rebellious, strong voice in her head argued vehemently. This was *not* how Kara Blum died. She wasn't going down without a fight.

So she fought some more, earning herself a reprimanding squeeze around her waist as he lowered her to the ground and spun her—still gently, disturbingly gently—around to face him.

"This time, I don't want you to struggle," he said.

She looked up at the man, whose body she knew so well, even though he was a complete and total stranger to her, because the man she thought she'd known had wanted to protect her, not torment her.

"Conor."

"It's been a while, clever girl," he mocked.

He looked different. Same rugged bone structure, same sculpted, perfect lips she remembered moving over her body, but where they'd once been quirked in an affectionate smile, they now were turned up in a sharp, mocking smirk. His dark hair, once buzzed close to his skull, was now a few inches longer, laying haphazardly around his head in short but thick, don't-give-a-fuck waves. And his eyes, once a warm, deep brown, were cold and calculating, something dark and dangerous moving in their depths.

They no longer were the eyes of a protector.

They were the eyes of a killer.

"Conor," she tried again, shoving down her fear and confusion, desperation making her throat thick as she searched his eyes for the compassion she used to see there, so long ago. "Please, tell me what's going on."

He groaned, the sound at once sexy and terrifying. "I forgot how hot it is when you say please. Say it again."

Fuck that.

But Kara quashed the rebellious streak, listening to her gut which was yelling that this man wasn't someone to fuck with.

"Please," she whispered.

He shook his head. "I don't think you've earned an answer yet."

Micah chuckled. "You didn't even let her wear a towel? That's harsh."

"She was trying to masturbate in the shower," Conor shrugged. "I was a little distracted."

"Trying?"

Kara curled in on herself, humiliated.

"Trying," Conor confirmed. "Couldn't seem to get herself off, but we'll fix that, won't we?"

Micah growled. Kara had only spent one night with the enigmatic man, but she'd never expected someone so self-composed to growl.

But then, she also hadn't expected him to break into her apartment. Either of them. Ever.

"She'll have to make it up to us," said Micah, taking a step forward, and Kara took a step back—directly into Conor's hold. She tried to pull away; he held tight.

Once, his arms had made her feel safe. Now, they messed with her head, made her almost hyperventilate.

Breathe, Kara, she urged herself. *Just breathe. Get them talking. Figure out what's going on. Figure out an exit plan.*

"I don't understand," she said, forcing herself to stare straight at Micah, even though it hurt to look at him. "Why are you both here? How are you both here? Do you—do you know each other?" A thought occurred to her, devastating in its likelihood. "Were you at the restaurant tonight? Were you watching me?"

Micah nodded, just once.

"You eavesdropped," she guessed.

He just raised an eyebrow, not saying anything.

Conor squeezed her waist. A warning.

"You won't be going out with that veterinarian again."

That did it. Kara tried to kick him, anger making her stupid. "Fuck you."

He squeezed her tighter.

"Try that again," he said, mean and cold, and she realized why she hadn't recognized him immediately. His voice was mostly the same, but there was something dark and flat and frightening in the cadence of his words. Something was different. This wasn't the mostly easygoing—if sexually controlling—guy she'd known, even briefly.

"We'll save story time for later," Micah interrupted. "Right now, we're leaving."

Kara took a deep breath—or as deep of a breath as she could, given Conor's tight grip on her. She needed to reason with them, but the combination of fear and shock meant her reasoning abilities were at an all-time low. Not to mention her anger, because how fucking *dare* these fuckers. There was no excuse for this behavior, no motivation that made this okay.

Still, she tried.

"Conor, Micah, you can't just show up after *almost two years* to my *home* out of fucking *nowhere,* basically *attack* me while I'm in the fucking *shower*, parade me around naked, and then expect me to go with you somewhere without any explanation."

"We *can* just," Conor said, his flat tone dangerous.

"I will call the fucking police," Kara stated.

"You will call fucking no one," Conor replied, his dangerous tone going tight with anger. At least she was getting a reaction out of him—which was really, really stupid of her.

"Conor," she tried again, aware she was flipflopping between escalation and de-escalation, anger and fear, incendiary and appeasing.

Micah shook his head. "This is a waste of time. Kara, you can make this easy for yourself, or you can make this difficult. The end result's going to be the same."

"And what's the result?" Seemingly incendiary, but she

wasn't going to let her fear control her. A terrifying question, but she needed to know. She needed to know if this *was* how she died.

Neither of them answered her.

Appeasement it was. She relaxed into Conor, who stiffened in surprise as Micah watched, a small smile tugging at his lips.

"Let me get dressed, and then we can sit down and talk about this," Kara suggested softly. "Please, Conor, I'm cold."

Conor began to release his hold on her, and Kara's heart rushed, keeping her eyes on Micah instead of the door in front of her. She calculated how many steps it would take to escape. Eight. Only eight steps, maybe ten at most.

Once again, Micah interrupted. "Clever," he said thoughtfully. "But you aren't going to play him this time."

"I'm not playing anyone," she argued. "If anything—"

He didn't let her finish her sentence. "We won't let you, will we, Conor?" Micah said, his eyes on the man behind her, who tightened his hold again in response, nipping sharply at her ear.

Pain, sharp and shocking, tore through her. She screamed. Had Conor broken skin? If he wanted to make her bleed, if Micah allowed it, what else would they do to her?

"You're never going to play me again," Conor whispered, then sucked where he'd bit. Aroused tingles shot through Kara, unwelcome and enraging.

"Let me go," she growled.

Lifting a hand from her arm, Conor tugged a lock of her wet hair. "No."

The room began to spin again. They were angry, or at least Conor was. Micah was...having fun?

Eight steps. She needed to distract them. Eight steps and she'd be out the door.

Eight steps and she'd be free.

"Are you looking for sex? What, you two met somewhere and compared war stories, realized you'd slept with the same person and decided to fuck with her head and get your rocks off? What, you needed to prove you're both big, scary men who can terrify a former fling?"

A look flashed in Micah's eyes at *war stories*, the slight smile falling off his face, but he said nothing.

It was Conor who spoke. "You have no idea what we need, do you?"

"Never took the chance to learn," Micah crossed the room toward her, tsking. "Fortunately, we know what *you* need."

Kara began to struggle again. Conor held her still. "You never found out what he did for a living, silly girl. Micah's a cyber security specialist. Expert hacker."

Betrayal cut through her. Micah had lied. He'd lied, and then he'd left.

Not that it mattered right now. Not now, with Micah standing a few inches from her, projecting heat. Not now, with Kara surrounded, trapped between the two of them, the air sucked out of the room. Not now, as Micah caressed her skin, his fingers whispering over that sensitive spot where her hip met her waist.

He spoke, voice a low hum. "Do you know how easy it is to hack into someone's computer, see all her accounts, every website she's visited, even the private windows? Everything she buys, everything she considers buying. Every kinky book she's ordered and read. Do you know how easy it is to follow her, break into her apartment and hide in the closet, listen to every phone conversation, every song she sings to herself, every time she cries? Read every text message, every email, every dirty, secret story she's written and saved in hidden folders on her laptop? You can learn a lot about a person that way. What drives her. What scares her."

Conor reached a hand down and gripped her between her thighs, squeezing until it hurt.

"What gets her off," he added, almost casually, like they were talking about vacation plans and not Kara's darkest kink. "But then we could've figured that out without the virtual paper trail or having to follow you. You love to be pushed. To be backed into a corner, and not let out again. Isn't that right, kinky girl?"

Kara took a deep breath and voiced her greatest fear. "Are you going to kill me?"

Both men laughed, the sound practically vibrating on her skin. For some reason, this, their laughter, was more frightening than everything they'd said.

Think, Kara, think. *There's a way out of this, you just need to think.*

Running wasn't going to work. There was no way she could free herself from their dual hold.

Stall them.

"Why me?"

"It would take another nineteen months to tell you 'why you,'" Conor said.

Nineteen months. The amount of time since she'd seen him last. She could deliberate over it later. Kara's eyes scanned through the room, landing on the Google Home on the TV stand.

"Okay, I'll do whatever you want," she said, forcing herself to arch her back against Conor, offering her bare breasts up to Micah, whose eyes dropped to her nipples, hard in the cold room. "You want to fuck me? Fuck me."

For a moment, surprise lit Micah's blue eyes, stretching his scar taut. The calculating asshole hadn't expected that, had he?

Now, Kara.

She took advantage of that moment to yell.

"Hey Google, call 9—"

A hand covered her mouth before she could get the next digit out.

"You shouldn't have done that, clever girl."

Something stung the back of her neck. Not teeth, this time. A needle.

"You're going to take a nap, good girl, while we take a little trip," Conor said.

Micah stroked her hip, his face going blurry. "Don't worry, you'll like where we're going."

Her body felt weak, her brain foggy. From far away, she thought she heard the Google Home saying, "Sorry, I didn't understand. Who would you like me to call?"

"What do you want from me?" she begged, and just as the room went dark, she thought she heard someone say:

"Everything."

4

———————

Kara came to, slowly. Her head ached like a vise was squeezing it, her throat was dry and scratchy, her muscles stiff. And the bedding was all wrong. The pillow was too firm, the sheets too silky. They slid across her skin. Her bare skin.

Kara very, very rarely slept naked. Even alone, it left her too vulnerable.

What the fuck was going on? Her head felt foggy, and she'd had the most disturbing dream, but what was it?

The pillow under her head shifted. Because it wasn't a pillow, it was a thigh.

Someone lifted her head and put a plastic bottle to her lips, which she opened automatically. She was so thirsty. Why was she so thirsty?

More importantly, where had the person holding the water bottle come from? Had she gotten drunk and booty-called the veterinarian?

Kara forced her eyes open. Conor was leaning over her, holding the water bottle. A large, tan hand was splayed over her stomach—Micah's. It was his thigh.

Everything came rushing back, the memory of the last time she'd been awake bright, bold, hypnotic.

It hadn't been some fucked-up dream.

She'd been kidnapped by two men she'd once fucked, who shouldn't know each other.

Hey, at least they hadn't killed her.

Yet.

Fuck.

Kara spat out the rest of the water, not caring when it splattered all over Micah's thigh and her chest. They'd injected her with some drug that knocked her out—no way was she letting them get the advantage again.

"It's just water," Conor said mildly, his hand stroking absently over her collarbone, making her shiver with helpless rage and something else Kara refused to name. "You're dehydrated from the GHB."

She swatted him away with her hands—her free hands, to her relief. He didn't respond.

"Why?" she choked out the words. It hurt to ask again, especially when she doubted she'd get a straight answer. "Just tell me why."

"Would you believe us if we said we're trying to protect you?" Micah asked.

"Protect me from what?"

"Bad people. Dangerous people."

Kara considered this for a second. She knew bad people, knew one particularly well. But not anyone dangerous. Not to her. Not until now.

"No."

Conor chuckled. "Smart girl."

Kara ignored him, focusing on her rage, tending to its tinder almost obsessively, wanting nothing more than for it to burst into destructive flame and fire. Until it turned this secret, shameful feeling into ash.

"The only bad people I know, the only dangerous people, are you." Kara enunciated each syllable slowly and carefully, lifting her head to cast her accusing gaze at both men.

Conor nodded, accepting the accusation.

Micah said nothing.

Kara still didn't understand how they knew each other, or why they'd taken her, or what they planned to do to her. She desperately wanted to understand, which was a mistake. Part of her had hoped this was some mission in protection from the SEAL and the hacker. It would mean she was safe, that she'd been right to trust them at one point, at least with her body.

But that wasn't the case. They weren't trying to keep her safe: They wanted to hurt her. There was no other plausible explanation. The truth felt almost impossible to accept, but the faster she could, the faster she could get herself safe.

Once again, Kara calculated how many steps lay between her and the door. What mattered was that she had to figure out how to get out of here—wherever *here* was.

At that moment, something in the room started beeping —loudly. A robotic female voice said in a creepy, singsong tone, "Boy Scout home."

Behind her, Micah groaned. "Fuck, he's back."

For the first time since he'd reappeared in her life earlier (*today? Yesterday? How long had she been out?*) the flat, implacable look in Conor's eyes shifted, something like worry in their depths.

"I thought we had another week."

He?! Who the fuck was he?

A rescuer? Or another tormentor?

Thuds sounded, wood planks squeaking slightly—shoes on stairs. They came closer, and Kara stilled, closing her eyes, praying for the former.

Until a familiar voice called, "Honeys, I'm hoooooooome. Did you miss me?"

And for the second time in god-knew-how-many-hours-or-days, Kara's entire equilibrium upended again.

Because she knew that voice. She had missed that voice. She had trusted that voice, with more than her body, at least until the end.

Her breathing increased rapidly, and she started chanting to herself, *please, no. Please, no. Please no pleasenopleasenopleaseno—*

A knock on the door. "Assholes, why is this locked? Are you two boning in there? Am I not invited?"

Conor pinched the bridge of his nose. She was momentarily distracted and curious to see if this was a joke, or if Micah and Conor were really lovers. But she remembered both men telling her they were bi (individually). Maybe kidnapping and terrifying women was foreplay for them.

"Let him in," Micah said quietly.

Conor grumbled something under his breath, getting off the bed and sauntering to the door. He squared his shoulders, looking back at Micah.

"Time to face the fucking music. Jesus fucking Christ," he muttered, unlocking the door and opening it.

And Kara's worst nightmare was confirmed when a familiar giant of a golden-skinned man with freckles across his face and a shock of orange-gold hair stuck his head in the door, and froze, staring at Kara like she was *his* worst nightmare.

For a moment, they just stared at each other, Luke's throat working in silence as a barrage of old feelings and memories flooded Kara. Dangling from the side of a climbing wall, having a panic attack, Luke coming to her rescue. Luke carrying her into Cave of the Winds on a hike and spanking and then fucking the shit out of her, until they both came so hard they could've brought the cave down. Luke laughing as she tried to keep up with him on a run. Luke's green-gold eyes, bright with pain, as he begged her to be brave and open up to him, then going a dark, shuttered green when she refused and left.

In the present, Luke's eyes were green-gold at first, confused, surprised, maybe excited, but they shuttered fast to that forest green, like he was hiding an emotion he didn't want her to see.

"Luke," she whispered. It was a plea.

He shook his head violently, like he was in denial.

"Luke?" Her voice broke this time.

"Oh, sweetheart," he murmured. "I'm so sorry."

He looked away from her, glaring first at Micah, who still held her, then at Conor, who toyed with the half-empty water bottle.

"What did you two dumbasses do?!"

The water bottle crackled in Conor's hand. "Careful, Lucas. Remember who's in charge."

"You fucking douchebag," Luke said.

"Call me a douchebag again," Conor said, stretching his neck. "See what happens."

"Both of you, stop," Micah warned. "If we're going to talk or fight this out, we need to do it privately."

He squeezed Kara's shoulder meaningfully. Kara didn't even bother to flinch away, still stuck on what Conor had said. *Remember who's in charge.* Like they were a team, one that Conor led and Luke followed.

Luke, who seemed apologetic and angry, but hadn't

pulled her away from Micah and Conor and said, *C'mon, I'm getting you out of here.*

He wasn't her hero.

There were no heroes here.

She wasn't prepared for the panic attack. The men's arguing turned muted, like they were outside of the fishbowl she was trapped in. The room went blurry. Her growing, flaming anger had temporarily abandoned her, leaving her alone with the sense that reality had warped.

"Kara? Kara." Conor said sharply.

The fog of panic cleared, at least a little. Kara couldn't let herself panic. She couldn't get distracted. She couldn't let what was happening fuck with her head at all. Wasn't that what they wanted? As long as she concentrated on escape, the confusion, terror, and those other emotions she couldn't name would remain deep inside where they couldn't hurt her.

"I want to go home," she said, shocked and ashamed at how quiet her voice was. She tried again, louder this time. "I'm going home."

Conor sighed, placing his hand on her bare thigh. Because she was still naked.

"You aren't in the position to make demands, willful girl."

At that, the terror overwhelmed everything else, releasing every negative emotion she could think of and some she'd never considered. She began to scream and thrash. Not because she thought someone might rescue her. No way would they be stupid enough to leave her un-gagged where a stranger could potentially hear her. No, she screamed because those emotions, which had been pent up for years in her own version of Pandora's box, came pouring out and needed to be expressed.

"Shit." Micah placed a hand around her neck, ignoring her slapping hands and kicking feet. "You're okay, baby," he soothed, and she felt her body being moved and turned into Micah's chest. His arms, massive and implacable, wrapped tight around her and rocked her side to side.

"Kara?" Conor's voice swam toward her. "Kara, calm down."

As if the order would do anything. All it did was add to the panic, wave after wave of it that sucked Kara down and thrashed her around in waves of her new terrifying, helpless reality.

"Goddamnit, have neither of you seen her have a panic attack before?" Luke appeared in the fog of Kara's vision, shoving Conor out of the way. "Micah, give her to me."

Conor grunted and Micah's hands stilled. Kara felt herself turned into a new pair of hands. Familiar ones, long slender pianist fingers that had once delivered so much pleasure to her body and so much calm to her mind. Luke didn't pull her close, just stroked those hands gently up and down her arms.

"Breathe, Kara. Just breathe with me," he murmured to her. "Okay? You don't have to do anything else right now, all you have to do is inhale and exhale." He breathed with her, moving his hand to rub her back. Exhausted, she stopped fighting him, collapsing against his chest, her throat squeezing as her screams turned into sobs.

After a few minutes, her head cleared and she looked up. Conor stood on one side of the bed, one hand in his pocket, the other crushing the plastic bottle in a clenched fist. Kara wasn't sure why he was so angry, but she documented the reaction and filed it away for further perusal. Micah sat on the corner of the bed, thumb and forefinger clasping his bearded chin, like he was documenting *her* reaction and filing it away for the future.

And Luke just held her. She leaned back, looking into his eyes, green-gold again, finally focusing on his words.

"Breathe, sweetheart. Just breathe. You're safe. I promise you're safe. I won't let them hurt you. I won't let anyone hurt you."

At that, Kara shoved him away. "You goddamned liar. How the hell am I safe? They came into my home, scared me, injected me with drugs, and took me *somewhere* without my consent, and without my clothes. I haven't been less safe in my whole fucking life."

Luke's hand tensed against her back before he released her. The second he let her go, cold air and panic rushed back in.

"Nice work," Conor commented caustically before leaving the room, the door wide open.

Kara crawled off the bed, wobbling on shaky legs toward it, air stinging her lungs.

Safe, she repeated to herself. *You're going to be safe, soon. Just leave.*

Surprisingly, no one tried to stop her. They only watched, Luke's green eyes troubled, Micah's blue eyes calculating as she reached the doorway, only to stop short when Conor reappeared, his chest all she could see.

She collapsed again, the room spinning, the panic attack winning, once again. Helpless. Helpless against everything and everyone, including her own mind.

Conor caught her with one arm, steading her. He held out his other hand, which still held the half-empty, now half-crumpled water bottle—and a small blue pill. Kara recognized the Ativan for what it was; it would knock out her anxiety and knock her out, too.

"She doesn't need that," Luke said sharply from some-where behind her.

"From what I can see, she's still panicking. She could hurt herself."

"What do you care?" Kara gasped, a distant part of her bemused.

In answer, he held the pill to her mouth, which she squeezed shut.

"Kara," he warned. "It's this or another shot."

A shot would fuck her up. The Ativan would clear her head.

Reluctantly, she opened her mouth for the pill and the water, swallowing it down. After a few minutes, her heart calmed, then her mind. But the combination of the adren-aline crash and medication made her sleepy. And maybe that was for the best; a panic attack wasn't going to get her out of here.

When Conor swept her up into his arms like a bride, she didn't fight him. It became too hard to keep her eyes open, and when he ordered, "Sleep, anxious girl," she obeyed him.

5

Conor stood with Kara in his arms, enjoying the feeling of her, naked and vulnerable—and safe, from everyone and everything but them—against his chest.

He caught the scent of her shampoo. Her hair still smelled like his childhood. Bee balm grew like weeds on his family's farm, and his mom would fill their home with jars and jars of the stuff, until the small farmhouse looked like a conservatory. When was the last time he'd smelled flowers like that? When was the last time he'd thought about home without his chest hurting? What was it about this woman? How did she manage to wipe away all the horror from the past two years?

He leaned in to kiss the spot on her forehead where her vibrant red hair curled in loose, sweaty wisps. He paused with his lips a millimeter from her skin.

A forehead kiss? Who the fuck was he, some fool poet?

"You okay, boss?" Micah asked, canny as ever. The jackass was too tuned into him, and the nickname, which his friend and lover saved for when he was about to suck

Conor's cock, itched right now. "You're gripping her hard enough to bruise her, and from what we know, that's Luke's show."

Luke laughed, bitter and strained. "Don't drag me into this, asshole. I didn't agree to any of this shit. I told you, you can't take someone without their consent. I told you to talk to her. I told you to seduce her, if you had to. I told you to ask."

"Where's the fun in that?" Micah asked mildly, but he was watching Luke like a hawk.

As if you could ask a woman who barely knew you and had left you once, *want to be in an indefinite four-way exclusive sexual relationship with us, even though all we can offer you is our cocks and our protection?*

She's going to hate us.

As if she could ever *not* hate them, once she found out what they'd done.

Shaking himself out of his navel-gazing bullshit, he addressed his literal partner in crime.

"How long will she be out for?"

Micah shrugged, stretching, his eyes still on Luke. "Who knows? If we're going to talk, we should go in the office. Unless you want Kara to know everything."

Conor wasn't ready for that. He wasn't sure if he would ever be. She couldn't know the truth; she would hate them more than she already did.

Maybe that would be better. What did it matter if she hated them? He hated her a little. She was the last reminder of who he used to be before she walked out the door, took his heart with her, and left him to nothing but his friends and his job and that final, horrible mission that took his soul.

Two young, orphaned boys staring at them with wide blue eyes.

What did you do to daddy and mommy?

"Boss." Micah's voice was edged with concern.

Conor shut his eyes, forcing his mind away from the memory, focusing on the bee balm smell of Kara's hair, the feeling of her in his arms, the way she sighed in her sleep as he lowered her onto the bed and Micah gently tucked a blanket around her.

"Come on, let's go in the den," Micah murmured to him and Luke.

But Luke stared, distracted. "So fucking gorgeous, it makes my chest hurt, you know?"

"And just imagine, you could've gone the rest of your life without seeing her again, if it weren't for us," Conor said dryly.

Catching himself, Luke averted his gaze from the sleeping siren.

"Luke—" Conor started, but stopped. He had no idea what to say. But he didn't want to be at odds with one of his best friends. He was sick of the conflict between them, sick of the fighting. The awkward silences.

Luke shrugged, the big man's usual fluid movements jerky. "I don't know who you are anymore."

"The other room," Micah repeated, walking to the door. Luke followed.

Conor took a moment, watching as Kara breathed easily in her sleep, feeling...feeling content, fucking *content*, for the first time in almost two years. He had everything he wanted, right here in this bed, and no one was taking it from him.

Not even Luke.

He followed them—his brothers, his partners, his friends, his... yeah, lovers, what-the-fuck-ever—out of the room, keeping an eye on the man in question, ready to jump him if he tried to pull a fast one, grab Kara, and make a run for it. Kara couldn't get out of the house on her own—the security system was set up to only recognize himself, Micah, and Luke as viable entrants and exiters—but Luke could get her out of here.

He wouldn't though. Conor wouldn't let him, and neither would Micah. Conor had the usual uncomfortable sensation that even though he was "the boss," Micah was, once again, secretly running the show, but he shrugged it off. As long as Micah wanted what Conor wanted—which was Kara, here, with them, for whatever the fuck they demanded from her, whenever they demanded it—it didn't matter if he was topping from the bottom. Micah was what Luke affectionately called a *chaotic switch*, and the shorter man used his chaos—and his muscles—to get away with the shit he wanted to get away with.

Conor shook his head like he had a bad case of swimmer's ear. He was ruminating, and he didn't usually ruminate. He followed Micah and Luke into the den and sank onto the large, leather couch next to Micah. He found at least a little amusement when Luke didn't sit in the chair across from them but instead closed the door and leaned against it, using his height to ostensibly gain control.

"Nice power play," he acknowledged.

Luke ignored him.

"I must be losing my mind. Two weeks ago, we were in this exact room, when both of you *promised* me you wouldn't kidnap this woman. I thought we agreed we'd leave her alone to live her life, instead of fucking stealing her from it. Tell me this isn't happening. Tell me I imagined her, *naked*, in the bedroom down the hall."

"Can't," Micah said with a sigh. "Because imagining her

naked body is nothing like seeing the real thing again up close."

Luke abandoned leaning against the door, rising to his full height, muscles prominent, face red.

"Don't make me punch you in the throat," he warned.

This fucking jackass. Like he got to decide what was right for Kara. Like she was Luke's, and Luke's alone.

When she'd been Conor's first, and never should've been Luke's at all.

"And *I* thought," Conor said, teeth gritted and fists fisted so he didn't rise to his feet and throw the first punch, "that you knew better than to get involved with the woman I wanted, and yet there you were, mere months after I fucked her, fucking her yourself—while I was off on a mission."

"Jesus fuck," Luke said. "Are we really still fighting about this? Micah was keeping an eye on her to make sure she was safe, but he couldn't get the job done so I subbed in. And yeah, I should've kept my hands off her, but she *needed* me."

Needed. So proud of himself because he'd had Kara for a month instead of the two-day fling she'd given Conor. "If she 'needed' you, why did she leave you?"

"She left you too, asshole."

Micah interrupted. "As the man who left *her*, I should have a say in this. Luke, we took her for her own good."

"Bullshit," Luke said.

"She's drowning in Chicago," Micah added.

"That lie going to help you sleep at night?" Luke asked.

"She's miserable. Lonely. Going to do something reckless soon."

"More reckless than kidnapping a woman who hopped on your dick once?"

Micah pounded his fist against his hand. Conor smiled

to himself; regardless of his chaos mode, Micah was the eye of his own storm. Not today, though.

"You don't know her as well as you think you do, Luke."

This stopped Luke in his tracks.

Micah continued. "I'm the hacker, remember? I'm the one who knows what she really wants and needs. And she needs us. Now, that us can just be me and Conor, or that us can include you."

"Not if I take her home," Luke threatened.

"And what, then you get to be her hero? You think that's what's going to win you the girl?" Micah full-on snapped.

"More than kidnapping her to some cabin in the Tetons and not letting her leave. How'd you get her here, anyway?"

"The cabin we built for her, remember?" Conor interjected.

Both men ignored him.

"Marcus's private plane," Micah said lightly. "He owed me a favor."

Enough of this shit.

"Three things," Conor interrupted, using his quiet, don't fuck around voice, the one that had made him "the boss" in the first place. Both men stopped, turning to look at him.

"One. We're not trying to win the girl. We have other plans for her."

Plans that included her screaming his name, begging for his cock, and realizing she didn't get to have the rest of him —not anymore.

Because there was no rest of him.

"Two. No one is her hero. We're her villains. Even you, Luke."

A fact that killed Conor a little bit more every day, especially when he thought of those two orphaned boys, and the knowledge that he had orphaned them.

"Three. You *owe* me. Both of you. Micah got on board, you haven't. This is how you make it up to me."

Luke shook his head. "You've got to let that shit go, man."

Conor shook his head, too. Just once. Because both of them owed him. Both of them had gone after the one thing he wanted, while he was living a nightmare.

Micah cleared his throat. "Fourth thing, if I may."

Conor had no idea what Micah was going to say, but he never did. After a moment, he nodded.

Micah spoke. "You're either part of this team, or you aren't, Luke. You either get to have her with us, or you don't. It's your choice, in or out. But as a man who used to pride himself on never lying, can you really say you don't want Kara badly enough to keep her?"

Luke grunted but didn't say anything.

"You agree to this now, Boy Scout, that's it. No second thoughts."

"Of course I fucking have second thoughts," Luke said. "Don't pretend for a second this isn't wrong."

"You're drawing the line now?" Conor asked, incredulous. "What haven't we done that society views as wrong? What's one more thing?"

Luke nodded. "There's one line I won't cross," he warned.

Micah shrugged. "She'll come to us. She won't be able to resist."

Once again, Conor imagined Kara, naked in the other room. Except this time she was covered in sweat, writhing against the ropes that tied her to the bed, begging for him to fuck her.

That one image, and look, his cock was hard. And the nightmares from the past faded.

"Agreed?" he asked Luke.

"Agreed," the taller man growled.

It went quiet again, each of them lost to their own thoughts.

"Alright, we should get some sleep," Micah said. "Long day today, longer days ahead."

Conor imagined Kara asleep in the next room, but the idea of holding her made his chest go tight in a way he hated. He wouldn't hold her. She would never have that power over him again. She was his now, but in ways he could manage.

Theirs, he reminded himself harshly.

Better that way. Maybe Luke, the fuck, could give her what she needed, and Conor only had to force the helpless envy away—before it swallowed him.

We're not trying to win the girl. We have other plans for her.

Kara tiptoed quickly back to the bedroom. She'd heard enough.

She'd woken to find herself alone, the bedroom door unlocked. Wary of her supposed luck, she'd started to make her way down the stairs, but stopped at the sound of raised voices down the hall. Escape may have seemed smarter than eavesdropping, but Kara was certain that she wasn't going to be able to leave the "cabin" that easily. She didn't even know where the cabin was. She desperately needed to do recon.

She didn't like what she'd learned. She still had no idea what Conor's other plans were for her, but these three men clearly—somehow—all knew each other. In fact, both

Micah and Luke had been plants when she'd met them, and that knowledge stung.

So did the realization that Micah had been watching her, that he thought she was "drowning." Kara lived a good life, and loneliness didn't equal misery. She had Lola and a home of her own, a job she was good at. She was getting a basset hound. Who could be lonely with a basset hound? So fuck Micah. Fuck the lot of them.

Except she wouldn't be fucking them. Micah might think she wouldn't be able to resist and would come to them for sex, but he was in for a harsh surprise. She didn't need them, either.

What she needed was to escape.

And Luke was her way out.

Even though he'd agreed to keep her here, he was the weak link of the three, and Kara would use that to her advantage, pick at him, manipulate him if she had to, wedge at that gap between him and Conor until it was too wide for them to bridge and she could escape this nightmare.

She still had so many questions, like how these fuckers knew each other, and of course, what their plans were for her, and what mission had gone so terribly wrong, why they were so convinced they were already bad enough that kidnapping her was nothing compared to what they'd already done. Conor was a killer, she knew that, but she'd always believed that he saw himself as a hero.

Something had happened. Something bad enough for Micah to now have a tattoo when he'd once wanted to be buried in a Jewish cemetery; enough for Luke to be lying, at least to himself. Something to have completely changed Conor.

She swallowed, some weak, emotional part of her

wanting to go to him and soothe him, soothe them all, use her body and her words to make whatever it was okay for them.

We have other plans for her.

So a bad idea, all around.

Hearing the door open down the hall, she hurried her pace, slipping back into the bedroom and arranging herself on the bed, closing her eyes just in time for the door to open.

"She's still asleep," Conor noted.

"Of course she is," Luke said, voice wry. "She had a whole panic attack and then you made her swallow a pill that knocked her the fuck out."

Apparently the two were getting along. For now. She'd change that.

Someone yawned. She heard footsteps as they approached the bed.

"I'm ready to crash," Micah said.

A zipper, then clothes landed on the floor. The bed dipped, shifting. Heat radiated as a warm, hairy chest, so broad it had to be Micah's, moved in behind her, his thick arms rearranging her until he was spooned around her.

"Well, which of you is joining us?" he asked.

Kara kept her eyes shut, willing herself not to speak.

Finally, Conor said gruffly, "Should be Luke. I'll go sleep in my own bed."

Her stomach dropped at his words, and she was instantly angry at herself. How could she feel rejected when she shouldn't want him to touch her or want her?

Micah coughed. "How about it, Luke? You always say you miss holding Kara as much as you miss fucking her. Or does cuddling cross the line for you?"

Silence. Kara waited to see what Luke would do. She heard a pair of shoes being toed off before the bed dipped on her other side. His simple, comforting smell of fresh laundry detergent and some mild spice soothed her, and she felt herself melt into the mattress. He lay there stiffly, space in between them, before he finally sighed and she felt herself being lifted and rearranged until her head lay on his clothed chest.

As she adjusted to the feeling of familiarity, and also the alien sensation of two men she'd dreamed of holding her close while a third watched, Micah dropped a kiss on her shoulder, then inhaled.

"God, I missed this fucking shampoo," he said. "Come on Conor, I know you did too."

"I'm going to bed," the man in question said, voice cracking.

He wasn't so unaffected after all, Kara thought with some satisfaction, then instantly berated herself.

Enemies, she reminded herself. She couldn't forget that.

But it was hard to believe when she felt so safe and cared for, wrapped in between the two men.

The door opened and shut as Conor left. The room went quiet, and Kara listened as their breathing evened out, the light snoring on her right as Luke's chest moved—he'd always been a snorer.

She didn't sleep, not at first. Instead, she shifted closer to Luke and away from Micah, hoping that her choice would aid her plans.

And as she plotted, thinking of ways to escape and then dismissing them as either too outlandish or too impossible, she tried to ignore how good this felt, how if it had been her choice, she might have embraced it with open arms.

I didn't choose this, she told herself. *I choose to leave.*

I choose me.

The words echoed in her head, a lullaby, a security blanket.

A buffer from this pretend dream.

But when she finally slept, she dreamed of them.

6

———

The next time Kara opened her eyes, it was day.
Midmorning light streamed in through bay
windows, sending knives through her brain.

Even though they'd made her drink water last night, she
was still dehydrated from the GHB and foggy from the
Ativan. Her head pounded, her throat was dry, and her neck
and back ached—not unsurprising, given that she'd been
wrapped in Micah's and Luke's arms all night.

Her brain slowly came back online. No one was in the
room with her. Which made it the perfect time to explore
the cabin, see if she could figure out where she was, and get
a sense of what their security system was.

First step was to find clothes. Being naked when they
were clothed put her at a distinct disadvantage, one she was
desperate to rectify. Immediately.

Not to mention it put sex in their heads. She may not
know what they wanted long term, but based on the men's
argument the night before, sex was part of it. They still
wanted her.

You want them, too, that one part of her brain whispered. She'd managed to silence it for so long—almost a year, in fact—but here it was again, the bitch.

Didn't matter. She was getting the fuck out of this rape-y, kidnappy popsicle stand and moving somewhere else, maybe another country, so she'd never have to see these assholes again.

Which meant keeping her mind on task.

Climbing off the bed, she searched around for something to wear. There was nothing of hers, of course, but there was clothing that she'd never actually wear: lacy nightgowns in multiple colors, some lingerie thing that just looked like a ton of straps you wound around your body in some confusing way, and a robe that was practically transparent, it was so sheer. She *did* find a pair of slippers in the closet, which would've been a sweet touch in any other situation.

After rifling through a few drawers, she landed on a navy blue SEALS t-shirt that dwarfed her body and ended at mid-thigh. She considered a few pairs of men's sweatpants, but two pairs were two tight in the hips, and even the loosest pair dragged at the feet.

Goldilocks, she wasn't.

Chuckling at the absurdity of her situation—it was that or scream, and she didn't want anyone to come running—she accepted that she would only be wearing a t-shirt for now. It was probably Micah's since it was loose in the chest and short around her thighs, which made her abdomen wind tight with remembered longing. She shoved the feeling away. It was the ghost of Christmas past, when she and Micah had spent the night together.

She slipped into the adjoining bathroom and peeked

inside, hoping she'd find some sort of weapon. Luke had taught her how to shoot a gun when they'd been together. They'd spent countless hours at the shooting range until it became second nature. It would be really fucking lucky if one of them was stupid enough to leave one like, sitting next to the toilet or something.

Of course, there was no gun to be found. Still, Kara gasped at what she saw. The bathroom was the stuff out of a Pinterest dream: Concrete countertops, copper fixtures, dark wood walls with a living plant wall, and a huge, white soaking tub in front of a window that overlooked the forest. Her stomach twisted in confusion. Why did this bathroom match her ideal master bath? How long had these assholes been planning this? Was this part of the torture? *A life you could've had with us, but instead we'll dangle it in front of you before we do something even more evil like lock you up in some freezing basement dungeon cave and make you shit in a bucket.*

To make matters worse, all of her favorite toiletries were there, including supersized bottles of her shampoo and conditioner. Kara hadn't even known the expensive brand came in such large sizes.

Where did they get the money for all of this? And for that matter, how had they gotten her here, wherever here was?

Unwrapping a toothbrush from the plastic that covered it, she brushed and rinsed the post-drugged dry and sour taste from her mouth, before leaving the bedroom.

The hallway from last night greeted her. She passed the room she'd eavesdropped outside of yesterday. Ahead of her was a loft that looked out onto a great room and huge floor to ceiling windows, which in turn, looked out over a mountain range.

She knew those mountains. The sight of the Tetons made her chest ache—her favorite place in the world, and here they were in front of her. She'd dragged Lola with her here on multiple hiking trips, Lola complaining about how stupid being outdoors was each time.

Lola. Her friend must be terrified by now—they texted all day, every day. She missed her so much it was like a stab wound in her heart. When would she see her funny, acerbic, supportive friend again? Would she ever? She needed to go back to Chicago—to go home.

But if she dwelled on that now she'd descend down another panic spiral, so she focused on the view in front of her and what it must mean. It was too much of a coincidence that the house she was captive in had the only view in the world that usually settled her soul.

Luke had known how she felt about them. He must have told the others.

Had they gotten this house for her? There was no way, right? And if they did, didn't that mean Luke had been a part of the planning initially?

Why hadn't they just *asked* her to come?

What did they have planned for her?

She needed to find out, and she'd have to eavesdrop or manipulate—likely both.

Fortunately, she was good at both.

She heard voices downstairs somewhere, the faint sound of male laughter and a thump, like a body hitting a mat. It shook her from her thoughts and she continued down the stairs. If she was going to figure out their security system, now was the time.

It didn't take her long. The entrance to the "cabin" (try a fucking chalet) was like some combination of Fort Knox and the Louvre. In the bright morning light, Kara could barely make out red laser lines sweeping the floor, walls, and ceiling. If she went near them, she'd trip the alarm system, and it wasn't like there was a code. It was a fucking retinal scan.

Where did they get the money for this shit? And why were they guarding her like some precious painting? She was no Mona Lisa, just a formerly reckless, troublemaking homewrecker with a lot of latent guilt and a constant hum of longing for the open road.

She continued exploring. Maybe there was a mudroom. Maybe the kitchen had a backdoor. Maybe she could just go back upstairs, open the window, and jump two stories and pray she made it. Maybe—

She was smarter than this. Desperation and fear were making her stupid and reckless. And even though she had once been reckless, Kara wasn't stupid.

She forced herself to take deep breaths before the panic took over again, because having a panic attack would be useless, even if Luke could talk her down from it. She wasn't about to take more Ativan.

Luke. *God.* She tried not to think about that day, when he climbed up the wall at her climbing gym like fucking Spider Man and rescued her from passing out. He'd seemed so *decent* then. What the hell had happened to him?

What had happened to all of them?

Luke was the weak link. He certainly wasn't the sexually sadistic mensch she'd once thought—if he were, he would've gotten her out of here last night instead of giving in. But she could play on that guilt she'd heard in his voice.

That was her in. She needed to work it, work *him*, until she broke the link and could escape. As long as she didn't let her emotions take the wheel, she could do this. She had to be smart, and clever. *Smart girl, clever girl*, she could hear Conor saying in her head.

Yeah? Well, fuck Conor. Fuck the way he thought he could control her with his deep, crooning voice and the ever-changing nicknames that implied he knew everything about her, even the dark and scary parts, and he liked all of them. Fuck all three of them. She wasn't going to let them overpower her, physically or otherwise. She just needed a plan.

Her stomach grumbled at her. For now, she needed to eat so she had enough energy to keep hunting for the truth.

Kara sighed. *Stupid human body.* Time to locate the kitchen.

It was down the hallway, past a bathroom and a locked door. When she entered the kitchen, she stopped still. Concrete countertops that matched the bathroom, black appliances, more copper fixtures, beams every-fucking-where... it was like they'd reached inside her heart and plucked out the design for Kara's dream kitchen, just like they had with the bathroom. She reminded herself that Micah was a hacker, that it would've been easy for him to log into her private Houzz and Pinterest accounts and see what she'd favorited. Kara ran her hands over the textured countertop, cool to the touch, before ripping them away. This was what the men wanted. It didn't matter that they'd built her a dream house in a dream location. They were trying to fuck with her head. A gilded cage was still a cage, even if it came with an eight-burner Viking stove.

Don't fall for this bananas shitbag.

She wiped an errant tear from her eye. How many times

had she and Lola perused home improvement stores while Kara loudly and emphatically denied she wanted a home— a real one—to call her own?

Stop that.

There was a plate on the island covered with a lid. A post-it sat to its left, a slim vase with one single peach strawflower to its right. Kara remembered the tulips the veterinarian had given her on their date. It was always roses or tulips, and no one had once bothered to ask her if she even liked them.

Except Micah.

I bet you're the strawflower sort of girl, he'd told her the night they'd met.

Yeah? Why do you think that? Most men don't even know what a strawflower is.

He'd ignored that. *Lucky guess. On the surface, you come off prickly and apathetic, like no one and nothing matters to you. But in the center, you're soft and loving. Want to prove me wrong?*

Kara tried to shake off the memory. It didn't matter that Micah had said the right thing, he'd probably seen her post something about strawflowers on her Instagram, for all she knew. He'd played her then, so maybe they were playing her now. What for, she had no idea, but the tightness in her throat told her she didn't *want* to find out.

She lifted the lid—poached eggs, toast, and a few slices of avocado. Also her favorite. The eggs were still warm. She began to eat, reading the post-it.

I promised you breakfast. — M

Kara spat out the eggs.

Forget escape.

She was going to kill him.

Sitting on the weight bench on one side of the gym, Micah relaxed, watching as his friends beat the shit out of each other and trying not to smile.

It was fairly commonplace, Conor and Luke so pissed they were ready to tear each other's throats out. The two men would catch a bullet for each other, but they were both hotheaded jackasses who were constantly battling for the spot of top dog in their little trio. When you shoved two dominant fuckers in a room together, they were inevitably going to butt heads and horns over everything. Throw a girl they were both obsessed with in the mix, a difference of opinion over how to handle her, and blood would inevitably spill.

They probably would've killed each other by now—if it weren't for Micah.

Micah didn't kid himself. He was as dominant as his friends. The difference was that the lessons they'd learned in the military had actually stuck with him. He knew that cooler heads always prevailed, and if he didn't keep a cool head their trio would have fallen apart by now.

And now that they were a foursome? Even more important he stay on top of his game. Or they *would* kill each other and that would leave Kara and Micah on their own. And while he wasn't above threatening the other two men with that potential future, it wasn't one he wanted. Micah knew on a gut level this only worked if it was all four of them. They were all parts of a whole, and Kara was going to be the glue that held them together.

Whether she liked it or not.

"You fucking motherfucker," Luke growled, drawing

Micah's attention back to the mats. Luke was bleeding, a cut on his lip and a swollen eye.

Conor punched him again, this time in the gut. Luke retaliated with an uppercut to the face. Conor grunted, cheek cut open.

Micah straightened. He really should be watching the video on his phone to keep track of Kara. He'd already been alerted by the alarm when someone reached the bottom of the stairs. He wanted to watch her, but Luke and Conor were at a new level of rage; they might really damage each other this time.

"Stop, you jackasses," he said lightly. Both were grunting too hard to hear him.

"Fucking stop for a second," he shouted this time.

They both froze.

Better.

Micah knew he had power over them. He knew they didn't understand why, but didn't question it either. If Kara was the glue, Luke was the spokes, and Conor was the wheel, then Micah was the one steering.

He grimaced. Shitty mixed metaphor. He was off his game. Funny how a curvy little redhead with big angry eyes could do that to him.

"What," Luke spit.

"Let's make this more interesting, huh?" Micah said, careful to take control of this situation again. "Less like you want to murder each other, more like you're trying to win."

"And what's the prize?" Conor asked, interested but obviously wary. Conor knew Micah's games, but he let them slide—for now. "If you say it's Kara's sweet pussy, I'm going to have it around my cock soon anyway."

"Not without her consent, you fucking won't," Luke said, punching Conor again.

Before they could start up again, Micah said. "He's right. We need to wait. Patience is a virtue we could all work on."

Or something like that.

Conor scowled—he'd gone to a dark place in his head and Micah knew even though his friend wouldn't actually fuck her without consent, he'd slipped down the slope and could easily convince himself she wanted it. And he wasn't wrong. Kara wanted it—but not *yet*. If they were a little patient, she'd play right into and under their hands, which was where they wanted her.

"Why do you think we're about to kill each other?" Luke commented, sounding like he found the whole thing funny, even though that couldn't be further from the truth.

Micah didn't even touch that. "First one to hit the ground and stay there blows the other. Neither of your cocks have had much play for a while other than your hands, why not take the prize?"

"Or I could shove my cock up your ass," Conor suggested. Micah hardened—that didn't sound bad, especially when he topped from the bottom. But he ignored his cock for now.

Luke laughed, a real laugh, something Micah hadn't heard in a long time. In fact, the reluctant kidnapper seemed lighter than he had since they'd been dishonorably discharged from the SEALs.

"Micah wants that, anyway, don't you, Tech Geek," he said, using the military nickname Micah also hadn't heard in a while, making Micah feel lighter as well.

His plan was working.

"Nah, today I want to watch." Making sure both men's eyes were on him, he unzipped his pants and pulled his hardening cock out, slowly stroking.

Conor swallowed, throat moving. Good prep since he'd likely be swallowing Luke's long-ass dick in a second.

"Alright?" Micah prompted.

Luke's eyes had glazed over. "Alright."

For Conor's part, he swung at Luke again, and then they were down on the mats, wrestling with each other. The tone of the fighting had already changed from tearing each other apart to tearing each other's shorts off. Micah kept an eye on them; ready to intercede if things went too far. It wasn't that he was against watching some ass play, but it was too soon for what he had planned.

He glanced down again at his phone. Kara was in the kitchen now, stroking her fingers lightly over the strawflower he'd ordered for her off a website under an alias. It had been a pain in the ass, but seeing her now made it worth it. Even though buying flowers was more Luke's gig, softening her up, *caring* for her, was his role, too—and Conor's, not that that fucker would ever admit it. She looked stricken about something, before she squared her shoulders and started eating her breakfast.

The breakfast *he* had made her. She was eating the breakfast he had made her, standing in *his* t-shirt. Possessiveness and satisfaction roared through him. They were so close. So close to what they wanted and she needed. All the puzzle pieces were there, they just had to figure out how to fit them together.

See, what Luke and Conor were struggling with wasn't actually To Kidnap Or Not To Kidnap. It was this whole sharing thing. Micah was just as possessive, but unlike them, he didn't feel territorial. She could be his, privately, and theirs, collectively. *Both and*, not *either or*. But he had a fight ahead of him.

Speaking of fights. Conor was straddling Luke's chest on the mat.

"Maybe I'll make you suck me off like this, fuck-ass," Conor growled. "I can tea bag you while I'm at it."

"I'm going to fuck *your* ass," Luke rasped from underneath him, then shoved his elbow into Conor's neck, knocking the stronger man off him. The two grappled for a bit, but this time, Luke ended up on top, twisting Conor's arm.

Conor probably could've flipped him over. They were evenly matched. So it was interesting—although not unsurprising—when he slapped his hand on the mat instead.

Looked like someone else wanted a little more peace. Micah had called it right.

Luke climbed off him and helped Conor up. The two men kissed, and Micah worked his cock harder.

"Voyeuristic perv," Luke laughed, then grabbed Conor's head between his hands and went at his mouth. Shirts flew off, and Conor worked Luke's shorts off his hips before lowering himself to his knees and grabbing the taller man's cock in his hand. He gripped it tight—tighter than Kara would ever dare to—but the hint of pain made Luke's ass cheeks clench.

Luke groaned, pushing Conor's hand away. Conor resisted for a second, but then opened his mouth and let Luke shove his cock into the more dominant man's mouth. It was mostly quiet, the sounds of Luke's groans and growls and Conor's sucking echoing off the small gym as Luke went to town on his throat.

They didn't usually talk when they were fucking—while they'd shit talk each other, dirty talk was only something they'd done with Kara. They'd discussed it, once Conor had gotten past the betrayal. It was something about how her whole body blushed and her eyes dilated, and yet at the same time she looked ready to beat you up for forcing her to acknowledge what she wanted. She'd get so fucking wet, goddamned nasty wet, and—

A gasp came from the doorway. Micah turned his head to catch Kara's hooded eyes. Her little nipples were hard under the t-shirt—his t-shirt. It was one thing to know she was wearing his shirt, another to see it in person. It set off some caveman provider piece of him. He fucking loved seeing her in his clothes.

Even though he wanted to go over to her, order her to her knees, and gently work his own cock down her throat, he resisted.

All in good time.

"See something you like, baby?" he asked as he moved his hand over his dick. Her eyes were dark with desire, even though she'd deny it. Just looking at her, hearing the sound of Conor sucking Luke, was enough to make him almost come.

Gripping his shaft tight to calm himself, Micah watched the woman he'd worked so hard to get to this exact place. She clearly didn't know where to look. She stared at Micah's hand, only to move her gaze to Conor and Luke, as Conor's lips moved around the base of Luke's dick, his hands gripping Luke's ass cheeks. Even though Conor was on his knees, he'd taken back the power.

Until Luke caught Kara's eyes and thrust even harder, making Conor choke in surprise. Conor recovered quickly, but made a whole show of it for the woman watching them.

"Jealous, sweetheart? If you get on your knees and crawl over here like a good girl, I promise I'll let you have a ta— what the fuck, asshole? Why the hell did you bite me?" Luke yelped. Conor pulled his mouth off Luke's dick.

"She's *my* good girl, you bastard," he growled. Before Luke could argue, he worked the redhead's cock with his hand, twisting his head to watch Kara.

It was probably wishful thinking, but Micah swore he could smell her wet cunt. She was aroused by this.

Conor grinned wickedly. "But you are *my* good girl, aren't you? You're our jealous girl? If you behave, I'll put my mouth on you next."

Kara's voice was low and throaty, an intentional siren song.

"Fucking touch me, I dare you."

Interesting.

"Dare us?" Micah asked, rising to his feet, aware his cock was jutting out at her. She'd had trouble taking his cock that night he'd fucked her in New Orleans, but she'd wanted it so badly he'd made her anyway, and she'd come so hard she'd nearly passed out, so malleable in his arms, Micah hadn't wanted to let her go.

Kara took a step back before stopping and holding her ground.

"Luke gets his cock anywhere near my face, and I'll be the one to bite it this time," she threatened.

Micah smiled. He'd been a little worried that kidnapping her would fuck with her spirit, but she was spitting mad, completely herself. Based on the look in her eyes, he was glad they'd locked up all the kitchen knives the night before.

"Don't threaten him with a good time," Micah said, watching as her chest and face flushed. Fucking redheads. Gorgeous when they blushed, and none more gorgeous than the one who looked like she was halfway to orgasm, and might stab him anyway.

"Sweetheart, you know I like it when you use your little

teeth on my cock," Luke said. The man's sadism went both ways. "But if you bite me, I'll punish your ass for it."

She swallowed, eyes glazed, and this time Micah *could* smell how turned on she was. So did Conor and Luke.

"You're so wet right now, aren't you, dirty girl," Conor said. "I bet if I came over there and forced your legs apart, we'd find out you're dripping down your thighs."

She squirmed. Luke laughed.

"Poor sweet thing. That pussy is so turned on it hurts, doesn't it? It's okay sweetheart, if you ask nicely, we'll make it all better," Luke groaned as he redirected Conor's mouth around his cock, and Conor complied. Luke continued crooning at her. "Just say: 'Please will you make me come?' That's all you need to do."

Kara's mouth opened, her throat worked.

"Oh baby, you're so busy battling yourself when you could just let go," Micah murmured, walking over to her until he was so close she could've reached out and grabbed his cock.

She shocked the hell out of him when she did, gripping him tight.

Leaning over, she murmured, "I could get you off with my hand, *baby*." She worked him. Fuck, he was so close.

Right before he could come, she released him.

"Or I can leave you high and dry, just like you left me back in New Orleans," she tossed over her shoulder as she swayed out of the room.

Micah felt his chest tighten. Even though she sounded cavalier, there was anger and hurt in there, buried deep. He wanted to take her in his arms and tell her he'd never meant to hurt her, that he hadn't wanted to leave. He'd thought back on that night so many times with regret, dreamed about a life where he had stayed instead of sneaking out while she slept. He'd done it for Conor, and because, at the time, he'd been a stupid, shortsighted man and hadn't realize how much she'd come to matter to him, to all of them. He'd learned his lesson and he was fixing it now. What more could she want?

Probably her freedom, he thought dryly. Oh well.

"Kara," he said, voice soft. Despite herself, she turned.

"What, going to try to manipulate me again?" she taunted.

Micah paused, swallowing his apology. They weren't ready for a big, emotional moment; Kara wouldn't accept sorry from him yet. Instead, he slipped his hand back over his cock and tugged it once, twice.

"You can play your games, but you know we'll win. And you know why?"

She hummed a rejection, but her eyes were on his moving hand.

"Because you want us to win, baby girl," he said.

She licked those berry-red lips unconsciously, and that was all he needed. He blew, knowing she was watching him, and knowing she wanted him, and knowing she'd have what she wanted soon—and so would they.

He heard a groan behind him—Luke had also come in Conor's mouth. Micah didn't have to look to know Luke's eyes were on Kara as she began to back out of the room.

Conor wiped his mouth. He was as hard as a rock.

"Your turn," he told Micah. "Time to take one for the team."

Micah sighed. "I am nothing if not a team player," he said making his way over to Conor, knowing it was going to hurt, and relishing the potential pain—especially with Kara's brown-gold, lust-filled eyes on him. It was going to feel that much sweeter now, knowing how turned on she was by this, the little voyeur.

"You don't want to miss the show," he told her.

In response, she lifted her middle finger and turned, leaving the room.

"Let the games begin," he murmured.

"Think they already have," Luke said.

7

K ara could hear laughter and grunts as she made her way down the hall, dropping the exaggerated sway of her hips to stomp in irritation.

They were probably still laughing as she stomped her way past the kitchen. Probably still fucking, too.

Laughing while fucking—Luke's specialty.

She hated them.

She *hated* them.

Starting with Micah. How dare that fucking asshole leave her the way he did back in New Orleans, then bring it up like it was nothing after *kidnapping her*, and then, and then, and then—

Motherfucker. She was pacing and muttering to herself. He'd really done a number on her. She stopped, forced herself to take a deep breath.

That breath did nothing to calm her down. Neither did the next or the next.

Damn it! She held back a scream. She did *not* want them to hear her and investigate. Instead, she distracted herself by picturing the look on Micah's face. Leaving him wanting had been satisfying. Sure, he'd gotten the last word, but she'd get the last laugh when *he* woke up one morning to find *her* gone.

She just wanted to go home.

But how? The house was locked up tight. She wasn't getting out of here on her own. She needed help. No, what she needed was intel.

Yet here she was, like an idiot, walking away from where the intel was instead of using her eavesdropping skills to gather more information. So she crept back toward the weight room, careful not to make a sound.

Pressing her ear to the wall, and careful to keep out of sight, she focused on what they were saying.

"...talk about this before you fuck me," Micah was saying.

"There's nothing to talk about," Conor replied. "Now bend over."

"The boss has spoken," Luke said, sardonically.

"So have I," Micah said, and Kara imagined him gritting his teeth. "The two of you are letting her get between you. Conor, the last time you had sex with Kara, she turned you upside down. Luke, you were so wrapped up in her, you lied —and you never lie."

"Isn't that why she's here, Tech Geek?" Luke asked. "Because she turned our lives upside down?"

"Yes," Micah acquiesced. "But you—we all—need to be aware of that. Don't forget your nickname for her—"

"—kryptonite pussy," Luke muttered, so low Kara had to strain to hear him.

Kryptonite pussy? She couldn't decide if she was proud or offended.

"—Right. The two of you are hanging on by a thread. Don't let her figure it out and use her powers against you both, or this whole plan will fall apart. Speaking of..." fabric rustled. "We're going to have to fuck later. It's almost lunch time and I need to make sure she eats something."

"You're going to leave me like this?" Conor complained.

"You have two hands, and you have Luke. Our girl needs sustenance. And not of the cock variety—yet."

She could hear them kissing, a quiet, tender murmur.

Kara stepped away from the wall, hurrying quietly down the hallway. If they knew she'd been eavesdropping, she couldn't use what she'd learned to her advantage. Instead, she was going to have to rush to the kitchen and then play dumb for long enough that she didn't set off Micah's—she now realized—carefully calibrated bullshit meter.

Kara made it to the kitchen and dropped onto a stool, just as Micah strolled in.

"You didn't eat the breakfast I left for you," he tsked.

"How do I know you didn't poison it?" she countered.

"Now, why would you think I'd poison your food, baby?" he taunted. "Don't you trust me?"

She really, really hated him.

"Why would you ask a question you know the answer to?"

This made him laugh, a deep, musical laugh that stirred up her insides and made her chest go tight. She forced herself to breathe—he didn't get to affect her. Not anymore. Especially not now, when he had her trapped and under his control.

Don't let her use her powers against you, or this whole plan will fall apart.

He'd been speaking to Luke and Conor, but what if he meant it for himself, too?

Kara was distracted from that train of thought by Micah rooting around in the huge refrigerator.

"I unfortunately don't have any oysters for you, but how do you feel about a tuna melt?"

"What, have you been going through my trash?" she asked him.

He turned, wrinkling his nose and looking annoyingly endearing. "No, through your food delivery receipts."

"I'm not eating anything you serve me."

"Kara," he said patiently. "You can't cook for shit. You told me the story about how you tried to make rocky mountain eggs once and almost burned your apartment down. You may not trust me not to poison you, but I don't trust you not to set the kitchen on fire."

"Maybe I want to set the kitchen on fire," she tossed out.

"Oh, baby, we got you all riled up earlier, didn't we?" he crooned, pulling out bread, an onion, and sliced cheese and placing them on the island before sauntering toward her. When he reached her, he spoke in her ear, causing tingles to race over her neck. "If you want, I can feed you, and then you can be my meal."

Enraged by the effect he had on her, she headbutted him, satisfied when he groaned, taking a step back and rubbing at his jaw.

"Fuck," he said. "When did you get so feisty?"

"I've always been feisty."

"Here." He untwisted the bread bag, taking small bites out of two slices of bread, then doing the same thing with the cheese. Confused, Kara watched him stalk over to one of the cabinets and pull out a can of tuna, which he showed to her.

"See? Sealed shut. I took bites of your sandwich, and I'm fine."

No, he wasn't. He was pissed—she'd managed to piss him off. Kara's blood sang with glee, with relief. Her hunch had been right, she *could* fuck with Micah as easily as he thought she could fuck with Conor and Luke.

"Okay, I believe you," she said quietly, not wanting to give her thoughts away. He just grunted and set about grilling the sandwich.

"If you're not going to kill me, why am I here? Just for your amusement?"

He ignored her, flipping the already-bitten sandwich so it browned on both sides, and sliding it onto a plate which he pushed over to her. He stared at her, jaw working, as she took her first bite—intentionally around where his teeth marks were.

His eyes flared at the obvious challenge. "You're here because you're ours."

And with that, he left the kitchen.

Once upstairs, her mind returned to her thoughts from last night and this morning. She'd gotten distracted by Micah's mindfuck of a note and the further mindfuck of seeing Luke thrusting hard into Conor's mouth, Micah's hand working over his cock.

She knew how that felt, intimately. Luke's cock was average thickness, but it was almost painfully long... it had taken her awhile to figure out how to work him, and he'd never been as rough with her as she'd just seen him with Conor.

Damn it, her nipples were hard again. She rubbed a hand over one gently before stopping herself.

Her mind drifted back to the scene in the weight room. The way Conor had worked his mouth over Luke... she recognized that, too. They'd only had two nights together, but Conor had spent a large portion of that time with his mouth attached to her pussy like a magnet.

She felt her insides clench at the thought; her clit was tender just from the memory.

And Micah? Micah's cock was *thick*. Where Luke was long, and Conor was just big all over, Micah's cock had been so thick it had almost hurt to take him.

But it had hurt so good. Hurt the way she liked it, and worse, the way they apparently knew she liked it.

"Fuck!" she screamed again, slapping a hand against the dresser in the bedroom so hard it stung. What was she doing here? She was supposed to be plotting her escape from her, *hello*, kidnapping, not traveling down the smutty path of past great fucks. She owed it to Lola to get home, to that future basset hound of hers, and to herself.

Kara started pacing again. There was a way out of here. She just needed access to the internet, for god's sake. She could send out an SOS tweet to the FBI or something, they'd be here banging down the door in an hour.

She scoffed, imagining sailing into wherever they kept their tech and logging onto one of their laptops and signing onto Twitter. Sure, that would go great. Maybe she could offer a blowjob or an enthusiastic fuck for some computer time.

Wait.

Kara paused.

She thought back to *before*—to Conor's temporary vulnerability after he came, to the way Micah had opened up to her and held her as they slept post-orgasm, and, maybe most importantly, to Luke's confession of love after a particularly wild fuck and the devastation on his face when she immediately ended things. Ignoring the brief, sharp guilty pang, she tried to unpack the thoughts swirling in her head.

Her original plan had been to get Luke alone and appeal to his clear guilt and need to be a hero, but she was missing an important factor: Even though they both tried to hide them, Micah and Conor also had emotions wrapped up in this. It was clear from the conversations she'd eavesdropped on and the way Micah had reacted to her headbutt earlier.

Kryptonite pussy. What if it was true?

Kara scoffed at herself. Fucking them seemed like some bullshit porn version of a plan to escape your kidnappers, and maybe it was just an excuse to get back into bed with them, but what would soften them up, trip them up, further weaken this complicated link between Luke and Conor so she could work on breaking it, more than sex? What other ideas did she have? She needed to spend time with them, to figure out why they did this in the first place, convince them she wasn't planning on leaving, and tease out a way to escape. She needed to get inside their heads and fuck shit up in there, and she knew how. Talking to them or lying and saying I love you or anything along those lines would send their admittedly well-tuned spidey senses tingling, but giving (and yes, probably receiving) some orgasms? That plan held weight.

It was the best she had. Micah's manipulations were a risk, but she couldn't do nothing.

She ignored the fear crawling in her chest, the voice that was saying, *you can't get naked with them and keep your heart out of it*. She'd managed the last time around with them, hadn't she? Dug deep for that well of protective coldness within her and used it to build a wall of ice around herself. She could do it again—especially because now they no longer were three smart, gorgeous men she'd met randomly, but her kidnappers and tormentors. They didn't give a shit about her, she wouldn't give a shit, either.

She'd had plenty of sex in her life without feelings.

She'd never had sex with anyone who had decided to ignore her choices, agency, and will, but there was a first time for everything, wasn't there?

Out the window, the Tetons stood, perfect and still in their brutal beauty. But even those mountains weathered and changed over time.

She could do this.

She *could.*

While she thought, her eyes traveled around the room. There was a little flashing red light in the corner above the bathroom door.

Cameras.

Of course they had set up cameras.

Micah might think they were in control of the game, that she wanted them to win.

Kara smiled. She'd let him think that.

This was her chance—to get back at them, to use sex to prove that she was the one with the power, not them.

Just call her Kryptonite Pussy.

Before she could talk herself out of it, she turned to face the camera and stripped out of Micah's shirt, crawling onto the bed. Circling her nipples, she winked at the camera and mouthed, *come get me.*

"Shit," Micah said, staring down at his phone.

Conor watched impatiently, one hand fisted around the bottle of lube. He still needed to come, badly. His balls were tight and his heart was beating rapidly, and even though he tried to tell himself it was just his body, just sexual need, he knew it was Kara. Her presence earlier took his already active sex drive and revved it so high it broke the sound barrier. And left him wanting more than just a fuck.

Damn it. Conor growled. Micah ignored him. *Asshole.* Micah had promised him a fuck, and even though it was partially for Kara's benefit, a promise was a promise, and he wasn't delivering.

Like other promises Micah hadn't delivered on. Like that one almost two years ago, when Micah had offered to keep an eye on Kara without touching her—and look how that had turned out.

Conor tamped down his territorial jealousy. It was water under the bridge; his lust and frustration were fucking with his head.

"What's wrong?" a sated Luke asked from the floor, where he'd been laying the whole time Micah was making Kara lunch. "Worried your ass is going to hurt when Conor reams it? Should I get first aid cream just in case?"

"She's getting naked," Micah said tightly.

Conor's already hard cock went rock stiff, to the point of pain. He held his hand out for the phone.

Micah slapped his hand away.

What the actual fuck. Conor felt a growl leave his throat. Who the hell was in charge here?

"Fuck, sorry." Micah rubbed his forehead, passing Conor the phone. "This is too soon. She's up to something."

"Of course she is," Luke said, sounding almost proud. "She's a fighter, she's going to use whatever tools she has. We don't have to do anything about it."

Conor growled again. "Why not?"

"It's not right," Luke said simply.

Bullshit. Nothing was right anymore, except feeling good. Getting balls deep back inside Kara would feel good.

Conor stared at the phone screen, mouth going dry, cock so hard, so heavy, it felt like it was going to split in two. Kara was giving a striptease in front of the camera. It was hard to tell from the size of the video, but he was 90% certain that she was smiling an I-Dare-You smile as she slowly revealed her perfect tits.

"Fuck," Conor said, and this time Luke grabbed the phone out of Conor's hand.

"Fuck," Luke repeated, voice low, his hand trembling as he watched whatever Kara was doing.

"What?" Conor asked.

"We shouldn't be watching this," Luke said, but he gave himself away when he couldn't tear his eyes from the phone.

Conor forced down his annoyance. Luke had to stop with this flip-flopping shit soon, or Conor was going to make him stop. How would the sadist like it if he were the one getting his ass whipped for once?

Guess their truce only lasted as long as it took Luke to come.

Still, Conor tried to appeal to him. Logically. Or as logically as a man could when his cock was hard enough to punch a hole through the space-time continuum.

"You said you were part of this. You have to be fully committed. And that means communicating about what she's doing, and actively participating," Conor said.

"Fine." Luke shook his head but handed the phone back. "Seems like *our* good girl was pretty turned on from our show, earlier. She's working it out with her hand now."

Conor and Micah both held their hands out for the phone. Luke passed it to Micah, who did something to it. Before Conor could pull rank—if she was masturbating, he was going to see it, damn it—the flatscreen in the gym turned on.

And there was Kara, in 4K, flat on her back on their bed, one hand playing with a nipple, the other flicking her clit. Her mouth was open and she was panting and Conor was immediately annoyed at himself that when Micah had suggested they mic the house, he nixed the idea. If he had been more farsighted, he could hear her pretty little sounds right now.

Fuck it, he could hear those sounds in person. He just needed to go up there.

As he started to stand, Micah reached out a hand and stopped him. "Let's be smart about this. Plan a little before we descend on her."

Fuck that. Conor had dreamed about watching her orgasm for eighteen long, horrible months. Here she was, practically in his reach, and he was going to what, watch it virtually?

"I'm always smart," he told Micah and started to leave the room.

Neither man followed him. Luke's eyes were still glued to the TV screen, and Micah was shaking his head.

"What the fuck?" Conor exploded—because some part of him needed to. His cock was so hard he thought he might die. "And don't give me that *it's wrong* shit again. She wants it. Look at her."

"Oh, I'm looking," Micah said. "But we don't want to fuck this up. Maybe some delayed gratification is what we need to get her to toe the line. I'm the one who left her, remember? Not the other way around. I know how Kara's brain works. Trust me, we should wait."

Conor bit back a curse. It was a cheap shot, but it still hit where it hurt. Because Kara had left him, and Micah had left her; maybe Micah was right.

Surprisingly, it was Luke who disagreed.

"If anyone knows her, it's me. I'm the one who was with her for a month. I'm the one who spent more than one night with her in my arms. You spent a few hours with her; the rest of the time, you were no better than a stalker."

Micah glared at the taller man.

Luke shrugged. "I'm not saying that her heart is tied to her pussy, and if you control one, you control the other. But Kara craves submission, for control to be taken from her. If we want to mess with her equilibrium, to get her to obey? We should use sex."

Conor didn't want Kara's heart. Maybe once, when he'd been a different man. He wasn't that man anymore. But her loyalty? He pictured her kneeling naked at his feet, opening her legs whenever he nodded his head at her, because obeying him mattered more than her damn pride.

Or freedom.

"The way I see it, we've got one shot to make this work— we better do it right," Micah argued.

Micah was talking like he wanted more than a mostly-willing plaything. Conor knew better. They'd never have her heart, why even try?

"We've got forever to make it work," Conor said. "She's here and she's not going anywhere. I'm done with this conversation, Micah. You want to top from the bottom, fine, but you're going to have to be in the room to make that happen."

With that, he left, hearing a *fuck* from Micah as Micah and Luke followed him out of the weight room.

8

S he was so close.

Kara had originally meant this as a taunt. Getting naked and getting her own hands all over her body should've been like waving a red flag in front of a trio of bulls. So what was taking them so long? Did they not care? Had she misread the whole situation?

The door burst open and three huge, bullish men filled the doorway, startling her into stopping her strokes and pausing her mere moments before her orgasm.

"What did I tell you?" Conor asked, his voice like silk, and all the more menacing for it. "Don't you dare come without our permission."

Anger and desire disrupted her planning.

"I'll come if I want to," she told him, or tried to, but her words ended on a moan as she got her fingers back to work on her clit. Seeing the three of them, so big and strong, watching her, got her so much closer to the edge. One more circle and she'd—

Smack.

The sound hit her first, the feeling after, radiating against her boob.

Her boob. One of these fucks had just spanked her. On the boob.

She looked up at Luke, whose grin was almost as scary as Conor's voice had been—if she let herself be afraid. A smarter woman would've been, given Conor's career, Micah's skillset, Luke's propensity toward sadism, and their collective ability to read her mind. But right now Kara wasn't feeling particularly smart, even though this had been part of her plan. She was enraged, made even worse by the orgasm hovering just out of reach.

"Naughty sweethearts get spanked," Luke tsked, the lust in his voice battling it out.

"Cocky jackasses get blue balls," she retorted, and he laughed with delight.

"Oh sweetheart, I missed that dirty mouth," he said.

"Baby," she heard Micah say, and felt the bed move as he crawled over her body, temporarily blocking her view of the other two men. "The only person with anything resembling blue balls right now is you."

Do not hit him. Do not. Stick to the plan.

"If you'd scoot down a little," she said sweetly, "you could help me with that problem. Want to be a team player, Micah?"

Smack. The sting came from her thigh, and, as Micah shifted, she saw that the fucker who had spanked her this time was Conor.

"Good girls say please," he chided.

"I'm not a good girl," she informed him, trying to calm her breathing. This wasn't going the way she'd planned. They were supposed to be trying to fuck her so she, in turn, could fuck with their heads. They weren't supposed to be standing over her, denying her control over her own orgasm and making her even wetter.

Making her *feel* things.

Being with the three of them was like sexual and emotional quicksand. The more you struggled, the worse it got. But the problem was that when you were submerged in quicksand, you forgot how it worked, you just wanted to escape.

Which is why Kara did what she did next.

Shoving an unprepared Micah off her, she rolled to the side and bolted off the bed and toward the door.

The door that swung closed on its own with a click.

Fuck.

"App operated," Micah said, reaching into his pocket and pulling his phone out. "All the doors in the house are, by the way."

"Bet whoever invented that app didn't think it would get used for something like this," Luke said.

"I invented the app," Micah pointed out.

Kara backed toward the closed door, tried the knob, but she knew already.

Locked.

The three men stared at her, Luke amused, Conor impassive, Micah calculating. Kara stared back, letting them see everything she was feeling, all the anger and hurt and excitement and fear and who-knew-what-the-fuck-else.

If all three of them were going to try to lock her up tight in this madhouse, she was going to lean into the madness and turn it into pure chaos. Burn this shit to the ground. And if she burned down with it? Fine.

Luke swaggered toward her, pulling his cock out of his

basketball shorts and stroking his hardening length with each step. She was surprised: Kara hadn't expected him to be playing along, but she'd have to go with it.

"Are you really going to do this?" she asked him.

Luke froze. Micah leaned back on the bed, watching patiently.

But it was Conor's eyes that flashed. His next words stole her breath.

"You still have your veto, difficult girl. Are you going to play it safe and use it?"

Oh.

Oh.

Something bubbled up in Kara's chest. Many some-things. Fear, and doubt, and...giddiness?

"Do I ever play it safe?" she countered, watching Conor's lips quirk and his eyes darken even further with satisfaction.

He nodded at Luke without a word.

"No veto, huh?" Luke asked softly.

So he still wasn't sure. Good.

But Kara didn't say anything. *I'm playing them,* she told herself. She was a horny, lying bitch, but she was going with it.

Luke squared his shoulders and stalked toward her again, backing Kara up against the wall until there was no room for her to escape.

No way to escape, nowhere to go. What was she doing?

For a rare, honest moment, Kara admitted she had no fucking clue, but she wasn't walking away now.

The tall, redhaired man stroked his cock an inch from her naked stomach, eyes bright.

"You know what I jack off to, when I have to use my own hand? The way you screamed for me that day in the cave. I was fucking you so hard I knew it had to hurt, but you begged me for more. Conor shared how he told you to struggle while he was fucking you, and you did. Micah shared how hard you came after he teased and denied you, and how much harder you came after he kept at you. And you *loved* it. You loved all of it."

He was hard, but he sounded angry.

"Luke—"

He ignored her and continued. "Sometimes I imagine you struggling to get away from me while I tease you, and then fucking you so hard I force orgasm after orgasm out of you, while you still struggle against me. And sweetheart? That little movie in my mind is better than any fuck I've ever had with any other woman. Maybe even better than with these assholes."

Kara's body, already turned on from earlier, went tight and wet and nuclear, she was so close. Her nipples were so hard they hurt, and her thighs were soaked. She almost dropped to her knees, but she... she wanted *that*.

And she could have *that*.

She had her veto. She could stop this. So why not live out every dirty thing she'd ever wanted but had been afraid to fight for—and afraid to fight against?

Trembling slightly, she balled her hand in a fist.

"You should keep fantasizing about that movie," she said, daring him. "It's the closest you'll ever get to the real thing with me."

"Jesus fuck," Luke groaned, laughing. But he was looking at her thighs. "Even when you're about to punch me in the nuts, look how fucking wet you get. I thought I was remembering wrong." He reached his free hand down to gently swipe her.

Kara practically shook from the barely-there touch.

"Told you," Conor said.

From the bed, Micah watched, but this time he kept his hands away from his cock, seeming satisfied to watch without participating. "Never seen anything so beautiful," he added, but there was a warning in his voice that Kara didn't understand.

Luke seemed to, though. He grinned.

"It's like that, huh, buddy?" he asked. But he didn't touch her pussy again. Instead, he grabbed her balled up fist and unfurled her fingers.

"Never punch someone with your thumb inside of your fist, sweetheart. I thought I taught you that, like I taught you how to shoot. Did you forget my... lessons so easily?"

"What lessons?" she tossed back.

He laughed.

"You'll pay for that later," he promised, pushing her hand down and wrapping it around his dick. Kara recognized the way his skin there felt, the length and size of him. She knew this part of him so well.

She hadn't missed his cock, though. Not at all. She told herself that as he urged her hand up and down on his erection, so hot and hard, it made her hand feel like ice in comparison. He moaned.

"I missed you, sweetheart. I missed this," Luke said.

"I didn't," she lied, and he laughed again.

"You're only making it worse for yourself," Luke said, but negated his words when he moved in even closer and dropped a kiss on her hair without missing a beat with his strokes. It was tender and affectionate and everything Kara didn't, couldn't, want. While Kara tried not to react to the kiss, he grabbed her ass with his free hand and tugged her even further in until the head of his cock pressed against her abdomen, towering over her.

"I'm about to come all over you, sweetie, even though I'd promised myself I wouldn't participate. You broke the seal. How's that feel, knowing I can't resist that little sweetheart cunt?"

It felt like her heart was going to explode, was how it felt. It felt like she was trapped on a roller coaster. Overwhelmed, Kara tried to pull away, and his cock got impossibly harder as he groaned even more, tightening his grip.

"No you don't," he said, and she felt him pulse under their joined hands, wet heat shooting out of him and all over her. It felt like it went on forever, him holding her tight against him, his nose back in her hair, as he came and came and came and Kara had to force herself not to come with him.

Weak link, she reminded herself. This was about breaking the chain, and Luke was the way in.

So why was she the one who suddenly felt weak?

Finally, Luke sighed, and the room was silent except for their breathing.

"Goddamn I've wanted that for so long, and it barely took the edge off," he said, releasing Kara and standing back to admire his handiwork.

"I've never seen you orgasm that hard in your life, and I've seen you a lot," Micah remarked from the bed. Kara wouldn't let herself look at Micah. She refused to let Luke's praise affect her, either. She was revved up and so close and if she orgasmed now...

She wasn't going to orgasm now.

Luke laughed, eyes still on Kara. "Sorry, man. Guess I'd been holding a lot in storage for her."

Luke dropped a light kiss on Kara's lips. It had been a

year since he'd last kissed her, and she shook from the sweetness of it. Tears welled in her eyes and she turned her head, blinking them away.

Was she crying?

What the fuck?

"Are you crying?" Luke asked, sounding worried.

"No," she lied.

"She knows she has her veto. She's just feeling a little overwhelmed," Conor offered from where he was busy propping up the wall on the other side of the room. "Poor girl needs to get off."

Luke chuckled. "Oh, sweetheart. Are you close?" He kissed the tears off her face, sliding his fingers into the come in their hands and rubbing it all over her stomach and breasts. When he circled her nipples, Kara's whole body jerked.

"You'll cry a whole lot harder than that, later," Luke said. "But I promise I'll go slow and build you back up to where you can take it. It's been a while."

With a swat on her ass, he pushed her back toward the bed and headed into the adjoining bathroom. Kara couldn't take it anymore. Reaching a hand down, she started rubbing circles around her clit. She needed to get herself off so they didn't get the chance to. She was too vulnerable right now, and she needed to be clearheaded when Conor and Micah took their turns.

Micah was up and off the bed so fast her head spun. He pulled her hand away from her clit.

"I think we've been pretty clear about this, baby," he said. "You don't get to finish until we let you."

Smack.

Her ass burned. Craning her neck around, she saw Conor staring at her, a stern negation in his eyes.

Smack.

Conor spanked her again, this time leaving his huge hand against her ass to absorb the heat.

"Now you *are* being a bad girl," he chided her, that silky-menacing tone back. "What do bad girls get, Micah?"

Micah didn't say anything. He was thinking through something. Kara swallowed. In the very brief time she'd known him, it was clear that Micah thinking meant scary things, unless you were on his side—and they were on opposite sides now.

It was Luke who answered though as he reentered the bedroom. "Oh, I know this one."

Micah chuckled. "I think this needs to be an interactive... what did you call it? ... lesson. Full participation."

Conor laughed too, more of a gruff bark than anything else. "I'm glad you agree," he said, weight behind his words.

Kara was too hot, too sticky, too on edge to try to dig into whatever was going on there. She forgot it when Conor pressed up behind her, reaching a hand down, spreading her open, and tapping her clit with one finger.

"Bad." Tap.

"Girls." Tap.

"Get." He carefully trapped her pulsing clit between his finger and thumb.

Close.

She was so—

"Punished," Conor said, withdrawing his hand.

Damn it.

Kara's whole body shook in need. As she felt herself being bent over the bed, she went a little feral. Wiggling her body, trying to pull her arms free, she was acting like a hellcat and she was fine with it.

In response, someone—Micah—grabbed her arms

tighter, stretching them up over her head. Someone else—Conor—grabbed her by the hips and moved her so she was on her knees, ass in the air. He squeezed, holding her still.

"You fucking assholes." She spat the words, could hear the tremble in her voice. "Make me come or let me go."

Before she lost hold of the cold wall around her heart.

"You don't really want us to, baby," Micah chided. He kneeled in front of her, legs slightly spread, thick cock in hand and pointed at her mouth.

"You know what to do," he told her. "Scoot up."

"I'll bite it," she threatened.

"Save it for Luke, you know he likes that shit," Micah told her. "No teeth, baby. We'll go slow."

"Back on board?" Kara heard Conor—had to be Conor with those hands—say from behind her as he moved her further up the bed, sliding her over smooth sheets.

Was he talking to her?

"I—" she started to reply, but Micah slid his cock into her open mouth, effectively shutting her up.

"Your way has its perks, boss," Micah sighed, wrapping a fist in Kara's hair and working her mouth up and down over his cock, aided by Conor's hands on her hips, urging her forward and moving her back.

Her almost-orgasm roared back to life. Even though she'd never admit it, she had missed Micah's cock. She'd never managed to get her mouth on him their one night together. Even though she'd tried to brush off their fuckfest as a hot fling with a complete lying douchebag, she'd still regretted not doing more when she'd had the chance.

He was a lot to take. Her mouth was stuffed full, especially as he started pushing his cock deeper so it touched the back of her throat, his satisfied sighs turning into harsh groans.

"Breathe through your nose," Conor advised. "Swallow around him. That's it. Good girl. He's so thick, isn't he?"

She tried to say, "I've got it, jackass," but all she could do was mumble around the cock making its way into her throat as Micah said:

"Fuck, baby, that's so good. You're so good."

She was supposed to be in control here.

Kryptonite pussy, she told herself desperately, but it was too late. Micah had twisted her up inside and around his finger—and his cock—again, and like a horny idiot, she'd gone along with it.

He'd get off first though. She could take some satisfaction in that.

She started working her mouth around him, deep throating his cock, feeling him harden and thicken even more in her throat as he began jerking on her hair to get her to move faster.

He was close. She could pay him back for the edging earlier, leave him wanting. He fucking deserved it.

She tried to pull back, fighting his grip on her hands.

"Conor," Micah gasped, releasing Kara's hands only to lace his fingers through hers and squeeze.

It was such an innocuous, innocent thing, but the movement and implied intimacy in the hand hold made the cold wall around her heart disintegrate and her arousal shoot back up into the stratosphere.

Nonono. She couldn't let herself feel anything for them.

"Conor," Micah groaned. He raised his hips and pushed his cock deep in her mouth, robbing Kara of all thought.

Conor moved one hand back to her pussy and started working her clit again.

Fuck.

One, two, three circles, and Kara's vision went white as

she came, screaming around Micah, who erupted into her mouth with a roar.

"Don't swallow yet," Conor was saying when she came back to the present. Micah was withdrawing from her mouth and she was being lifted up into a kneeling position.

"Open your mouth, baby, and show me," Micah coaxed and Kara complied, not caring at this point, even as his come dribbled down the sides of her mouth.

"Fuck, that's so hot," Luke said. He crawled onto the bed and leaned over to lick the escaping seed off her lips.

Kara squirmed, the sensation and the complete filthiness of the act making her clench in aftershocks.

"*That's* hot, Jesus," Conor muttered.

Micah ignored them. "You want to orgasm again, don't you baby? You can swallow when you come for the three of us," he crooned at Kara, and then six fucking hands descended on her, tweaking her nipples and circling her clit as Kara shook.

Someone worked a finger inside of her soaked pussy, rubbing at her g-spot. It was all too much. She screamed as she went over the edge.

Distantly, someone said "swallow." Kara gulped down what she could, uncaring that she was following orders or that she was making a mess all over herself and the bed and them.

Finally, they released her, and Kara collapsed face first into the bed, wet and sticky and gasping.

Micah stroked her back, sighing.

"My heart is about to pound its way out of my chest," he commented. "Baby, nothing feels like you. No one in this entire world is like you."

Kara ignored his words, the way they made her heart

want to leap out of her own chest and directly into his hands. She needed to recover and recalibrate, that's all.

Except she felt herself being flipped onto her back, Micah and Luke now on either side of her.

"What are you—" she started.

Conor interrupted, prowling onto the bed and over her. Naked, he straddled her thighs with his, looming over her so his face was the only thing she could see.

"Did you forget, generous girl? It's my turn."

Conor was hard enough to drill a hole through the ground.

He'd let Micah lead. Even when he, Micah, and Luke were fighting, they could practically read each other's minds and take direction from each other. It had served them well when they had been SEALs together, and it served them now.

He'd had a second to think when they'd gotten upstairs. It was clear Micah was confident in how to handle this, so even though Conor's cock had been ready to explode for the past however-fucking-long, he went along with his partner's silent tells and instructions. And it had been hot as fuck to watch Luke and Micah get off with Kara, to see their come in her mouth and all over her body, to deny Kara her orgasm while directing her as she sucked Micah, and then to make her come so hard.

But he was at the fucking edge of his control, and if he didn't get inside her immediately, he was going to Hulk out and destroy everything in his vicinity.

All he really wanted to destroy right now was Kara's wet, wanting little cunt.

Two years. It had been almost *two fucking years* since he'd been inside her. It couldn't be as sweet as he remembered. That would be a good thing, wouldn't it? He'd still keep her, but maybe she wouldn't have the same fucking hold over him.

Kryptonite Pussy, Luke had called Kara's magic, and he had to agree.

Luke, who had participated—sort of. Who'd let Kara get him off but had stopped shy of penetration, as if that would keep him from being a full participant, and fully complicit.

"You're missing out," Conor said to the ginger man, who glared, like he knew exactly what Conor meant.

To demonstrate, Conor stroked Kara's pussy, grinning as she jerked, her eyes dark with helpless lust and annoyance. She *thought* she wanted to control this, but what she wanted —what she always wanted—was to fight for control, only for it to be taken from her. He'd figured that out about her their two nights together in Coronado, and Luke and Micah had confirmed as much based on their own experiences with her. Even if they hadn't, her responses so far told the same story.

Kara liked to be forced.

"Don't you want my mouth?" she asked in a purposefully sultry voice.

Conor laughed, lightly circling her nipple.

"I want that, too, but later. I've been dreaming of getting back inside this greedy little cunt for fucking ever, sweet girl," he said.

He couldn't wait any longer. They knew she was on birth control; he knew they were both STI-free. Forcing her still-trembling legs apart, he angled her hips and shoved into her in one brutal, perfect fucking thrust that almost had him seeing a supernova.

Tight as fuck.

Wet as fuck.

Hot as fuck.

Perfect as fuck.

"Fuuuuuuuck," he growled in her ear. She deserved to know how perfect she felt.

It was as amazing as he remembered. That bee balm scent, even stronger from her sweaty body, teased at his nose, making his throat go tight. In retaliation, he pulled out and thrust deeper, creating a fast, uneven rhythm that Kara clearly appreciated, based on her writhing body and chorus of moans and sexy little cries.

Holding himself in a pushup with one arm, he used the other to grip her chin.

"Look at me," he ordered. "I want to see your face when you go over again for us."

He didn't have to look at Micah and Luke; they knew what the *us* meant. Luke and Micah were using their hands on her—he wasn't really paying attention—but it was working, because her moans got louder and her cunt got even tighter around his cock.

"Please," she begged him.

"What, needy girl?" he asked.

"Use your words, sweetheart," Luke said, back on Conor's team. For now.

"Kiss me," she gasped.

Triumph shot through Conor's body and lit a fire in his balls. She wanted him for more than his cock. He dove in, sucking at her mouth, pressure building in his spine as he swallowed up her cries.

Luke worked a hand under Kara's ass, and he did *some-*

thing. Whatever it was made Kara rip her mouth away from Conor's mouth as she clenched around him, wetness coating him.

"Luke! Conor! Micah!" she screamed.

The last bit of his control snapped. He drove into her, gripping her tight as almost two years of built-up tension and need and, fuck it, *longing* poured out of him and into her.

He was pretty sure he did see a fucking supernova.

Jesus fucking Christ, he was *fucked.*

He relaxed his body, covering her and sharing sweat. The way her chest moved made his heart beat even harder than it had moments ago. He kissed her sweaty forehead again, and the smell of bee balm made him squeeze her tight to him.

"Conor," she protested. Since he didn't want to bookend the most incredible sex of his life by suffocating her, he rolled off her body and against Micah, who stroked Conor's waist and kissed his ear in approval.

Conor chuffed a laugh.

"Good enough for you?" he asked his partner.

"Him?" Kara complained, laughing too. "Shouldn't you ask me that question?"

Teasing him. She was teasing him. As if this was normal and she'd chosen to be here with him. If he let himself, he could pretend he was a good man who deserved teasing from her. It was so sweet it hurt his chest.

"Clearly it was good enough for you, sweet girl," he said, kissing her lips softly. "Thank you."

The soft look in Kara's eyes disappeared like he'd snapped his fingers, a chill descending in its place. Ignoring the way she began to struggle, the empty ache he felt from the way she distanced herself, Conor pulled her deeper into his arms, tucking her head into his chest.

He was so fucked. They all were. But it would be okay.

He had her now. She'd let him back into her body. It didn't matter that he was a bad man who didn't deserve her —he'd taken her anyway. She was theirs. What else mattered?

9

Well that *had not gone as planned.*

Covered in a film of sweat, a mix of hers and Conor's, as he kept her locked in the cage of his arms, Kara ruefully considered the one flaw in her plan: She'd forgotten how sex with them fucked her forward, backward, upside down and inside out. It had been too long, and she'd blocked out the way they dragged her emotions out of her when they made her orgasm; how them orgasming with her, on her skin, *inside* her, unlocked the box where she stored all her vulnerability so it came leaking out—the way Conor's come was leaking out of her. Which was a gross metaphor, when she considered it, but felt true.

As if Micah had heard her thoughts—and at this point, Kara wouldn't put mindreading powers past him—he chuckled and said, "Two years ago, if you'd told me seeing someone else's come spilling out of a woman's pussy would make me hard, I'd think you were full of it. But now that Kara's full of *you,* I'm starting to see the appeal."

Kara looked at the broad man. Micah's eyes were a deep,

sea blue, as if lust and satisfaction, and not just of the sexual variety, had tinted them a bolder color.

"Well, baby, how do you feel?" he prompted.

How did she feel? Exhausted. Weightless. Broken. Whole. Like she'd purposefully cut out essential parts of herself a long time ago to stop hurting and the men had found those parts and were determined to put them back. She didn't want them. She had a solid, steady life, with a ride-or-die best friend, a home, and the potential to build so much more. And if she was still so lonely she ached in bed at night, staring into the dark and wishing for something else, then at least she was safe. And free.

She wasn't safe here. She wasn't free.

So she didn't respond.

Micah laughed again. "That good, huh?"

Oh, fuck that bullshit. She wasn't going to let him win.

"I've had better," she lied, keeping her voice cool.

Micah raised an eyebrow, and Luke coughed from wherever he was in the room, but Conor was silent, his arms going stiff and squeezing around her before he suddenly released her, rolling away and climbing off the bed.

"Boss," Micah started.

But Conor was already across the room, not even sparing a glance for Kara as he stepped out of sight. As if looking at her was a waste. As if she meant nothing.

"Move," Conor barked at Luke.

Kara couldn't see the two men from where she lay on the bed, but there was a pause before Luke came into view.

"Unlock it," Conor barked again—at Micah, it seemed, because after a brief pause Micah did something on his phone and the door opened again.

Footsteps, and then Conor was gone.

Kara tried to focus on this new knowledge, that the

doors locked based on an app on Micah's phone, so she could avoid the absurd pain in her chest at Conor's departure.

Or the further pain when, with a chiding look, Micah murmured, "bad move, baby," and followed Conor out. As if she was the wrongdoer in this scenario.

That left her with Luke. The man she should trust the most. But he had let her down by participating so easily, and at the same time, not participating at all. Convoluted, to be upset both that he took part and also that he kept himself out of it, but then Kara's whole brain was topsy turvy right now, synapses firing wrong and making her yearn for things she shouldn't and feeling hurt and rejection where she should only feel rage and the need to escape.

She opened her mouth before she could stop herself. "Why is he so angry?"

Luke looked at her, like he'd briefly forgotten she was in the room.

"Conor's always angry."

"He didn't use to be," Kara pointed out.

"Yeah well, a lot of shit has happened since you last saw him. Saw us."

Now Luke looked angry, square jaw prominent in the granite of his features. Usually his face was soft, easy. She'd only ever seen him angry once: When she'd decided to leave him.

"What happened? To make him do this? To make you all..." Kara trailed off. Accusing Luke of being part of her kidnapping seemed like it wouldn't help her get on his good side, even if it was true.

Luke shook his head, jaw still tight. "Not my story to tell. Or not only my story. And why would I tell you, Kara, when I don't think you have much empathy for us?"

That pissed her off, but she kept her voice soft. "Do you really expect me to have empathy for you, when Conor and Micah took me from my life, and none of you will let me go back? I had a life, Luke. I *have* a life. I have close friends, a good job, an apartment I love. Maybe my life isn't perfect, but it's my *life*. You owe me my life back."

Luke ran a hand through his hair. "Let's just go to sleep."

"Avoidance isn't going to get you anywhere with me. One of you needs to tell me the truth."

Luke hesitated, but Kara knew which button to push.

"What happened to hating lies and hating liars, Luke? Or was that its own lie?"

He sighed, rubbing a hand through his hair again. Like the others, his hair was longer now. "I won't go into too much detail—it's not safe to—but all three of us are SEALS together." He stopped and corrected himself, even stiffer now. "Were SEALS together."

SEALS.

Were.

It felt like the bed, the floor, the entire room had disappeared, right out from under her. Her center of gravity was gone. They'd *all* been SEALs. They'd known each other. They'd *played* her. She'd been played. There were other facts of note here, that they were no longer SEALS, for instance, but Kara set that aside for later scrutiny. What was most important was that the three organic flings she'd had... at least two of them had been planned.

"So you all knew me from the get-go. Were you and Micah there the night I met Conor at the bar?"

Luke nodded.

"Was this all some game? A bet? *Who can fuck her the most*? Well, congrats Luke, I think you won." Kara spat the words.

She was hurt. Somehow, and god knew why, this was worse than being kidnapped.

"No." Luke was emphatic. He came to sit on the bed, grabbing Kara's hand and ignoring her taunt. "You were Conor's. Even when you left him, you were his. Micah was... worried about his focus, and what it might do to our bond, so he offered to keep an eye on you for a while when Conor had to go fill in a spot on another team for a mission. And then Micah couldn't keep his hands off you, even though he promised he would. He fucked up, so I offered to take over." He shared a wry, self-deprecating half-smile. "And you know how that went. It was never a game, Kara, I promise. Not for me, not for any of us."

Kara digested this, letting Luke hold her limp hand. Could she believe him? Luke claimed he never lied, but he'd lied to her by omission, what was one more?

This was important, she knew that much. For them to have broken their promise to Conor, Kara had to have had some power over them. *Kryptonite pussy.* If she had weakened the link between them before she'd even known she was doing it, she could do it now. She just had to get back in touch with the woman she'd been and use that version of Kara against them. Tough, painfully honest, with a hidden sweet side, right? That's what Luke had said to her when they were together.

"Let's say I believe you. What happened to make you all like this? Because you aren't the men I remember." Kara made sure to look him in the eye when she delivered the blow, needing to say it, regardless of how he took it. "None of you."

Luke closed his eyes. "Yeah," he acknowledged. "The men you knew...they're gone. I'm sorry."

The apology was for more than that, Kara knew. One

piece led to the other. Luke, the man who had saved her on a climbing wall once, and had wanted to save her from herself, would never have gone along with a kidnapping, weak link or otherwise. They'd changed, and Kara felt that loss keenly, and not only because she was trapped in a house with these strangers who wouldn't let her leave for god knew what reason.

And she still didn't know why.

"Luke," she said quietly, lacing his fingers with hers. She told herself it was only a strategy to get him talking, but the feeling of his fingers intertwined with hers settled something in her chest that had ached since Conor left the room. "Please tell me. You once said you'd never lie—by keeping this from me, you may as well be lying."

He closed his eyes, then opened them. Nodded.

Playing with her hand without looking at her, he spoke. "We were sent on a mission. I can't give you the details, it's not safe. We were supposed to kill someone—an enemy of the state, someone truly bad. And we did, but our intel was wrong; his wife and sons were supposed to be gone and they came home and..."

Luke trailed off. Kara squeezed his hand tight, her heart beating rapidly. However this story ended...she wasn't sure how she could live with knowing.

"...the wife jumped in front of him to save him. She died, right in front of her two young sons. And since our directive had been to kill her husband, Conor shot him, so their kids saw their parents die, one after another. They're both orphans now, and it was our fault. And what's worse is we learned the guy we were sent to kill was a good man. Just Uncle Sam playing power games and using us as pawns. When we tried to report it, to do something, all three of us were dishonorably discharged. We've had to go into hiding;

we know the people who sent the orders down the chain are after us. Taking less than savory hit jobs to be able to build this cabin and—" he cut off. "That's enough for you to know."

The brutality, the violence, the sheer tragedy of it... no wonder Conor thought he was evil. No wonder why they'd gone so nihilistic.

"Where do I come into it?" Kara asked him.

"Conor decided if we were already this bad, we should take what we want. And he wanted you."

Wanted. Like she was a pair of sneakers or a video game.

"I'm a person," she reminded Luke, as if he'd forgotten. "You don't get to just want me, and take me."

His green eyes had gone dark, looking almost black in the moonlight. "But we did, anyway."

"And you're okay with this now?"

He didn't say anything, instead shifting his body so he lay down beside her and turned her, pulling her back against him, so he spooned her from behind.

"That's enough storytime," he said, his voice gruff. "I need to crash."

At first Kara held herself stiff in his arms, but then she remembered the woman she needed to be to win, so she forced herself to soften against him. With a satisfied groan, Luke pulled her tighter. She tried to stay awake, but the warmth of his hard, naked body layered against her cooling back, and his strong arms wrapped around her waist and right breast as he breathed, slowly lulled her brain into sleep.

He'd hold her this way, but he wouldn't fuck her.

"Luke," she started to say on a yawn, "why didn't you have sex with me?"

But she was asleep before he could answer.

Luke had forgotten that Kara was a snorer.

A loud one.

She'd been asleep for a while. Luke listened to the sounds she made as she slept and dreamed, thinking over the last question she'd asked before she passed out.

Why didn't you have sex with me?

Why, indeed. He'd barely taken the edge off—even though Conor had sucked his dick before he'd used Kara's hand and body to get himself off. But watching her with Micah, and then with Conor, had made him hard all over again. Then Kara had started asking questions, the deep probing kind that Luke hadn't wanted to give her answers for, and his dick had lost the urge to fuck.

He shouldn't have answered any of her questions, but she'd called him a liar.

He couldn't answer the last one, because he was a liar.

Luke hadn't fucked her because if he had, he was just as bad as the others. If he had fucked her tonight, he may as well have kidnapped her, too. He was complicit.

And he was a liar, because she'd still gotten him off. He'd shoved his dick at her and rubbed it all over her. And fuck, it had been hot. Fuck, had he been angry. Fuck, had it felt good to have her in his arms and use her body as an easel. To reconnect with this woman he'd once thought he loved. Which made him no better than Conor or Micah. He was a liar—the worst kind—because he was lying to himself.

He closed his eyes, playing with her breast. Kara moaned in her sleep, and Luke considered waking her up and taking her right now.

But no. It was a slim line, but he couldn't cross it. Not unless she asked him to.

Fortunately, or unfortunately, depending on how he looked at it, the bedroom door opened.

"That did not go well," Micah said as he approached the bed and pulled his sweatpants off. "Looks like it's just us again."

"And Kara," Luke pointed out.

Micah stared at the sleeping woman, his worried face softening. "And Kara. Thank fuck."

Luke waited as Micah climbed under the covers, then gently lifted Kara, lowering her back down so her head rested on Micah's chest. Even that tore him into two pieces, because sharing her felt so right, but doing it while she was sleeping and couldn't consent felt so wrong.

Kara liked when power was taken from her, but she needed to be conscious for it.

"You're having second thoughts," Micah guessed.

"Of course I am." Luke could hear how harsh the words were. Kara's breathing stilled for a moment. Had he woken her? But then the snores started back up again, and Luke relaxed.

"That's some sound," Micah commented.

"You never heard her snore?"

Micah's voice was quiet. In the dark, Luke could see the other man stroke Kara's hair.

"Never really got the chance to. She wasn't that deep asleep that night I left her. Sometimes I wonder..." Micah trailed off.

What would have happened if I'd stayed. Luke didn't have to hear it out loud to know that's what his lover was thinking. He thought something similar, all the time. What if he hadn't pushed Kara to tell him the truth about her past that day? What if he'd convinced her to stay with him? He would've lost Micah and Conor, but she would've been his.

Mindreader that he was, Micah caught onto Luke's thought process.

"This, what we have now? I know it isn't conventional, and I know it's unfair. But it's what she needs and what all of us need."

Was it though?

"She asked me why I didn't fuck her tonight. She also told me we owed her for taking her from her life."

"And what did you tell her?"

"I didn't answer the former. For the latter, I told her the truth. Some of it, at least."

Luke relayed what he'd told Kara, as the woman in question snored away. Micah listened. Luke couldn't tell what the other man was thinking, the dark room obscuring his expression. Not to mention that Micah had a good poker face. Luke waited for the admonition. There was no way that Micah and Conor were ready for Kara to know the truth about them, if ever, and yet he'd told her anyway.

Instead, Micah asked the ceiling: "Well, why *didn't* you fuck her?"

"That's all you have to say?"

Micah shrugged, and Kara shifted on his chest from his movement. She grumbled something in her sleep. Micah twisted his head to look directly at Luke.

"Here's the thing. You're trying too hard to be the good guy here. But we left 'good' behind months ago. Even if what we did in Frankfurt hadn't pushed us over that line, the jobs we've taken since to afford all of this sent us so far over, there's no chance of turning back. You're holding onto someone you used to be, and for what? This is who we are now, who you are now." Micah cleared his throat, lost in thought for a moment, before rubbing his chin against Kara's head gently, and continuing softly. "This may not be what Kara wants, but it's what she needs. She was lonely and emotionally starving and the fire in her was slowly burning out. Hurry up and commit to this. Otherwise you'll be left behind, looking in. Is that what you want? Because it's not what I want. It's not even what that jackass in the other room wants, even though he may pretend otherwise. We're one unit. Who are we, if we're not together?"

Each word was like a stab of honesty in Luke's chest. There *was* no turning back. This *was* who they were now, goodness be damned. As for what Kara needed...Luke remembered the first time they'd fucked. Kara had started a fight with him over nothing as they hiked to a cave in Colorado, goading Luke on until he carried her into the cave and thrust into her so hard she almost screamed the whole thing down. She hadn't wanted to ask, she'd wanted him to take.

When she'd asked him why he hadn't fucked her, there'd been hurt in her voice. Buried deep under layers of denial, and anger, and self-righteousness, but there. She'd wanted him to take her tonight. And like some asshole caught up in the past, he'd only half-assed it. He was on the outside looking in, by his own choice, and that had always been Luke's worst fear.

He wasn't going to be left behind. Even if it meant leaving his values behind instead.

Luke stroked a hand over her hip. Micah moved his own hand. Their fingers grazed, and Luke did something he'd never bothered to do, never even thought to do, and linked his fingers through his friend's, his partner's, his lover's.

Micah's mouth shifted in a smile. "Never out of the fight."

"Never out of the fight," Luke repeated, the old SEAL motto sticking in his throat.

Micah sighed. "And it's going to be a fight. Let's get some sleep."

But Luke lay awake and stared into the dark, trying to reconcile with leaving his past self behind.

Because if they were going to do this, at some point, he was going to have to lie. Not by omission. By commission.

But was that really worse?

Kara shifted again in her sleep, the snoring paused as she murmured something, something that sounded like his name.

She was his.

Theirs.

Luke's whole life was getting the short stick, playing second fiddle, being left with sloppy seconds, etc. Until he'd met Conor and Micah. He'd finally been a part of something where he mattered equally.

Kara wasn't sloppy seconds. He'd take her however she came, whenever she was willing, and whatever piece of her he could get. He just wanted every fucking piece.

Even if he had to take them by force.

And so, in the dark, Luke let his old self go, because he'd sacrifice any piece of himself to have all of Kara.

10

When Kara woke, the sun was high in the sky, sunlight bright and burning against her eyelids. There were no arms around her, and her head was on a pillow. At one point last night, she'd briefly woken to murmuring, only to realize she was lying on Micah's chest. But for now she was alone.

She opened her eyes and confirmed it. She was sore all over, and sticky, and gross. Luke's come had dried onto her belly, and she could still feel Conor between her legs. If she closed her eyes, she could picture the ways they'd fucked her. She'd been ridden hard and put away harder, and while there was some shame at the realization, mostly she felt satisfied.

None of that.

Shame wouldn't help her here, but neither would satisfaction. She'd forgotten last night why she'd taunted them into fucking her in the first place, so lost in their bodies on hers, the way they'd stared at her like they were desperate to have her, even the way they had talked about her to each other, as if they owned every part of her. But in the morning, she remembered. They'd kidnapped her so she could be a receptacle for their lust, nothing more, nothing less. Conor had proven that when he walked out on her and just left her there, when Micah had followed him. And yes, Luke and Micah had slept in bed with her, but that meant nothing. If she stayed here, she'd get even more lost in them. She'd lose all control, all sense of herself, become vulnerable again. And she knew what vulnerability meant. Exposing herself to them meant giving herself over to being hurt. Chris had taught her that.

And she was forgetting the most important part. It didn't matter that this house was like something out of her dreams, that she was in her favorite place in the world, that Luke and Micah and even Conor, briefly, had held her like she was something precious. It was all a lie. They had stolen her away from her life. There was no respect there.

There was no—

She dismissed that four letter word immediately, shoving it away.

Instead, she focused on what she would be doing if she were at home. Today was Sunday, the first farmers market of the year. She'd be at the volunteer tent, cold brew in hand, organizing the wooden coins that stood in for actual cash and chatting up the various vendors, planning out tonight's dinner with Lola and debating over who was cooking. (Lola was the better cook, she always won.) Kara missed that version of reality with a deep pang, and resolved herself: she was doing whatever she could to get back to it.

She needed to keep pushing at Luke, causing tension in the men's bond, until she could break it and get free. They were murderers, criminals. She needed to get out of bed, face what came next.

Sex, probably. How were they going to fuck her next? How was she going to fuck them back?

Well, first she needed to shower.

In the bathroom, she looked in the mirror and grimaced. There was beard burn from Micah on her cheeks, her jaw, her neck, her—yup—breasts. Her lips were red and swollen, her hair big and tangled and wild. *Rode hard, put away harder.* And she'd let them. More, she'd goaded them into it. Wanted it. Like the whore she'd always been, the whore Chris's wife had called her, once upon a time.

No. That wasn't her voice, and she didn't believe it anymore. Liking sex didn't make her a whore. She was healing, and she wouldn't be dragged backwards.

Besides, there was no time for self-recrimination and questions and emotion whatsoever.

Watch, listen, potentially manipulate, find a weak link, make a plan, escape. She could have an emotional breakdown when she was back home and her kidnappers were in prison.

She turned on the shower, waiting until it was near scalding, and bypassed the bodywash clearly meant for her, instead choosing the other bottle. It smelled like Luke, like sex. She was doing it for manipulation, only—not because she wanted to smell like him.

Who's the liar now? that voice in her head taunted.

She scrubbed down her body, and as she washed the men off her, she shoved away her wayward emotions—anticipation, lust, longing, and a curious sympathy for what had happened to the three of them that made them this hard and cold and angry and *wrong*.

After showering, she toweled herself off, squeezed some product into her hair, brushed her teeth, and went back into the bedroom, bypassing the closet of sexy clothes for another one of the men's shirts. It was beyond long and tight across the chest—clearly Luke's. She let herself feel some satisfaction, not sexual, not really, but at the knowledge that by choosing to cover herself in Luke's smell and clothes, she might be driving even more of a wedge between him and the others.

It wasn't because wearing his shirt made her feel safe. It *wasn't*.

Before that voice could call her a liar again, she slammed out of the—unlocked—bedroom and headed down the stairs to face her captors.

In the kitchen, Micah stood, back to her, scrambling eggs on the stove with one hand and stirring something in a small pot with the other. He turned, and something about what she wore made him chuckle and shake his head.

"Morning, baby. Don't worry, I know you prefer poached. Go sit down and Conor can get you coffee."

Conor was sitting at the counter. He glanced up at her. "Sleep well?" His eyes ran over her. "Luke, did you tell Kara she could wear your clothes?"

Luke shook his head. "She didn't ask permission."

Permission?!

"I don't need to ask permission to wear clothes. And I'm not about to prance around your house butt naked."

Conor's jaw went tight. Whatever he'd been pissed about last night, he was still pissed about. "If we want you to prance around our house butt naked, that's what you'll do. Bad girls don't get clothes. Strip."

The command made her bare thighs clench, and her

anger got the better of her. "No. You don't get to ignore me for almost two years and then take me from my life and everything that matters to me, for no fucking reason, lock me up without escape so you can treat me like some insignificant fuck doll, and expect that I'll bend over and let you."

Conor's jaw tightened harder. She thought it might snap.

"Ignore?" he asked, his voice dangerously soft.

"Ignore," she repeated.

"Kara."

And...she was wet. She thanked the heavens the shirt covered her thighs, which were probably glistening by now.

"Conor."

"Bad girl: I. Said. Strip."

She gritted her teeth. She wasn't about to lose. "Make. Me."

She stared him down and he stared back, their battle of wills going on forever.

Luke interrupted. "If they get stuck in this standoff, we'll be here all day and never eat. Boss, I'll strip her for you."

Kara jerked in surprise. Luke was going along with Conor's demands?

Conor seemed to have the same thought, because he released her gaze to whip his head toward Luke.

"Glad to have you back, bro," Conor murmured. He cleared his throat. "You won't strip her though. Kara's going to be a *good* girl and do it on her own. Aren't you?"

A fire flared inside her; a little angry, a lot turned on. He was engaging with her, and she didn't want to admit it to herself, but it felt good.

"And what happens if I don't?" she taunted.

"How's your cunt feel, sore? Did you wake up sticky from

us today? How about we edge you for hours and then leave you there, wanting?"

This time, her pussy clenched. She couldn't admit she needed that, especially when Micah hummed at the idea as he turned off the stove and scooped the scrambled eggs onto one plate, the poached eggs onto another.

Glaring at all three of them, she dragged Luke's shirt off her body. She wanted to cower behind her hands to hide how hard and tight her nipples had gotten, but she wasn't going to let them see her embarassment. Instead she stood, straight and tall, daring them to say anything.

"Satisfied?" she asked Conor.

"Hardly." He looked down at his phone and took another sip of his coffee, like she wasn't even there.

"Breakfast time," Micah announced.

Luke took a seat at the counter, leaving a third stool open. After a moment of confusion, she went to hop onto it. Luke's hand on her shoulder stopped her.

"That's Micah's seat, sweetheart."

An alarm bell screamed in her head.

"If you think I'm going to kneel at your feet like some fucking submissive puppy begging for scraps—"

She heard Micah chuckle, Luke practically choked with laughter, and out of the corner of her eye, even Conor's lip twitched.

"Jesus, you read some kinky fucking shit sometimes. I meant that your seat is here." Luke patted his lap. "Hop up."

Sit on his lap for breakfast? Something in her chest yearned to be cared for that way. Kara stifled it.

"I'd like my own chair, please," she said politely.

"Oh, baby, you know I like how you say please," Micah said as he arranged the plates.

Conor didn't even look up from his phone. "You haven't earned one."

She was being tag teamed. Again.

She shouldn't have to earn her own fucking chair. But it wasn't worth belaboring the point, especially when Conor was being so implacable.

She turned to Luke and put her hand on the bar stool, trying to navigate how to get on his lap without touching him anymore than she had to. He was being so different from yesterday; in some ways, like the confident man she used to know; in others, like he'd embraced the inner kidnapper he'd been trying to repress.

It wasn't hot. It wasn't.

She lied to herself as Luke lifted her up and settled her on his lap, her back to his chest, spreading her legs so she straddled him. When she tried to close them, he pinched her inner thigh.

"Keep them open like that, sweetheart."

She complied, her legs trembling with desire.

"Yeah," Luke growled. "Just like that."

Kara cleared her throat, determined to hide how turned on she was. "Can I get some coffee please?"

Without looking up, Conor pushed his cup over to her.

"I can't have my own?" she asked.

Conor just grunted.

"Fine." She took a sip and almost whimpered, the coffee tasted so good.

She did whimper when she felt Luke's hand snake up her leg and start teasing her inner thighs, almost spilling coffee on herself.

"Shit, fuck!" she complained.

Conor's lip twitched again. "Careful, you don't want to

burn that sensitive skin." And he reached over and tweaked one of her nipples.

"Damn it, Conor!"

In response, he pinched the other one. It hurt like a bitch. And what was worse, she felt herself getting wetter. There was no way that Luke wouldn't notice.

He did, although he didn't comment, just spread the wetness from her body to her sensitive clit.

"Oh my god," she huffed a breath, trying to wriggle away.

He slapped her thigh in reprimand. "Too much after last night?"

This was the Luke she remembered. The confident, controlling, slightly sadistic one, who could affect her so easily—and not only physically. He'd seen right through her in a way she'd both loved and hated, knowing when to be gentle and when to bring her to the edge of pain and over. He was fully participating now, and it sent a thrill through her already tingling body.

She'd missed him. She loathed it, but she'd missed him.

He slapped her thigh again. "Sweetheart, I asked you a question."

"Yes."

"Good." He sucked an earlobe and rubbed her harder. She stiffened, willed her body to remain still and numb.

"Food's up." Micah brought over three plates and two bowls, balancing all the dishes perfectly. "I worked in my parents' deli when I was in high school," he offered in explanation. "Some things you never forget."

Placing the plates down—scrambled eggs, bacon, and toast for Conor and Luke, egg whites and chicken strips for himself, a smaller bowl with two poached eggs, toast, and a bowl of berries in front of her—he sat in the seat beside Luke's, so she was, once again, trapped in by them.

Also, there were only three forks.

Her stomach dropped.

"Can I have a fork?" She hated how small her voice was, but the idea of being fed like a child took something out of her. Made her feel small, in a way she hated.

"No, baby." Micah stroked a finger down her cheek before grabbing the bowl with poached eggs and turning to her. "Open."

"No." She echoed him and shook her head. Or she'd lose a part of herself, just like she feared.

"Kara." Conor was at the end of his tether. "Let Micah feed you breakfast, or I'll spread you across the counter and *you* can be breakfast."

Kara opened her mouth immediately. Luke laughed, his chest rumbling against her skin. Micah fed her a perfectly poached egg, careful not to spill any yolk on her bare body. She tried to ignore that poached eggs were her favorite breakfast food. Micah had not only known, he also seemingly cared enough to prepare an entirely separate meal for her. Under other circumstances, Kara would be touched by his gesture. No one had ever put that much thought into Kara's desires and needs—and they seemed determined to fulfill them.

Except for her most essential need: freedom.

They all ate silently, Micah pausing between feeding himself to feed her. She was starving, and she just didn't have it in her to argue. She tried to ignore the way that Luke was touching her, two fingers stroking inside her while his thumb circled her clit. She tried to ignore the way this care for her warmed something inside her. She was about to come, and from the way even Conor was watching her now, they all knew it.

"Open, baby," Micah said, a strawberry between his fingers and a glint in his eye. She glanced under the table, confirming that he was hard.

"Taking care of you gets me off," he said by way of explanation, not looking the slightest bit embarrassed.

"Here's what gets me off," Luke retorted, lifting her off his lap for a second. She heard the zipper on his pants open.

"Luke, what, you can't," Kara protested.

But he'd already dropped her over his dick, and she was so wet by now it didn't take more than two thrusts and a steady push on her hips until he was fully seated inside her.

He sighed, resting his chin on her head, pulling her back against his chest. "Much better."

And then he continued eating.

She'd forgotten what he felt like, so long and curved she could practically feel him in her throat, hitting her in just the right place, even though he didn't move at all. She clenched around him, she couldn't help herself. And her chest clenched, too, because there was no question he was fully participating, and the part of her that wanted to be taken without being asked loved it. There was something about being desired this much, and that along with the sureness and entitlement that they seemed to feel as they touched her and tasted her and fucked her...

Belonging. It was belonging. The one thing Kara had always promised herself she didn't need, but god, did she want to belong to someone.

And here was this false promise, of belonging to them. Sparkling and enticing.

But it was nothing more than fool's gold.

She needed to turn the tables on them. Get her emotions out of this, and fuck her way to freedom.

Before she could try, Micah tapped her lips with another strawberry.

This was...this was—never in a million years, never in her kinkiest dreams, had she imagined something like this. One man penetrating her with his cock, her seated on his lap, while another fed her breakfast, and the third, the third...

She glanced at Conor. His eyes were dark, pupils dilated, even though he didn't move a finger to touch her. Just watching, and—even though Luke had barely moved inside her, hadn't thrust even once—some combination of Conor's dark, lust blown eyes on her and Micah coaxing her to eat another strawberry, and Luke just fucking *sitting* there with his cock inside her and his chin on her hair, pushed her over a precipice she hadn't even realized she'd reached. With a muffled moan—her mouth was still around the strawberry —she came, clenching around Luke. And it almost hurt— she was still sore from Conor fucking her last night, and it wasn't only her pussy that felt rubbed raw. Every time they touched her, every time they fucked her, it was like the heart she'd numbed to pain on purpose began to feel again. And like anything long dead brought back to life, it fucking hurt.

Kara must have been a masochist, because she rode out the orgasm and thought:

More. Please, more.

Luke squeezed her hip once and groaned but otherwise didn't move. When the aftershocks stopped, Micah fed her more poached egg.

"How did that feel, sweetheart?" Luke asked, voice hoarse. "Good? Or hurts?"

Physically? Or emotionally?

She answered anyway. "Both."

He kissed her neck. "Good." And then he just. Kept. Eating.

"Um, I have a question," she asked in a tight voice, careful not to move.

"Hmm?"

"How long am I supposed to sit like this?"

Conor moved his hand to her face, tracing her lips. She wasn't sure how she'd thought he was implacable, he was practically rippling with energy and emotion right now, the cold, harsh look gone from his eyes. Even his chin had relaxed.

"Until we've finished breakfast. So I suggest you get to eating, hungry girl."

He moved his hand, only for Micah to pass him a cut up strawberry, which he placed between his teeth and *oh god* he was leaning in.

"Let him feed you, baby," Micah said on her other side, and transfixed, she opened her mouth, Conor kissing her and feeding her the strawberry, and the flavors—him and the fruit—exploded in her mouth.

"Fuck, she's clenching around me, and she just got a hell of a lot wetter. Whatever you did, Boss, keep doing it," Luke said.

Conor couldn't answer, he was too busy kissing her. The strawberry was gone, and his taste—cinnamon, coffee, mint —filled her as he sucked on her tongue and licked at her mouth. In that moment, he owned her, all of her. Kara forgot her end goal, distracted by the way he both took from her and gave back. The closed off man from last night was gone, and the man who had challenged her to stay with him nineteen months ago was back.

He released her, staring into her eyes.

"Conor—" Kara began.

But he turned her toward Micah, whose eyes had gone a deep blue, a red, shiny strawberry between his lips. He fed it to her the same way, mouth to mouth. Micah's kiss was different from Conor's. Where Conor took, Micah teased. Where Conor conquered, Micah coaxed, his tongue a slow seduction but no less potent than his partner's, and he owned her no less.

Not to be forgotten, Luke breathed into her ear, making her shiver.

"Come, sweetheart," he said, and when he thrust up with his hips, Kara obeyed his demand and shattered again.

They continued like that, feeding and kissing and fucking her, giving and caring and taking again, until their plates were empty and Kara no longer was sure which way was up, what she wanted, what she needed.

"Still hungry?" Conor asked.

She shook her head, panting, and he laughed that low, smooth laugh and kissed her lightly.

"Greedy girl. Don't worry, we'll make sure you're satisfied."

"Always," Micah added, kissing her again, so softly it felt like she might break.

Taking that as his cue, Luke let loose, lifting her up, up, almost off of him, only to slam her back down, groaning as he came. He held her tight on his lap long after he finished, softening inside her as he sighed.

"Thank you, sweetheart," he said.

"Good girl," Conor said.

"You pleased us, baby," Micah praised.

Their words were like an echo, a united front of praise and gratitude that left Kara shaken and unsure.

Why had she let them take over? Why hadn't she tried to

control this? Why had she let them win? And why was she still sitting there, filled with Luke's come, his now-soft dick still inside her, like he owned her?

She'd let them all own her.

Who the fuck was she?

On that thought, Kara struggled to climb off Luke's lap, surprised when he lifted her off of him, pushing his chair back and setting her on the floor, a gymnastic feat of balance that seemed effortless.

Conor rose and blocked her.

"Can I please go now?" Her voice was so small, it was almost embarrassing.

"I'm still hard," Micah said. "Someone's gotta take care of me."

Luke lifted his hands in the air. "Not my turn."

Conor laughed, his eyes heating, seeming more relaxed. Not the man he'd been yesterday. And for a moment, she envied them. Conor, Micah, and Luke: they had each other. They belonged. Was she really so cocky she thought she could tear at that bond? Kara had always wanted that kind of connection. She had Lola, but not a family. This was a family, and she was an outsider, and some deep, secret part wanted *in*.

She needed to get out of there, now. Recalibrate. Regroup.

She coughed.

"Want to stay and watch the whole way through, curious girl?" Conor asked.

"I *want* to go take a shower."

Implacable Conor came back. "Ask nicely."

She growled. This was bullshit, but she'd play along anyway.

For now.

"Can I *please* go take a shower?"

He stepped aside and let her pass, and she scooted around him, ignoring the chuckles and murmurs, refusing to let herself turn around and watch them. It was a tempting trap, but she was stronger than that.

She was.

She *was.*

11

Conor was rock hard. What's more, he felt more relaxed than he had in months. Something had happened just now with Kara; after fighting him so much, showing him that fire he'd missed, she'd given herself over to them, and whatever had been keeping her separate had disappeared, like the fight had been fucked out of her. Like she was *theirs*.

He stretched, sighing, reliving his triumph. Before Kara had walked out—run, really, because his runaway girl was scared of losing control—he'd *owned* her. They all had. Luke might've been the one inside her body, Micah the one inside her head, but Conor had forced his way into her heart, because he'd been directing the whole thing. It almost made up for his case of blue balls.

Her heart. He didn't want it because he wanted her love, he wanted it because it was the way to have all of her, to keep her, and Conor wanted to keep her without having to fight her every step of the fucking way. And didn't he deserve a little light in his life after all this darkness?

Hell, he wanted to fuck her again. It had taken everything in him to let her go just then instead of ordering her to her knees and taking his cock out, wrapping a fist in her hair, and forcing her to deep throat him.

"If she's trying to control us through sex, it doesn't seem like she's doing a good job at it," Micah mused. His words popped Conor's good mood like a pin.

Had it all been a lie? Was she just fucking with them when they fucked her?

"I'm not an idiot," Conor barked, then instantly regretted it. It wasn't Micah he was pissed at, it was himself. Because he *was* an idiot. Of course she was using sex as a way to escape. They'd stolen her; why would she want to stay?

But for a moment, he'd forgotten how and why she was there. What was it about her fucking kryptonite pussy that made him such a fool?

He was going to punish her for it. Make her regret playing them. Make her—

Just make her.

Micah raised an eyebrow. "Did I call you an idiot? Or did I call all of us idiots?"

Luke laughed, shrugging. "I'm not too cocky to admit I fell for it. Worth it, though. Especially because we were the ones doing the controlling."

Conor growled. Suddenly Luke was on Micah's side?

"And you're okay with this? With fucking her, even if she doesn't *really* want it?"

Luke's eyes darkened, and Conor watched, throat dry, as the taller man's long dick started to go hard again. It was amazing, what just thinking about the woman upstairs could do to the three of them.

Fucking kryptonite pussy.

"Oh, she wanted it. She never would've come the way

she had if she didn't. She wouldn't have participated that way. And now that I remember how good it feels when she comes around your cock, gives all of herself in that moment, I'm not giving it up again."

"And so you're willing to participate fully?" Micah asked.

Any other time, Conor would've chuckled at how obviously Micah was manipulating Luke into confessing he was all in. But Micah wasn't the only manipulator in the house.

Luke just nodded, and although Conor didn't trust him, he didn't have time for that right now. He needed to get his cock sucked by a woman on a power trip with a bad attitude.

As if Micah read his mind, he said, "Don't you think it's my turn?"

A question. Because Micah never announced or claimed, but convinced you to claim it for him. Usually this would amuse Conor, but right now his cock was feeling territorial and his mind agreed.

And his heart?

Fuck that. He didn't have a heart.

Proving that, once again, Micah could read his mind, he approached Conor, wrapping his big arms around Conor's neck.

"You do have a heart you know," he said quietly, then dropped a kiss on Conor's chest. "You like to tell yourself your heart is dead and buried, but your obsession with Kara, your loyalty to us, they prove otherwise."

The light caress of lips against his t-shirt, combined with Micah's words, were like one huge, sweet stab wound followed by multiple smaller slices where said heart would be, if it existed.

The room was still and quiet. Conor's ears filled with his own rapid breathing. He slashed his head in negation, just once, tipping his head up so he didn't have to see Micah in front of him.

Conor hadn't felt fear in so long, but Micah's declaration —which felt more like an accusation—planted seeds of terror. Conor couldn't have a heart, not again, because he couldn't risk losing it. Not to Kara. Not to anyone.

"Okay," Micah said softly, stepping back, but he tilted Conor's head down with an implacable hand so he had to look the blue-eyed man in the eyes. "You're not there yet, but you need to get there. Both of you," he added, including Luke, who currently had his head bowed so no one could see the taller man's face. "This isn't only about Kara, you know. It's about all of us. Our unit. And I know it's a risk neither of you want to take, but if you want the reward..." Micah trailed off.

"The only reward I want is her sweet obedience and sweeter c—" Conor began to argue. It wasn't denial, it was the truth.

It had to be.

"If you say 'cunt' I'm going to punch you," Luke said from across the room. He'd finally raised his face, anguished humor in his dark green eyes.

Conor just shrugged. "And what? You're claiming you have a heart? What, you're going to write love poetry for her next?"

"No one said anything about that shit," Luke said quickly.

What else could they be talking about?

"Emotionally constipated, the both of you," Micah murmured, but released Conor and stepped back, disappointment clear in his eyes.

Conor flipped him off as he headed up the stairs. He heard Micah murmuring something to Luke behind him, and for a moment, wondered if this was how Kara felt every time she left a room they were in, like she was some out of control child throwing a tantrum and the adults were only indulging it.

It was shitty, but maybe he'd be kinder, gentler, when he fucked her.

Nah.

He didn't know how to be kind or gentle. Not anymore. That required the heart Micah wanted him to have.

Conor's jaw locked as he approached the bedroom.

Sometimes even Micah was wrong.

Somehow, she kept ending up back here.

In this bedroom. Running away from laughing, horny men. And asking herself the exact same question:

What the fuck am I doing?

She was kidding herself if she thought she'd been in control in the kitchen. They had taken control, and she'd been nothing more than pussy putty in their hands. They'd fed her and fucked her and made her feel precious and cared for, and at the same time used—in the best possible way.

In the worst possible way, Kara reminded herself.

She went into the bathroom and looked at herself in the mirror, forcing herself to really look. Was this what she wanted, to stay here, a hostage sex toy? Didn't she deserve more out of her life? Out of herself? They didn't respect her. If they did, they would've tried talking to her instead of kidnapping her. They didn't admire her, if they did, they wouldn't keep her here. They didn't—they didn't love her. If they did, this would be more than three assholes using her as a fucking come dumpster.

Even if it didn't feel that way. Even if she had felt precious and important to them, as Micah saw to her hunger and Luke saw to her pleasure and Conor saw to... saw to...saw to her mental satisfaction, that need to be taken.

But it was all a lie. God, could she stop flip-flopping like some pathetic lovesick heroine in one of those dark romances she read too many of? There was no HEA here, only destruction. She had to face it. Maybe her life in Chicago wasn't so great, but she had the opportunity to make it great, and they'd stolen that from her. Like she'd said to Luke, she had a life. She deserved to keep living it the way she wanted. In some ways, this was a wakeup call. When she got home—and she would—she was going to stop living this half-life where she was haunted by her past and uncertain of her future. She was going to be all in, create something she wanted. Something she deserved.

There was another, underlying reason why she wanted to escape. One she could admit to herself. This wasn't only about the freedom to build a life for herself, it was about freedom, period. End of story. She needed her freedom because giving herself to them, especially when it seemed like all they wanted was her body and her obedience, was too terrifying to contemplate, much less do. She'd lose herself in the process.

Especially to hot and cold Conor, who wanted her one moment and seemed enraged and repulsed by her the next.

Someone knocked. From the mirror, she saw the man himself standing there, his large body leaning against the doorway, like she'd summoned him.

Play this right, Kara. Remember your end goal.

Freedom to live her life. And if it meant more fucking, so

be it. She ignored the way her pussy clenched at the thought.

What she said was, "Knocking. How gentlemanly."

He laughed, but it was cold and bitter. "I aim to please."

She looked at him in the mirror. "No you don't. Don't lie."

His face hardened as he took a step toward her, but his voice was silky. "Lie? Who's the liar here, scheming girl? Because it's certainly not me."

Shit.

He'd seen right through her.

"Conor..." she started, but he shook his head and turned to go back into the bedroom.

Part of her wanted to just let him go, but that was the angry, childish part of her, not the wise part that knew doing what he wanted was more likely to get him to let his guard down around her. Right now it was a brick wall, and she needed to start chipping away at it if she wanted him to relax enough for her to escape.

Freedom. Safety.

Loneliness.

She dismissed that third word, which had come from absolutely fucking nowhere, and followed him out to the bedroom, where he was busy making the bed she'd left a mess that morning.

"Still keeping things neat, huh?" she observed quietly.

His shoulders hunched a bit, but he said, "Guess you can take the man out of the military, but you can't take the compulsion to make hospital corners out of the man."

Ouch. She had said that to Lola, hadn't she?

"I'm—" Kara stopped herself before she could apologize. Yeah, maybe she'd insulted him to a friend, but he'd spied on her in the first place. And was doing much, much worse.

He finished making the bed, then went to sit at the foot of it, pulling down his sweatpants as he went. His cock, long, hard as a stone and an angry looking purple at the tip, bobbed in front of her.

Kara swallowed, knowing what he wanted.

Conor grabbed a pillow and tossed it on the floor in front of him.

"You're about to make it up to me, manipulative girl. On your knees."

She stared at him, part of her wanting to fight, because how dare he call her manipulative...except that's exactly what she'd been doing. Manipulating him. And she was going to just manipulate him more, once she got his cock in her mouth.

"Unless you're going to finally use your veto?"

In response, Kara kneeled on the floor, leaned forward, wrapping her hands around the base.

Conor pulled her hand away.

"Hands behind your back. Mouth only."

Looking down so he didn't see how pissed she was, she obeyed his orders, running kisses up and down his hard length. Butterflies collided against each other in her stomach from his scent, musk and earth and sex.

"Eyes up here," he said, softly but no less commanding.

She glanced up at him. His eyes were dark, the pupils swallowed by his lust and need for her, and she felt momentarily triumphant until he wrapped her hair in one big hand and used it like a bridle, holding his cock in his other, and directing her so his cock slid past her lips and teeth and steadily forward until it hit the back of her throat. Her eyes watered as she stared at him, and a look passed between them as he released a groan, which tugged on something in her chest.

Overwhelmed with feelings, she tried to pull back, but he stopped her with a yank on her hair.

"Don't fight me," he ordered, and she let go of any physical control, giving it all over to him as he began moving her head back and forward over his cock so she swallowed and then released him, his thrusts in tune with her heartbeat. As if he could hear it.

As she sucked and swallowed around him, and he grew impossibly harder between her lips, he spoke.

"Fuck, Kara, how are you always such a perfect girl?" he asked, and the butterflies collided again, this time harder—this time, in her heart. Something cracked, and feelings released, let loose with those fucking butterflies she wished would just die.

He released her hair to stroke her cheek, and she flattened her tongue, taking over the blow job to suck and swallow around his cock, desperate to get him off so she could regain the control she had lost.

Submissive, I will be submissive, she reminded herself. *Let him think he's winning.*

She moaned around him, but it wasn't a fake moan. She could feel herself growing wet as she prepared for him to finish down her throat.

But Conor stopped, pulling out of her mouth and angling his cock down between her bare breasts.

"Have you ever been tit-fucked before?" he asked, almost casually—but she could see the possessiveness in his eyes.

Kara licked his precum off her lips. "Never."

"Good. Get on the bed, on your back. Push your tits together."

Well. This was going to be degrading.

Except if it was, why was she so wet, she was practically dripping on the duvet?

"You want this," he said, his voice thick with triumph and desire as he fumbled in the drawer next to the bed, pulling out a bottle of lube and showing it to her. "You want me to fuck your tits and come all over them, don't you? This is your punishment, filthy girl, and you're so excited you can't even keep still."

The sexy asshole was right. She was writhing on the bed, her hands pushing her breasts together like an offering, her chin tucked in, staring raptly at his huge cock as he crawled over her body and drizzled lube into her cleavage. Crouched over her, he nestled his shaft in the valley between her breasts and placed his hands over hers. But where she'd expected a harsh, painful grip leading to a crude, soulless titty-fuck she was prepared to suffer through—including ignoring how badly she needed to come—Conor surprised her by placing his large, callused hands over hers and lacing their fingers so they were working together to make a tunnel for his cock. As she stared, their hands, her breasts, and his cock blurred together into one moving, shaking unit, his cock sliding into the crevice they'd created as a team, up and down, up and down, up and down.

It shouldn't have been something she got off on; there was nothing he was touching that was particularly sensitive, but the way he used her, held her, squeezed her, cooperated with her, made her tremble with need. And when he began whispering "perfect girl, perfect girl, my perfect girl," everything in her went tight. She was overwhelmed by sensation: his earthy, raw smell, his voice above her, the blur of skin against skin, the feeling of her body trapped between his thighs and gripped by his hands.

On impulse, she began to kiss the tip of his cock when he slid upward. He shuddered over her, squeezing her hands and breasts even tighter.

"Yes, perfect girl," he groaned, so she did it again.

Conor's thrusts picked up speed, and she was sure this was it, but suddenly he released her.

"Conor?"

He still crouched above her, his dick hard and pulsing, but he was shaking his head, gasping for air.

"Conor, are you—"

"Can't punish you like this, gorgeous girl," he said. Then: "Fuck!"

Climbing off her, he grabbed her around the thighs and pulled her down the bed with him, then flipped her onto her stomach.

"Knees," he barked, and she scrambled to her knees and elbows, barely preparing herself before he gripped her hips in his big hands and shoved deep inside her, once, twice—

All she wanted was to let him come deep inside her.

Freedom. Safety.

Her life, the way she wanted it.

If she was going to drive in that wedge, now was the time.

"Conor, what could make a man who used to be a hero and once promised not to hurt me do what you're doing to me? I don't even recognize you anymore."

—with a snarl, he thrust one more time, then pulled out and came all over her. She could feel it, hot and wet and sticky, between and on her ass cheeks.

Conor wrenched himself away from her. "What the fuck was that, Kara?"

Trying to ignore the come dripping off of her, she rolled over to look at him. She hurt, she needed to orgasm so badly.

"I need to know," she asked, trying to keep her voice

warm and gentle. "I need to know what kind of man I'm letting inside of my body."

"Luke shouldn't have opened his damn mouth," he snarled again.

She waited.

"You want to know? You want to know? I'm the kind of man who takes a man and wife from their family, who makes their children orphans. I'm the kind of man who steals a woman I used to fuck from her life, just so I can keep fucking her. The kind of man who leaves his woman wet and wanting, because she's playing games and doesn't deserve to get off. The wrong kind of man. The irredeemable kind. Is that what you wanted to hear, cruel girl?"

Tears welled in her eyes. She needed to come; she wanted to cry.

Cruel girl.

Before she could say something—apologize? Defend herself? Insult him further?—he slammed out of the room, leaving her cold and sticky on the bed.

Was she winning? This didn't feel like winning. She was no closer to getting free. Instead, she felt shackled to the bed by confused emotions, misplaced guilt, and the outlandish wish that things had gone differently.

For the rest of the day, no one fucked her. No one came to her. No one spoke to her. She got herself off—a quick, frustrating orgasm that she prayed would be interrupted by one of the men, but ended up being as lonely an endeavor as all her other masturbation sessions had been until they'd kidnapped her.

And that night, she slept alone. Or tried to. Really, she stared out the window, barely able to make out the shapes of the Tetons in the distance, and let herself do something she hadn't done in years.

She cried.

12

"**Y**ou shouldn't have told her," Conor said into his mouthpiece, his jaw tight with fury.

But then he'd been furious since yesterday, when Kara had said *I need to know what kind of man I'm letting inside my body.* He wasn't sure who he was pissed at most: Luke, who was out of eyesight, up on the roof of the building across the street with his sniper rifle, the asshole; Kara, who was back safe in the cabin, likely making a mess of the place; or his own damn self.

Conor, Luke, and Micah were in downtown LA on a hit job. Their client, a corporate bigwig, wanted a competitor's principal researcher taken out before they could put out a product that would drive their client underwater. And their client had promised them more than money—he claimed to have answers, especially because the researcher in question worked for Johnathan Pharmaceuticals, a big pharma organization that was part of the conspiracy that had cost Conor, Luke, and Micah their careers—and souls.

Conor heard Luke growl. "I wasn't going to keep lying to her, and lying by omission is still lying."

Conor laughed. This hypocritical asshole. "Like you lied to me by omission a year ago when you didn't tell me you'd been dating and fucking her?"

Micah spoke up. Conor could see him; he sat on Spring Street outside a little café, sipping coffee and watching passersby.

"Not now, you two. We need to focus on getting eyes on the target."

"Fuck that," Conor said, recognizing the growl in his own voice. "We're talking about this now. Kara has no business knowing about that last mission. Luke, all you've given her is further ammunition against us."

And more of a reason to hate them, but Conor didn't mention that part, or the way it made something in his chest ache. Saying it out loud was too vulnerable, and Conor didn't do vulnerable. Not anymore. In that, he and Kara were disturbingly similar.

"Not everything is a fucking war, Conor." Conor imagined Luke grinding his teeth. *Good.* "That part of our lives is over."

"That's where you're wrong, Boy Scout. Everything is always a war, and the second you forget that, you've lost."

Luke's voice was so quiet, Conor could barely hear him in the earpiece. "I hate that you feel that way."

Before Conor could respond—and what could he respond with, really?—Micah spoke.

"Shit."

That was concerning. But Conor couldn't see anything that would've disturbed his friend. "What's wrong, Tech Geek? Do you have eyes on him? Were we spotted?"

"No."

But Micah wasn't even looking at the street; he was staring down at his phone.

"Micah." Conor's gut clenched, because that could only mean one thing. Visions of the house, empty, Kara long gone, tortured him. "Did she escape? Did someone take her?"

"Worse," Micah said, his voice strained. "She's having a panic attack."

"Fucking fuck!" Luke's exclamation rang in Conor's ear. "I *knew* one of us should've fucking stayed with her."

"We can argue and point fingers later," Conor stated, trying to remain calm. Impossible, as he imagined Kara writhing on the floor of the home they'd built for her, struggling to breathe. He'd been so angry at the way her accusation had hit its mark, he'd treated her like shit. And now she was in pain, and he couldn't help her. "We need to figure out how to help her."

"We need to abort the mission," Luke said.

"There's a million dollars riding on this hit, as well as answers. This is the closest we've gotten to Johnathan Pharmaceuticals," Conor argued, but even as he spoke the words he knew he didn't care. Even though it wasn't just a million dollars; it was a million, plus fucking answers to the mission gone wrong. "Not to mention that we'll piss off the client, and we don't need another enemy in the world."

They had plenty.

Which meant Kara now had plenty.

Kara, who was trapped in the house, alone, unable to breathe. Conor had never felt this helpless. The energy bars he'd eaten threatened to come back up.

"What happens if she can't find her way out of it?"

Luke spoke. "She'll be okay, physically. She might throw up or pass out, if she's hyperventilating. But it won't kill her."

"She's hyperventilating," Micah stated, his voice

reflecting the helplessness that Conor felt. "She's on the floor. She's shaking, it's so bad. Luke, what do we do?"

Luke was silent for a moment. "Nothing. Panic attacks usually don't last longer than an hour. We abort the mission and go home and do our best to care for her. And apologize for being assholes who left her locked up like a prisoner of *war* in the first place."

Conor knew prisoner of war was directed at him.

"I'm coming down," Luke said.

"Shit, I see the target," Micah said.

Conor watched as a man walked down the street, alone. He couldn't believe he was passing up on one more step to finding vengeance, but he knew in his gut that protecting Kara came first.

Except Luke, once again, displayed his competence. One second, their target was standing, the other he'd dropped to the sidewalk, face up. Blood spread below his head, where his brains leaked out. Once upon a time, killing a man created a sense of guilt, no matter how small, in Conor.

Now, he felt nothing.

"Mission accomplished," Luke said, his voice sardonic in Conor's ear. "Time to go home to our girl."

Kara woke that morning to find herself alone in the house.

There were three notes for her on the kitchen counter.

The first was in Micah's handwriting.

On a job. Food in fridge. Netflix password is taped next to the TV, but don't bother trying to get on the WiFi, it's fingerprint protected. Phone in the office if there's an emergency. House is

locked and alarmed, but if you're bored, you can try to break out.
😼

The second was in Luke's.

You have Netflix, and we loaded up a Kindle for you, but we also left you a notebook in the office. Maybe it's time to get back to what you love.

The third was from Conor.

Be a good girl.

Kara flipped off the camera above the subzero fridge, knowing they could see her. How dare Luke suggest she start writing again, when she'd left that dream long behind her? He thought he knew her so well.

"You know nothing, Jon Snow," she muttered to herself, then laughed. She and Luke had binge-watched *Game of Thrones* together, and Kara had teased Luke for being similar to the almost naively idealistic TV character.

She shook her head, dislodging the tender memory before it could soften her toward him.

It was recon time.

The office was unlocked. There were four desks, simple and clean, no papers, no nothing. Kara did her best to ignore the math, because the realization that there was a fourth desk—with that fucking blank notebook on it—was enough to send her into another rage spiral, and she wasn't going back down that path right now. What was she supposed to journal? (*Dear diary, today I was still kidnapped but had a lot of sex!*) Write an erotic short story about a woman who was kidnapped against her will and forced to do filthy sex acts with her captors?

Well, forced would be the fiction there.

Those assholes.

Next to the notebook was an iPhone. Kara tried her password to unlock it and did her best not to let it annoy her that Micah somehow had figured it out—especially because it was 0926, the date she'd first met Conor.

Ugh, ugh, ugh. She'd given herself and her inner longing away somehow. Stupid hacker.

She tried dialing out—911, her own cell phone number, her mother's—although Kara had doubts her mother ever answered her phone or even checked her voicemail—Lola's, but nothing worked. Finally, she scrolled through the contacts, already knowing there would only be three numbers: Luke's, Micah's, and Conor's.

Giving up on the phone, she turned to the other desks, trying drawers only to find them locked. Fortunately, Kara knew how to jimmy a lock—it was an essential skill when she lived in Brooklyn and forgot her keys, especially because the super charged fifty bucks every time she locked herself out. Leaving the office, she went into the master bath and dug through the drawers until she found a bobby pin, biting off the plastic coating and exposing the sharp edge, then unbending it so it was straight.

Returning to the office, she twisted the bobby pin in the lock on the desk closest to the door until she heard the lock click and the drawer slid open.

"Girl's still got it," she said, proud of herself. And then her eyes went wide at what was in the drawer.

Disturbing autopsy photos with the names Eric von Steuben and Miranda von Steuben on them. Coroner reports. Huge piles of paper with text blocked out, with dates and times and codes Kara couldn't decipher.

Kara stopped, her heart aching when she saw what was underneath the reports: A pile of computer printed photographs of two young boys with big blue eyes, some taken close up, some far away. They both looked miserable and lost.

Luke had told her about them, hadn't he? The two boys that Conor had orphaned in their last SEAL mission. The reason she'd asked him who he had become.

Guilt, thick like black tar, stuck to her chest and refused to let go.

He kidnapped me, she told herself. *He just took me out of my life, like my wants and desires didn't matter.*

It was why she'd dug her fingers into that fresh, gaping wound of his and messed around in there. Conor acted like he was invulnerable, like he was in charge, and she'd wanted—needed—to shake his foundation, make him doubt himself. He'd been so pissed he came on her instead of in her, and left her there feeling like trash. But in retrospect, maybe it was worth feeling like a used tissue if it meant she succeeded.

And yet. Even though Kara had told herself it was part of her play for freedom, it hadn't been that, not really. No, she was hurt that he kept rejecting her, that he kept himself separate as if all she was good for was a fuck, so she'd lashed out and hit him where it hurt.

And oh, had she hit him good.

And oh, did it feel fucking terrible.

Shoving away her misplaced guilt where it couldn't torment her with uncertainty, she carefully stacked the photos and paperwork in the order she'd found them and placed them back in the drawer, using the bobby pin to relock it before trying the other drawers on the other desks.

In the second one, all she found was a piece of notebook paper with a list of names on it, many crossed off. Most of the names were unfamiliar until she reached the bottom three. She recognized two:

Elliot Johnathan
Joshua Johnathan

And the final one made alarm bells go off in her head:

Christopher Johnathan

A name she tried not to think about anymore.

Elliot Johnathan and Joshua Johnathan were Chris's brothers. The three came from a wealthy, WASPy family and had gone on to make names for themselves: Elliot Johnathan was the founder and CEO of Johnathan Pharmaceuticals, Joshua Johnathan was the head of The Johnathan Group, a firm that had, among other unsavory deals, military contracts with national and foreign entities and who knew what else. Chris used to joke he was the creative black sheep of the family, because instead of running a billion-dollar-plus company, he wrote bestselling highbrow literary novels beloved by critics and litbros alike. Oh, and taught naïve grad students. And fucked around with some of them, behind his wife's back.

Kara shook that off. A spidey sense tingled—was she here as more than a reluctant fuck buddy? What did the Johnathan brothers have to do with anything?

The final drawer made her angry. It was piles of information about her: credit card statements, medical bills, a list of her favorite, filthiest romances, and photos, so many photos of her. Sleeping, running on the 606 trail, meals out with Lola, getting on the El, going on first dates. Close ups on her face, and lord, did she always look that sad and wistful? There was no way.

Lola. She hadn't thought about her, in what, days? Did her best friend think she was dead? Did everyone?

Her throat hurt as she realized she'd barely thought about the life she'd been forced to leave behind. But what had she told herself earlier? Even if she didn't love her life now, she deserved to build one that she did love. And these assholes had stolen that from her. And invaded her privacy.

They were full on stalkers, kidnappers, killers. Bad men, not the kind she should be feeling guilty toward.

But those boys' faces haunted her, and so did the bleak but thunderous look in Conor's eyes after he'd yelled at her before leaving her alone last night.

God, could she make up her mind? She still had to hate them, she had to escape. She wasn't sure how she could use this information, but there was a puzzle here, and it seemed to her she was at the center of it. If she solved it...

Then she'd have some leverage against these assholes.

But she didn't know enough.

She couldn't *do* enough.

She was helpless. Alone, and helpless, and as those words echoed in her brain, rage turned to panic and the room started to spin around her.

She had to get out of here.

She had to get free.

She tried all of the doors, growing more and more desperate and pissed off when they were all locked and the disembodied creepy robot voice stated, "Unsuccessful attempt to unlock front door, 08:06 a.m.", "Unsuccessful attempt to unlock kitchen door, 08:11 a.m."

She tried a number of windows, too—the huge bay windows in the great room, the windows framing the front door, the window over the kitchen sink, figuring that she could shove her body through one of them. She even considered the bedroom window, figuring that it wouldn't be too bad of a fall, all things considered, but all of them were sealed shut.

Full-on desperate now, she dragged one of the kitchen stools into the great room and slammed it against the window, only for it to practically bounce off and almost hit her in the head. She tried twice, a third time, before dropping the damn stool on the floor. *Fucking hell*, what were these windows made of? Were they bullet proof? Who and what were these paranoid assholes so afraid of?

Alone and without any hope of freedom, an indefinite future of being nothing but a sex toy stretched in front of Kara like a funhouse hallway of horrifying mirrors, reflecting her reality back at her. She'd tried so hard to avoid having a panic attack, but she felt her calm crack the way those mirrors in her mind were. Crouching on the floor, she inhaled and exhaled as carefully and mindfully as she could, trying to calm her mind, to tell herself *you are okay, you are okay, in this moment, you are okay.*

But she wasn't. Kara had lived a life of freedom, of never being stuck in the same place, of never having to face herself and accept who she was. She'd always embraced the metaphor of the open road, the horizon in the distance—and with it, the potential for the better life she'd *one day* live. Because for Kara, freedom mattered, and yet she'd been caught as surely as a butterfly on a pinboard. That knowledge swept over her like a wave before crashing over her head. Her breathing sped up and distantly she realized she was hyperventilating.

That would be funny, if her kidnappers didn't kill her, but her panic did. The thought was distant and muted, like there was a wall of glass between Kara and her sanity.

As her vision blurred and her heart raced, her arms went numb and that *oh god, I'm about to have a heart attack* feeling increased, an image came to her: three men, surrounding her, telling her to breathe. Luke, hanging by his hands on a climbing wall next to her when they first met, as he talked to her while she was panicking, until she stopped.

Luke a few days ago, holding her on the bed upstairs.

Breathe, Kara. Just breathe with me. Okay? You don't have to do anything else right now, all you have to do is inhale and exhale.

Micah, watching over her. Conor, angry because he was worried.

All three of them, caring. About her.

All she had to do was inhale and exhale.

So she did, taking deep, slow breaths and forcing herself to slowly let them out. In and out, eyes on the mountain range in front of her. The mountain range she loved, that these men had brought her to.

And slowly but surely, the panic attack dissipated, until she was able to shakily stand and stretch her shoulders.

There was a difference between trying to outpace a panic attack until it caught up with her, and actually being able to work her way through and over it. The undertow was gone, the waves of fear weren't threatening her anymore. The room no longer felt claustrophobic, and her mind returned to her.

Thank god.

And thank those fuckers, too, Kara thought ruefully. Annoying as fuck that the men who had caused the panic were the ones who cured it, even when they were absent.

She wasn't ever going to thank them.

13

———

Kara was lying on the bed, staring at the ceiling and constructing a mental murder wall when she heard the alarm go off and the disembodied voice announce that "Boss, Tech Geek, and Boy Scout have arrived back on premises."

At the announcement and the realization that she wasn't alone in this fucking house anymore, Kara's heart leapt before settling contentedly in her chest, because her heart was a stupid idiot that had no idea what was good for it. She had missed them, but she shouldn't have missed them. She'd been anxious and lonely without them, when she should've been relieved to have them gone.

Moments later, feet pounded up the stairs.

"Kara, baby?" Micah sounded terrified.

"Anxious girl, we're here," Conor called, sounding like the man she used to know. His voice was kinder than the last time she'd heard him, when he'd bitten out his words and come all over her before leaving her a just fucked and put away mess.

"Sweetheart," was all Luke said. A plea.

The bedroom door opened, the three of them crowding the doorway. Kara lifted her head to see them, desperation clouding all three men's eyes, making their faces sharp with worry. They glanced at each other, then Luke pushed his way through to join her on the bed.

"Sweetheart," he repeated, "how bad was it?"

How bad was what?

And then she remembered.

The cameras.

There must have been one in the living room she'd missed. Which meant while they were out on their "job"—whatever awful shit that must have entailed—they'd still had eyes on her and had witnessed her at her most vulnerable, most helpless. Weakest.

And if that wasn't enough to make her wish they were gone, she didn't know what was.

And yet. She was still glad they were here.

"It wasn't that bad," she said finally, avoiding Luke's gaze, because how could she tell him, tell any of them, that thinking of them was what had calmed her down and helped her through the panic and over to the other side?

"You scared us, baby," Micah said from the doorway, and for once there didn't seem to be anything calculating in his eyes. Maybe he actually wasn't storing this weakness away to use against her later.

Conor slowly approached the bed, and a lump filled Kara's throat as he dropped to his knees at the foot of the bed, reached his arms forward, and dragged her down until her legs hung over the sides.

If he was about to try to fuck her after what happened last time...

But instead he kissed her hip and lay his head in her lap.

It felt like an apology. Like a benediction of some kind.

Like he was so relieved to see her, he'd gone weak at the knees.

It felt like power. Like hope. Like...

The four letter word whispered in her head, but Kara dismissed it. It couldn't be love. Not when she still hated them.

But it was certainly something.

"Baby," Micah said, his throat tight, "We're sorry. We never should've left you alone here. What do you need? What can we do?"

Be with me, just be with me, a tiny voice whispered in her head.

She ignored it.

"You can let me go," she said softly.

Conor lifted his head from her lap.

"Not that," he said, his voice husky. "Never that."

He kissed her hip bone again.

Luke cleared his throat. "Have you had any water or anything to eat? After an episode like that you must be starving."

She was, but not for food. She was starving for this sense of being cared for. Had been for so long, she admitted to herself. She didn't want it to end.

But that way lay madness.

If she was going to stick to her plan—and she needed to —then she needed to get Luke alone, so she could take advantage of this moment of guilt and play on it so she could get more answers and get what she wanted.

Which was freedom.

Wasn't it?

"I'll make you something to eat," Micah said, but didn't move, still watching her. "We *are* sorry, baby, okay? We'll take care of you from now on."

And why did his gentle declaration sound like a threat? A dangerous one, but to her heart, not her body. She was in so much trouble.

Especially when Conor said, "We'll never leave you alone again, we promise."

Because the ominous promise should've terrified her instead of calming her more.

You wouldn't have had a panic attack in the first place if they hadn't kidnapped you, she reminded herself. *And if they never leave you alone, you'll never be free.*

Freedom. Her reason for existing, and her end goal. No matter the price.

"Conor," Micah called.

Conor didn't move.

"Conor, let's give her some time with Luke," Micah said, and reluctantly, Conor rose to his feet, dropping a kiss in the middle of her abdomen and leaving tingles in his wake.

"I'm sorry too, poor girl," he murmured, an anguished look in his eyes as he followed Micah out, leaving her alone with Luke.

Who sat next to her on the bed, but didn't touch her. She could feel the distance between their bodies like an unwelcome weight, and she wanted the weight of his body instead.

So she rolled over to him.

"Were you worried about me?" she asked softly, stroking a hand down his arm, entranced by the way his chest worked at her touch.

"Sweetheart, I've only been that worried one other time in my life."

"When?" she asked, curiously.

"When we first met and you were dangling from the

climbing wall and having a panic attack up there and your fucking climbing instructor was yelling at you."

She remembered that day, the way Luke had talked her down. It was a memory that had comforted her through the months in between seeing him. It had protected her only a few hours before.

"That's the only thing that's scared you this much?"

"Sweetheart, you're the only thing in the world that has the power to scare me that much."

Kara's heart skipped like a stone and sank, sank, sank.

She wanted him in that moment, badly. Not because she needed to play him to get free, not because she needed to drive an even bigger wedge between him and Conor, but because she'd never felt so seen or wanted before by someone, and she loved that feeling.

Could she have that, if she stayed?

"Maybe you should get some sleep, sweetheart," Luke said, starting to stand. Kara put out a hand and grabbed his wrist, stopping him.

"Luke, I need you."

He stopped and turned back to her. "Then I'll stay with you," he said simply.

"No." Kara cleared her throat, surprised by how tight it was. "I mean, I *need* you. I need you to help me feel like I'm here, and present in this moment. Like I'm okay. And…"

His eyes deepened to a green as dark and vibrant as the forest surrounding them. "And what, Kara?" His throat also sounded tight, the words delivered on a rasp.

She swallowed. "Like I'm in control. I think. I know that's not how we—how you—usually fuck, but…"

He smiled, boyish and sweet, and for a moment Kara forgot how she'd wound up here in the first place. "Sweetheart, I can do that for you."

But then she remembered how Conor had refused to let her go, and Luke had said nothing, and remembered why she was here, and what she was trying to accomplish. Maybe taking control during sex would get her there, or at least keep her in the right mindset to get back some control when they weren't deep inside her. Trying something new was worth it, and it would settle her, and test him. Luke didn't give up control. Luke liked to dominate. More than that, he liked to inflict pain.

She swallowed. "Can you be gentle?"

"Sweetheart, I can be whatever you need right now."

Except her rescuer.

As if to emphasize his point, he tugged off his cargo pants and t-shirt, lifting his hips so his pants fell to the floor, and revealing his perfect chest, tan and speckled with freckles like confectioners' sugar. He lay back on the bed, propping his arms behind him.

"Is this where you want me?"

Kara gulped, fire shooting through her at his semi-hard cock. She could still feel him inside her from the other morning, the way he just held her on top of him, so he touched all of her.

"Lie back," she murmured, rolling toward him and kneeling in front of him, placing a kiss on his cock as he obeyed her. It twitched, once, twice. Then she descended on it, licking a trail up one ridge and down the other, before blowing on him. His cock twitched again, and Luke groaned. She looked up at him, and forced herself not to get lost in the green depths of his eyes.

"More," he demanded.

"Say please," she teased.

"Kara," his voice warned.

"You promised."

He nodded, his head jerking like it took effort.

"Please, sweetheart. Please give me your mouth."

So she gave it to him, opening her mouth and sucking him in deep, working his base with her hands, because he was too long to fit the whole way down her throat, especially on the first go. She bobbed her head, making sure to suck, and when he hit the back of her throat she swallowed around him.

"Fuck, sweetheart, so good," he groaned, thrusting his hips up to push even further.

In response—and punishment—she released him and sat back on her heels, winking at him.

"What did I do?" he gasped.

"No moving," she said, drunk on power. Was this what it was like, to be the one in control?

Luke nodded, shutting his eyes, face strained as he tried to control himself, and Kara went back to sucking. She remembered what Micah had said about Luke liking a little bit of teeth, so she carefully, gently, gently slid her teeth along his cock as she deep throated him. He growled and became impossibly harder, filling her mouth and throat and taking most of her air. She pulled back and licked up precum, and he swore.

"Kara, sweetheart, please, I need more, I need—"

She cut him off by straddling him and sinking down, down, down on his cock, until she was full of him, so full.

"I need *this*," she told him, insistent. "You promised."

"Sweetheart," he said, removing one hand from behind his head to reach for one of hers, placing it on his chest above his heart. "I need *you*."

And *god*, if those three words didn't pierce through her.

"Do you feel it?" he asked, as she lifted and lowered over him, grinding and using his cock to hit her where it felt good, every time. "Do you feel how hard you make me, sweetheart? You can fuck me, you can do anything to me, and I'll always come back for more, because I'm a sadistic, masochistic, greedy bastard and all I want is you. Do you feel the way we're connected? My heart is beating—for you. Take *me.* Take *it.* Just don't stop."

His words powered through her, making her feel shaky and weak, even as she rode him, harder and harder, ready to bring them both to completion.

"Are you going to come?" she taunted.

"Are you going to ignore what I'm saying?" he challenged.

Once again, she punished him—punished both of them —by rising off his cock and hovering over him, even as her thighs and calves screamed, and her pussy quaked with need and the loss of him.

He swore. "Fuck. You're a secret sadist, sweetheart."

"Takes one to know one." She lowered herself back onto him, and she was so soaked he slid in easily.

And she was done with being in control. Had she really thought she was in control? She might be in charge of his orgasm, but his words, his words...they controlled her, and she wanted him the way she'd always had him.

"Luke," she said.

"Sweetheart, I'm about to come, and I swear to god if you tease me more I won't be able to control myself," he warned.

"So don't," she said. "Take me the way you want to."

A moment slid by, sticky-toffee-slow. And then he was no longer inside of her and she was being lifted into the air and lowered onto his face, practically smothering him with her soaking wet pussy. Luke groaned against her, the sound vibrating through her, and she writhed on top of him as he licked and sucked and ate her, pushing on her hips in a silent order to let him in. He thrust his tongue deep inside her, and everything in Kara tightened. And from the rumbling of his chest, he was roaring, or saying something, some soft sweet love words of filth against her pussy, holding her tight as he tortured her with his mouth.

Moments before she thought she was about to come, he *bit her.* Right on the clit, no warm up, no nothing.

Kara screamed, distantly aware that she was coming all over his face. As she did, something in her chest shifted, lifted, loosened, and was gone. Luke had taken part of her heart. She was losing. Lost. In him, in them, and the worst part was *she didn't fucking care.*

Then she was being lifted again, and Luke moved out from under her so she was dropped on the bed.

"On your knees," he said, his voice like sandpaper. Kara turned her head to watch him, hard cock, almost purple from how hard he needed to come, bobbing as he walked into the closet to grab something.

He caught her watching.

"Head on the bed. No peeking."

She lowered her head to the duvet, and the smell of sex —his sweat, her desire—overwhelmed her. She was sinking into the scent of them, but before she could drown, she was brought back by a *thwack* and then a stinging burn on her right ass cheek. She shrieked into the cover, and then there was another *thwack,* evening out the burn. He continued, the sound of a leather belt (because it had to be a leather belt, that's what he'd always used on her), singing through the air before landing in a perfect arc of pain on her ass or upper thighs.

"Spread your legs," he ordered, and she rushed to comply, her whole body singing along with the sound of the belt.

She'd forgotten how much she'd loved this, the way the pain chased away her fear, the way it tethered her to the ground, and to him. It left some fear behind, though, especially now. It terrified her, the way each hit tied them together, like Luke understood the way her heart beat, could see to the inside of her, and liked every bit.

And then he hit her between the legs, right on her pussy, and she forgot how to think, the burn taking her somewhere perfect.

The belt hit the floor with a clamor and then his mouth was there again, soothing away the sting.

"Luke," she mumbled against the cover.

His mouth was gone from her pussy.

"Sweetheart, it's time," he said.

She didn't get a chance to even ask what he meant. There was a small *click* and then cool gel dripped between her ass cheeks, and he was working one finger inside her hole, then two, then three, and it burned like the spanking had. But better. Anticipation made her chest go tight.

"Don't tell those assholes I got back in your asshole first," he joked, and Kara laughed breathlessly as he removed his fingers, and she was empty, so empty, until he was back, working his cock into her this time.

"It hurts," she moaned, as he slowly, so slowly, pushed deep into her ass, lighting up a fire within her.

"I know, sweetheart, that's the best part," he murmured, pushing deeper still, until he bottomed out inside her and groaned.

"I'm going to fill this hole up, aren't I, baby? You're so tight and hot and perfect back here; you're so tight and hot and perfect everywhere," he was groaning as he reached a hand underneath her and started strumming her poor, overworked clit with his fingers, like she was an instrument he'd always known how to play. And hadn't he? Didn't he know how to play her, even though she was the one who was supposed to be playing him?

She was supposed to be saying something. Doing something. She had a goal, beyond getting off. But as he started to pump in and out of her, muttering filthy words like *perfect, beautiful, good, you're so good sweetheart, our good girl, aren't you?* she was too close to coming to care.

So good.

That's what it was. That's what she needed in this moment.

With superhuman strength, she forced words out of her mouth. "You're good too, baby. I want to be good for you, because you're so good to me. You're a good man, Luke."

His hips stuttered, then he pressed deep, bathing her insides with his come as he roared on top of her, and the heat and wetness of him, the feeling of him doing what he'd promised lit her up inside and she was coming, coming, coming with him.

He collapsed on top of her for a moment, then rolled to the side, pulling her with him so she was in his arms.

"Did you mean it?" he demanded.

Her brain was a fog of spent desire and sexual satisfaction. "Mean what?"

"When you called me a good man, Kara. Were you being honest, or were you playing me, like Micah thinks?"

Fucking Micah.

She looked him in his eyes.

"Luke, you *are* a good man."

"How?" he rasped, his voice still hoarse. "How can you say that, knowing what I've done?"

"And what you're still doing?" She sat up to make sure he was looking in her eyes as she traced light fingers over his face, doing what she could to relax the strained muscles there.

"And what I'm still doing," he acknowledged.

"Because a few bad choices don't determine who we are. It took me a long time to realize that. Too long. And it was because of you, although it took me longer to admit it to myself."

"The professor in New York," he said softly.

Kara nodded, the memory not hurting the way it used to. It was on the tip of her tongue to ask him why he was calling Chris "the professor" when he obviously knew his name, but it didn't feel like it was the time to confess she'd gone snooping through their files. Instead, Kara took a deep breath, ready to break the weak link, knowing it would get her closer to freedom and hating herself for it at the same time. The look in Conor's eyes, in Micah's, when they'd found her today flashed in her mind, but she shoved away the regret. They'd taken her, they deserved this.

"But Luke...you are a better man than your current choices. You're a better man than this." She inhaled one more time, forcing the words out of her mouth and praying they were true. "You're a better man than *them*."

His hands, which had gripped her waist, squeezed tight, so tight it was hard for her to release her breath.

Then he was moving her off him, her body growing cold as he pushed off of the bed and stalked out of the room, without bothering with his clothes or even a backwards glance.

"Luke," she called.

"You know how much I hate liars," he said without even looking back at her, and then the bedroom door slammed shut, and she heard a click, because he had locked her in.

Alone.

With his come leaking out of her ass.

It was an echo of the previous night, as she lay there alone on the bed, sticky and sore, the small satisfaction in winning and getting closer to achieving her goal and finding freedom leaking out of her as self-loathing and loneliness flooded in, and all she wanted to do was to crawl to him, to them, and beg. Plead for them to stay so she wasn't alone.

When had lust become longing?

The thought filled her with fear. Because she was alone. And moreover, she was good at being alone—she'd honed it like a survival skill. After a while, Kara forced herself off the bed, feeling weak and broken, cheap and worthless. She stumbled into the shower, turning the water to scalding, and stood below the showerhead, letting the stream pummel her body into submission and accepting the burn on her bruised and mottled ass, the sting between her cheeks, as punishment, as if Luke was still there, beating on her.

He'd done it preemptively, hadn't he? Punished her for the words she hadn't said yet? And she wasn't lying. He was a better man than Micah and Conor, no one would question that. He had a moral compass the other two lacked, he just needed to be gently steered back toward it again. But he'd reacted like she'd slapped him. He was the one who always stayed, she was the one who left, and yet here he was, flipping the script on her.

And he'd *locked* her in. It wasn't like she was going to be able to escape, so then why had he done it?

As the water turned cold, Kara turned colder, realizing.

He'd locked her in because he'd needed a locked door between them. Because he couldn't be near her, not for another second. She'd done that. In her rush to drive a wedge between him and the other men, she'd driven one between him and her, instead.

Fuck.

Kara sank to her knees in the cold water, wondering how she kept fucking up so badly, and unsure how to fix the messes she made. But wasn't that her whole MO?

She didn't even know if she wanted to fix this specifically so she could achieve her goal and escape this funhouse of fuckery, or because the idea that she'd hurt Luke hurt her. Even if he deserved it (and he deserved it).

She was so fucked.

14

———

"What are you so pissed about?" Conor asked Luke as the taller man entered the kitchen.

Micah could feel angry energy permeate the room. He was busy stirring kale and white bean soup in front of the stove, but he glanced up. Luke, who was usually the most lowkey of the three of them, had a thunderous expression on his face. This couldn't be good; Kara had done something, and Conor was clearly still too angry at Luke to help him get to the bottom of this.

"Not now," Luke growled at Conor, who laughed darkly.

"She got to you too, huh? She's great at finding buttons," Conor taunted, proving Micah right.

Micah sighed inwardly, resisting the urge to tell both these fuckers to shut up. Sometimes he just wanted to pull rank by pummeling them both into submission and hopefully knocking sense into their dumbass heads in the process. But he knew better. You could rule with force of will, or you could rule with cunning, finding a way to guide the people who thought they were in charge in the direction that was best for them—and for you. So even though it almost physically hurt Micah to watch these two fucking knuckleheads get into it, *again*, he let them.

Although for a moment, he wished for romantic ease instead of constant fighting. He loved the two of them—he could admit that to himself—and he knew they loved him and each other. But despite his...persuasion skills, he wasn't sure if he'd ever get that declaration from either of them. Not because of internalized homophobia; but because Luke was broken and Conor was emotionally constipated and neither of them knew how to say I love you.

Micah hoped Kara would help with that, one day—but she was nowhere near loving them herself.

He dismissed his wishful thinking and turned back to the conversation.

"Do you have to be an asshole right now? Really Conor, let it up," Luke was saying as he dropped into a stool and buried his head in his hands.

The way to fix things, to progress their relationships, wasn't to get them to stop fighting on their own. It was to get in Kara's head, so she would finally stop picking at the scabs between them and let them heal.

Micah couldn't help but respect the woman, who always seemed to be one step ahead of them. She'd figured out the rift between Conor and Luke quickly, just like she'd figured out that Micah was, well, not pulling strings, per se, but was using what he knew of the people around them, pushing those buttons, and using it to push them in the direction he wanted. Kara had figured it out because she saw the similarity between the two of them. She was doing the exact same thing.

The difference was that Micah was doing it because it would serve everyone best. He was thinking about the long term, was trying to build something here, even if he recognized he was starting with a shaky foundation. Kara was acting from panic, from *should* mode, and it was selfish and in the end, bad for her, too. And was causing even more damage to his foundation.

Okay, so he was a lot domineering. But she liked it.

Fuck, did she like it. Micah got hard just thinking about it. He wanted to fuck the woman upstairs, not referee. Hold her afterwards and bask in the contentment he knew was somewhere around the corner.

Speaking of which.

"Luke, where's Kara?" Micah asked.

Luke kept his head buried in his hands. "I locked her in the bedroom."

Conor laughed again. "That's the first smart thing I've heard you say in a while."

"Fuck off, Boss," Luke said.

Micah dismissed this, placing the spoon on the ladle holder and turning to Luke, who sat across from him. "Why did you lock her in the bedroom?"

Luke looked up and stared at him. "Because she's dangerous, and a liar, and I needed some peace for a second."

Conor started laughing again.

"Seriously, you motherfucker, do you want to get beaten to shit in the weight room again? Because I've got some energy to kill." Luke's eyes were filled with anger that needed an outlet.

Conor shook his head. "What, sexually frustrated? She might have pissed me off, but at least she didn't leave me high and dry."

"No, I'm sexually satisfied," Luke drawled, winking at Conor. "She let me fuck her in the ass, and god, it was sweet. She wanted it bad. She ever let you do that?"

Oh, shit.

Micah ignored the feelings Luke's confession stirred up in him. He shoved away the lust at imagining the feeling of sliding his cock between Kara's big and bouncy ass cheeks and thrusting deep into her, feeling her that way, knowing her that way. And he breathed away the jealousy at learning that Luke had been the first one. This was *good*. It meant that she was finally trusting them, letting them in, figuratively and literally, because Kara didn't leave her soul behind during sex, not with them. She shared it, even if she didn't want to admit to being so vulnerable. It didn't matter who it was, because they were a team, a unit.

But they weren't fucking acting like one, damn it. Conor had risen from the banquet in the corner and was stalking toward Luke, eyes flashing, veins popping out in his neck with jealousy and pent-up rage. They were going to beat the shit out of each other again, and this time it wasn't going to end in one of them blowing each other. This time it was probably going to end in someone's death, which would ruin Micah's long-term plans for all of them.

Which meant he needed to referee after all.

"Don't you see what she's doing? Come on, you two. Stop hulking out and let some of that blood go back to your brains. Think. Kara's smart; she saw that wedge between the two of you and she's chipping away at it every day. And you're *letting* her."

Conor froze. Luke's eyes went wide.

"Jesus, fuck."

"Damn it."

These dumbasses. They were lucky he loved them.

"Conor, what did she say to you that made you so angry at Luke yesterday when we were in LA?" Micah asked.

"She asked me who I had become and why I had

changed. She knows. She knows what I did." Conor's voice sounded thick. The man never cried, but this was the closest he'd ever sounded to it.

"What we all did," Luke said slowly. "So when she told me I was a good man, a better man than the two of you—I knew it was a lie."

And Luke hated liars.

What Micah hated was this idea of good man versus bad man. They'd done good things, and they'd done terrible things, and he was sick of his two partners judging themselves based on it, forming and reforming their identities around it, and then planning their actions in reaction to it. The world was a dark and terrible place, Kara had brought light into it, they brought her what she needed, and that was it. So they'd maybe stolen her away from her life, so what? He knew they could give her a better one. If only she'd start writing in that damn notebook. If only these two—no three —idiots could get in touch with their feelings and express them to themselves and to each other.

But he didn't say that to them; being direct was never the best way.

"She's playing you both. She's trying to escape. She's angry and lashing out and she knows how to push your buttons," Micah said as rationally and calmly as possible. "You need to stop letting her."

Luke's shoulders hunched. "She'll never forgive us. She'll never want us. We shouldn't have taken her."

"Luke." Conor's voice, for once, was gentle. "We didn't have a choice. We're in hiding from the Johnathans, and if we had showed up one day and asked her to date all of us, we would have brought danger to her door. And she was already in their crosshairs. We can't live in the light with her, Boy Scout. Are you willing to live without her?"

Luke's shoulders sagged, and Micah watched in shocked delight as the two men approached each other and hesitantly put their arms around each other. Luke buried his head in Conor's neck. They were quiet for a moment.

Kiss. Kiss and make up. Say those three magic words.

But Conor coughed and ruined the moment.

They pulled apart jerkily and avoided each other's gazes.

Emotionally repressed idiots.

"This is never going to work," Conor muttered, and the mood spiraled even lower in the room.

Micah squared his shoulders, determined, and, frankly, angry. Kara was topping from the bottom, and Micah was the only one who got to do that. Instead of being the glue to pull them together, she was a sledgehammer breaking them apart. It couldn't stand. She needed to be punished, she needed to be persuaded, but Luke clearly wasn't up for a good spanking session, so Micah was going to have to step in. For her sake.

For all their sakes.

"Finish stirring the soup. Don't let it burn."

"You know I know fuck all about soup," Luke protested. "And Conor will set the house on fire."

Conor laughed, the sound unhappy.

"Just do it," Micah said, walking out of the kitchen, anticipation lighting his veins.

It was his turn, and he dared Kara to try to fuck with his head, too. He'd fuck with hers right back, right before he fucked her into submission.

His cock went fully hard at the thought as he plodded up the stairs, his big body making the wood planks groan, ready to face his match.

This was a battle, a war, and he would win.

He always did.

The lock clicked and the door opened. Micah stood in the doorway, his broad shoulders barely fitting. It wasn't that it was a narrow doorway, that was just how big he was.

And Kara, who'd come hard with Luke less than an hour ago and was caught in a mental and emotional nosedive, felt her pussy clench and go wet. Just at the sight of this cunning man. All it took was looking at him and everything revved into action. But part of her was terrified, too, because sex with Micah was like being taken apart from the inside out, and then being forced to look at and memorize every part of herself, even and especially the darkest and most secret parts, and she hated every bit of it.

Except this time.

This time she would do the same thing to him.

"Am I free to go?"

He chuckled, not bothering to answer her.

"Out of this room, I mean," she clarified, angry all of a sudden. That's what he did to her: made her horny and angry and thrum with energy, all at once.

"Nope." He pressed something on his phone, and it triggered the door to shut and lock again, leaving her trapped with him.

"I was worried about you," he continued. "We all were. How long have you been having panic attacks?"

"You've been stalking me for almost two years, you should know," she shot back.

"There's a lot we don't know about you from before those two years," he answered easily, tugging at his sweatpants so they began to slide below his ass, revealing his adonis belt and a gathering of hair that led to his hard cock.

It was tenting his sweats, thick and massive and Kara's throat went dry, she wanted it so badly, even though she also wanted to punch him in the face. It was a toss-up which she wanted more.

"I'm sorry, do you really think you're about to get your dick sucked again?" she asked, huffing in false indignation.

"You'd like to do that, wouldn't you? Feel like you're in control for a second? No, Kara, I'm going to fuck you, get so deep inside that pussy you won't know where I end and you begin, and what's more, you won't want to know."

She swallowed, throat going even dryer at his tempting, provocative words. She was aware of how naked she was, bared to him, her nipples hardened into needy peaks.

"I don't want you."

"Little liar," he said, and she winced. But unlike when Luke had said it, so cold and accusatory and with such pain, Micah said it with fondness and even respect.

"But first," he said, "Let's talk about what it is you think you're accomplishing with your cruelty."

It felt like she'd been stabbed in the chest. She curled forward, almost jerkily, in order to protect herself from his words. Even though they were true. Maybe because they were true.

They deserved her cruelty. They deserved all the cruelty from her. She forced herself to meet his eyes.

"Ah, I see that does have an effect on you. So why are you doing it, hmm?" He pushed down the left side of his boxers over his hip, one inch, then two, stopping there, the tease.

"I'm speaking the truth," she said, forcing her eyes back up to his face.

At least Micah was having the same struggle. He tried to keep his eyes on hers, but they kept slipping down to her breasts. In response and as a dare, she uncrossed her legs and widened them, so he could see her pussy.

He shook his head, like he could see right through her. "And that's it? No purpose, beyond radical honesty? Why don't I give you some radical honesty, Kara." Stalking slowly toward the bed, Micah pushed down his sweatpants as he went, until she could see the shadow at the base of his cock.

She forced herself to look up at him. His eyes were a deep, troubling blue.

"How about you don't? How about we just hate fuck instead?" she suggested.

He paused at the foot of the bed, looming over her.

"Hate fuck?" For a moment, he sounded angry, his eyes going storm-cloud blue-grey, but then he laughed, his eyes clearing. "Oh, baby, you really are leaning into this lying thing, aren't you? You may want this to be a hate fuck, but you know that's not what's happening here, and it terrifies you. See," and at this, he pulled his sweats down the whole way, revealing his thick, hard cock in all its terrifying, tempting glory. But nothing was more glorious or terrifying than his eyes. "I know you, Kara. I know what happens when you try to brat your way into being dominated. You may tell yourself you're trying to fight us, that you hate us, but that line is thin, isn't it?"

"Fuck you," she spat at him, but the curse was breathy and desperate.

"Oh, you're gonna," he promised, his eyes a brilliant blue as he climbed on top of her, doing a pushup with one perfect, huge arm and stroking her pussy with the other.

She shuddered.

"Soaked." He grinned, showing her just how wet she'd made his fingers before sucking them between his lips and groaning. "You may be a pain in my ass, but you taste fucking perfect. Kryptonite pussy, like Luke says."

There it was again. But they didn't know she'd eavesdropped.

"Kryptonite pussy?" Kara snapped the words, because she was still fucking offended. Not by kryptonite pussy, but by his declaration, as if he knew her. "There is a line, you're right, Micah. And you crossed it, you and Conor and even Luke."

She waited to see any change in his expression at her words, but his face was smooth, his eyes bright with lust but clear of any misgivings. It was different from Conor, who believed he was a bad man and so had gone complete nihilist with masochistic pleasure. And then the realization came to Kara.

"You don't care, do you?" she said. "Good, bad, it doesn't matter to you—as long as you get what you want."

He angled his hips, nudging up against her slit, then pushing slowly but mercilessly into her with his too thick to be real cock, and *god,* she'd forgotten how fucking good it felt when he was inside of her. "As long as *we* get what we *need,*" he corrected, staring at her as his face went tight with pleasure, as he lit up everything inside of her like a pinball machine. She tried to ignore it, to ignore *him*, but it was impossible as he bottomed out in her and began to stroke in and out, touching every part of her, and hitting her every time in that perfect spot that tightened everything inside her, like he'd played the game that was her body a million times before and was the reigning champion.

He wasn't going to win this time.

"You're kind of an enigma, aren't you, Micah? Or you try to be," she gasped.

He only hummed as he watched her, pulling out and

shoving back in and lighting her up all over again. "You feel so good, baby."

Kara forced herself to stay on task. "You like it that way, don't you? Being a mystery to everyone, the man behind the curtain, pulling everyone else's strings. But no one ever really sees you, do they, Micah? What's that feel like, to go without being seen?"

He stilled inside her, stretching her wide, veins in his arms and neck prominent, his eyes back to that storm-cloud blue-grey as he slowly pulled out. For a moment, Kara thought he might leave her entirely, her body and then her, she'd pissed him off so much.

Instead, he said silkily, "You've been paying attention."

But his next thrust was anything but silky. He shoved back into her, hard and fast, sending the ball in the pinball machine careening out of control, like he was trying to smash the whole system. Kara cried out from the shock and heat of it, from how good it felt and how much it threatened to destroy her.

He continued. "Ballsy words for the woman trapped underneath me and writhing on my cock."

Kara shoved at his chest and wrapped her legs around his waist, trying to get enough momentum to roll them over. She failed, of course: Micah was as unmovable as a mountain.

But maybe, just maybe, not as certain.

"Easy words for the man who never has to worry about being the physically weaker one. But that's not really winning, is it, *baby*, when you can rely on your body and not your brain to make someone do what you want?" she asked.

His eyes flashed, electric blue now.

"You want to be on top?" He rolled them so she straddled him, his hands clasping her to his hot, hard body. He kept speaking, moving his hands down to unwind her legs from around him and dragging her up his body. "You want to call the shots?" She was halfway up his chest now. "Be the one in control?" He lifted her in the air like it was nothing, so she dangled over him, her pussy an inch from his chin. "Except you don't, do you baby? You *like* it when we're the ones in control. You want to tell yourself it's fucked up and that you want to leave. But you're lying to yourself. Giving us the control is what you want. What you *need*. And we'll do anything to give you what you need, and make you like it."

With that, he dropped her directly on his face and went to town on her, sucking and licking and biting her pussy until she was a wet, writhing, screaming, out of control mess, proving him right. She was going to come, and she still hadn't figured out what was the right button to press with him.

"And what do you want, Micah?" Kara cried out above him, her words running into each other as she struggled not to orgasm. "What are you lying to yourself about? You must want something, otherwise why go through all this trouble to kidnap me? It can't just be that that's what Conor wanted and you were just obeying orders, because you never really obey orders, do you, *Tech Geek*?"

His mouth stilled underneath her, then delivered a sharp bite to her clit in reprimand, and when Kara came, it was with the satisfaction that she'd finally found his button.

Just like Kara told herself she didn't want them to take control, Micah told himself he didn't want to be seen. But if Micah had nailed it on the head—she badly wanted, *needed*, them to take control—then she had found his secret too— Micah *badly* wanted someone to truly see him.

He lifted her off him and dropped her on her knees on the bed next to him, sitting up. "And what, you see me?"

he said like he'd heard her thinking, and who knew, maybe he had. "You think you know who I am, sweet baby girl?"

He'd stolen Conor's and Luke's nicknames for her and woven them seamlessly together. It was a statement, a reminder that there were three of them dominating her right now, her lovers and her jailors. The unit mattered to him.

Before a recovering Kara could take that thought further, he was rolling on top of her, pulling her legs out so she lay flat and layering his body on top of hers, sandwiching her legs between his.

And then he was thrusting back inside her, and he was big and hard and hot and everywhere, and Kara could feel herself close to coming again.

"Guess you don't want me to see you," she said, the words muffled by the bed beneath her.

But he had heard her, because he pressed his mouth to her neck and then bit down, hard. "Oh baby, it's you who can't handle looking at me, right now. I'm just giving you what you want."

He punctuated the last word with a thrust that sent her tumbling over the edge of an orgasm again, chuckling against her sensitive ear and neck as he continued fucking her through her second orgasm and into her third.

"Micah," she moaned.

"Kara," he countered with a croon.

"What are you scared of," she said on a gasp, the breath knocked out of her by her last two orgasms.

At that, he pulled out of her and she was so, so empty as he rearranged their bodies so he was sitting straight up and he was lowering her down onto his lap, until they were wrapped around each other, so close that she had to tilt her head back to look at him as he bounced her, still pulsing on his lap, and stared at her.

"Baby, I'm not the one who's scared," he said.

Maybe she had to give a little vulnerability to get the truth out of him. "Okay," she admitted on a moan, "I'm scared. I'm scared that you're right and this is how I want sex, and what that says about me. But you're scared, too."

"Of what?" he asked, his voice gentler now.

The unit mattered to him.

"That you've built a house of cards here and it's going to come crashing down around you. Because that's what you really want, isn't it? One happy little family to what, replace the one you don't have? I know nothing about your past, do I?"

His body froze and strained.

Kara 1, Micah 0.

So then why did she feel she was the one who'd lost?

And then he was powering his hips into her, lifting and straining, and coming hard.

"Yeah, one happy little family to replace the family that disowned me because I didn't conduct myself to their standards," he agreed, his voice tight and rasping. "One unit, and you're our happy little family's happy little fucktoy, our woman, the *center of our universe*, and you're going to fucking stop fighting us and admit you *love it*." And with that, he shouted her name and thrust so, so deep it almost hurt, and was filling her up, pressed tight together, coming so hard Kara could feel it leaking out of her.

When he finished, he groaned, nipping her ear. "That was fun, trying to one up each other, wasn't it? Did you like being on top for once, baby?"

At those words, Kara expected to be dumped on the bed and abandoned the same way she'd been abandoned by

Conor and Luke earlier, but instead Micah lifted her up and off him, climbing off the bed with her in his arms and carrying her into the bathroom.

"Micah, what are you doing?" she asked, surprised and discomfited by how much she liked being carried around like a doll.

Or a bride.

She dismissed that thought as Micah placed her on the floor and turned on the shower before ushering them both into the steaming stall. But her brain was whirring out of control as Micah began washing her body, slapping her hands away when she reached for her shower gel and lathering her up with soap, his eyes clear.

"You're so fucking sexy, baby, especially when you're wet," he growled.

Kara laughed and slapped lightly at his head, the fight temporarily fucked out of her.

"You're incorrigible," she told him.

"You're mine," he responded simply, casually, but his tone brokered no argument.

And for once, Kara was too tired to argue.

"Your fucktoy," she said, both teasing and acquiescing as she repeated his earlier words.

He was quiet for a moment.

"More than that," he said. "I'm sorry."

"For kidnapping me?"

He shook his head, a wry smile on his face as he began to wash himself under the starting-to-cool water. "Never for that."

"Of course not."

"No, I'm sorry for ever making you feel less than what you are," he said.

Kara cleared her suddenly-thick throat, almost afraid again. To ask. "And what am I?"

His eyes were so, so blue.

"Everything."

After, they lay in bed together, Micah remaining still as Kara hesitantly played her hands over his body until she reached his tattoo that circled his left bicep.

She'd never looked at it closely before. It was hard to pay attention to, when she was being controlled with orgasms. And maybe a part of her had avoided it because it meant learning too much about what mattered to him, which could lead to caring.

But now, after seeing into him, after realizing he *wanted* to be seen, she had to know.

She traced it, really taking it in for the first time. Before, it had just looked like a gun. Now she saw it was a military grade rifle made of zeroes and ones that curved around his arm. But instead of shooting bullets, a long, green stem extended from the barrel. There was nothing at the end of the stem, as if it had been cut off for some reason, like the greenery had never been given the chance to flower.

For some, inexplicable reason, seeing the Banksy-like tattoo closely for the first time filled Kara with anticipation.

"What's it mean?" she asked him.

"That's really more of a third date kind of conversation," he told her.

She lightly smacked him on top of the tattoo. "I think we're far past the third date."

"Are we?"

Kara didn't respond, because how could she? This wasn't dating, but it was far more intimate than that, another terrifying realization she tabled for later consideration.

Micah chuckled lightly. "I joined up the day I turned eighteen. After that, everything in my life was ugly and violent, even later when I became a SEAL and spent a lot of time behind a computer screen. For years, I told myself that my relationship with Conor and Luke was enough, that I didn't need anything peaceful in my life. But all we did was destroy, when I wanted to build something.

"And then, on one Christmas Eve, I met a woman at a restaurant in New Orleans. One who saw me more than anyone ever had. I'd been tailing her for some time before that, but she was a stranger, one I was sure was as destructive as me. But when we talked, when we *fucked*, I realized that she was trying to build something too—even if she didn't realize it. And she loved strawflowers. I looked into them, and they're interesting, because they seem fragile, and in some ways, already dried out. Too rigid to be beautiful. But they're hardy and when they have enough support, can withstand anything. They just have to be willing to bend, first."

Kara's throat was tight, heart beating fast, tears gathering in her eyes from his words. He knew her better than she wanted him to know her, and yet, just like that night in New Orleans, some part of her yearned for him to know all of her —and want her even more.

No. He was right about her—she did want to build now, not destroy. But the life she wanted to build wasn't, couldn't be, with them.

"Then where's the flower?" she asked, pressing the edge of the tattoo.

He kissed her forehead again, saying quietly, "It's not complete yet."

They fell silent then, and for the first time, the silence felt comfortable. And Kara, who had tried so hard for so long not to be fanciful, felt like the distance between them was shrinking, that something in the silence was tying them together and it would be near impossible to tear that apart.

In the process of trying to find and chip away at the weak links between the men, had she bound herself to them?

He'd been played.

Micah lay on the bed—a bed he'd had specially made so it could fit three large men and one curvy woman comfortably—and chuckled to himself as he stroked Kara's wet hair and listened to her snore. She hadn't quite read him like a book. More like she'd read him like a book in a language she was fairly new to but picking up on quickly. It was humbling and sexy and terrifying, to be fucking honest. That she had figured out that he wanted to be seen. For all his plotting and planning, for all that he loved Conor and Luke, it sometimes felt empty to do so much work with so little notice.

Oh, he knew that Conor and Luke realized what he was doing. He assumed they even knew why, on some level. But what they didn't know was that it mattered to him that they saw him, that he needed to hear the words.

And yet Kara had figured it out after having spent what, one week in his presence? She'd seen him tonight, just like she'd spotted him sixteen months ago in New Orleans when he'd paused in tailing her to give a homeless veteran some money so the poor man wasn't stuck outside and starving on Christmas Eve. Because Micah knew what it was like to have no home. Had Kara sensed that about him?

She murmured something in her sleep, nuzzling into his chest.

She'd scared him, scared all of them, when she'd had that panic attack. But even though knowing they may have set it off didn't sit well with him, he still knew that having her here was for the best, for all of them. She was right, he didn't have much if any guilt over what they'd done. It wasn't that he was a sociopath by any means, it was that the end *justified* the means, and in this case, having her with them, forming a family with her at the center, was what they all needed, badly. Including Kara. If only she would admit it.

It seemed like she was coming around, but Micah knew not to trust that. Kara was clever, and more than that, she was stubborn and terrified of emotional intimacy, which made any capitulation on her end untrustworthy. And yet, as she snored on his chest, the weight of her against him the most grounding thing he could remember feeling since ever, he felt himself slipping into a state of hope and partial belief. That one day they could take the locks off the door, turn the alarm off, and she would stay. By choice.

And he could finally complete the tattoo.

He'd do anything to make that hope reality. Lie, cheat, steal.

He'd even kill for it.

15

She'd lost her fucking mind.

She shouldn't want to stay. But somehow her plan to fuck them into trusting her, feeling guilty, and escaping had turned into them fucking her into submission, sexual *and* emotional.

When Kara was young, she was terrified of heights and anything to do with them, especially roller coasters. So her then-divorced parents who didn't believe in weakness insisted on an exposure therapy trip to Six Flags. The thing that Kara had hated most about roller coasters is that as you rode up to your doom, you could see the stairwell where you had one last chance to disembark, but her parents never let her off, despite her begging. Instead, she had to hold on tight and try not to throw up as she plunged to what she assumed would be her death.

As Kara lay in bed, alone again—Micah must have cleared out at some point, and she was going to pretend she didn't miss him—she remembered those rollercoaster exits. She wanted one, badly. Wanted to get off this thing before it descended, taking her with it. She could feel that pulse as she neared the top of whatever this was between her, Luke, Conor, and Micah, and she knew she wasn't ready for whatever came next.

Was her plan even working? So far, she'd only managed to piss off Conor, alienate Luke, and let Micah get under her skin. And the clock was ticking—the longer she stayed here, the harder it was to emotionally distance herself from the men. She was getting *attached*, and she couldn't even fucking blame it on Stockholm Syndrome, because Stockholm Syndrome was actually a fake syndrome created to discredit a woman.

Ironic.

She needed to take a different tactic. But what?

The door banged open, interrupting her strategy session.

Conor stood there, face a blank mask.

"Come downstairs." he ordered.

Kara felt her back go straight. "Since when do I do what you say?"

He grinned, slow and sinister. "Since you don't want to be tortured with edging and orgasm denial all day."

That got her moving. She went to the closet to grab some clothes, but Conor stopped her.

"Did I say you could get dressed?"

"You're such a jackass."

He grinned again. Kara had to stop herself from scuttling backward into the closet. He hadn't seemed this dangerous since the night they'd kidnapped her.

You're stronger than this. Don't let him see he scares you.

They stared each other down, neither willing to give. Finally, he shrugged. "We were going to take you outside so you could get some fresh air, but if you'd rather stay up here, locked in the bedroom with sealed-shut windows..." he turned to go.

The temptation of fresh air, of feeling closer to the mountains and getting out of this beautiful prison was too enthralling to consider what she might be signing up for if she went with him. She wasn't stupid enough to think this would be an opportunity for escape.

But seeing the open sky and not feeling like the walls were closing in around her, feeling free for a moment—even if that moment was a lie—she needed it. Even naked.

She followed Conor out of the bedroom and down the stairs, bypassing the living room for the foyer. Conor stood in front of the retinal scanner, and then with a beep and a click, the behemoth of a wooden door swung open. For the first time in days, Kara smelled it: crisp, fresh mountain air. She followed a silent Conor out the door, filling her lungs with the smell of false freedom, standing still on the porch and letting the cool air bathe her bare skin in comfort. She stretched, aware of Conor's eyes on her. Covering her eyes to block the sun, she gazed at her surroundings. Sure enough, she wasn't escaping. Long prairie grass danced in the breeze. In the distance, at least a mile away, an easily 10-foot tall cement wall surrounded the property, with no gaps she could see. Beyond the fence, the Bridger-Teton National Forest reached back far, a collection of generations-old pines providing shade and privacy. And beyond the trees, the Teton mountain range rose. The view was stunning, breathtaking, and drove home just how alone and trapped she was.

How could her absolute favorite view, her favorite place, have become so treacherous, so unfamiliar?

"Micah and Luke are waiting," Conor said, and she followed him, careful to stay on the path so she didn't cut her feet on the sharp blades of grass or get stuck with a burr.

Growling with impatience, Conor turned back to her and lifted her into his arms, carrying her around to the side of the house. Kara didn't even bother protesting, just heaved a sigh and let him cart her around like the doll he so very clearly wanted her to be.

He lowered her onto a patio. Luke and Micah sat across from each other at a large picnic table, made of a high-glossed pine. They watched her, Micah expectant. Luke whistled.

"I know what I'm having for lunch," he called, and the other two men laughed.

Conor lowered her to her feet. "You should be fine now," he said gruffly.

Kara was angry at herself for blushing. By now, she shouldn't be embarrassed anymore by either her nudity or their double-entendres, but they made her feel so vulnerable she reacted to them like an uptight virgin. Fighting that inclination, she thrust her breasts out and swaggered toward them, moving her hips in an exaggerated sway to call attention to her body. She'd fight fire with fire.

It worked. As she approached them, Conor following her close behind, she saw both men swallow.

Captive: One; Kidnappers: Zero.

Micah patted the spot next to him. Kara ignored him.

He shrugged. "Alright. Better view this way, anyway." He cleared his throat. "You're here so we can have a conversation about attitude adjustment," he said.

Kara's insides boiled. *Attitude adjustment?* She'd give Micah attitude adjustment. She'd shove it so deep up his ass, none of them would be able to fish it back out.

But she tempered her tone, instead saying, "I'm so sorry,

I didn't realize I had a bad attitude. Why don't you tell me how your other captives behaved, and I'll try to emulate them." Her voice was so saccharine, it hurt her throat. But god, she was angry. How fucking dare they attack her attitude after everything?

And oh, they did not like that. Conor smacked her ass, *hard,* one cheek and then the other. She jumped, covering her ass and pivoting to glare at him.

"Just try it, bratty girl," he threatened. "See, Luke and I had a simple suggestion for how to adjust your attitude. It consisted of beating your ass until you couldn't sit down without screaming—"

"—and locking you into this ingenious chastity belt I found with a built-in remote-controlled vibrator, so we could edge you forever and you would never, ever, get off again," Luke finished for him, staring at her breasts. His eyes, filled with lust, had gone to a dark green that matched the surrounding forest.

Micah shook his head. "See, these two neanderthals didn't realize that you were reasonable, so I wanted to try talking this out. You've disappointed us, baby." He tsked, and Kara wanted to punch him in his self-satisfied face. "We thought you'd understand that we're doing what's best for you. We want you to be a part of this family. Instead, you're trying to rip it apart, and that won't stand."

To emphasize his words, he rose from his spot on the picnic bench and came to stand in front of her. He raised her now quivering chin with one finger so he could look her in the eye.

"We're giving you everything. The mountain home you've always dreamed of. An escape from your doldrum life. Something more, something greater, the adventure you've always wanted. Great sex, the kind you can't get anywhere or with anyone else. A way to express your submissive needs—safely. And, most importantly, we've given you what you've always secretly wanted: A place to belong. A family."

Kara's heart sank, his words ringing painfully true. Everything he listed, she desperately wanted. But her freedom was too high a cost.

Because that was the most important thing to her. More than building a life. The freedom to choose one. That's what they'd taken from her, she finally realized. Not Chicago, but her own agency to create, wherever that was.

Even if they gave her a damn notebook.

"A gilded cage is still a cage," she told him. "Maybe I wanted those things, but I don't want them with you. Not with cold-hearted, selfish killers."

The heat at her back disappeared, Conor's sudden absence like ice.

Micah tsked again. "You tell yourself you're against violence, but our violence turns you on."

"Especially when we use it to take down your enemies, starting with Chris Johnathan," said the last man she expected to hear those words from. Luke's eyes, usually clear with purpose and what she'd once decided was an earnest goodness, were still dark—but this time, with vengeful purpose.

"What does Chris Johnathan have to do with any of you?" she finally asked. She couldn't tell them she'd snooped, but maybe this would finally give her some more pieces of the puzzle.

"He hurt you. He could hurt you again. Therefore, he has to die," said Conor, coming around her to drop onto the picnic bench next to Micah.

"As painfully as possible. Should be fun," Luke added, his inner sadist coming out.

"There's more. There has to be more," she prompted them.

Conor sighed, rubbing his forehead. "We can't tell you everything. But the man I killed—"

"—we killed," Luke interrupted.

It seemed like they were getting along again. Kara filed that away.

"The man we killed had worked for Johnathan Pharmaceuticals on a very hush hush project. He left the company, but he escaped with some essential formula their CEO was desperate to get back."

"Elliot Johnathan," Kara said.

Conor nodded.

Luke jumped in. "Of course, the government didn't tell us any of that, just that he was an enemy of the state with a dangerous weapon that could destroy all of America. After we killed him, something felt off. Before we could look into it, we had been dishonorably discharged and threatened with our lives if we let anything out. So, of course, we investigated."

"That's where you came in," Micah said. "Because when we were doing recon, we realized the other members of the Johnathan family were tied to you, one in particular. Seemed there had been a big literary scandal in New York... you can fill the rest in. The Johnathans are powerful, and they decided to kill two birds with one stone."

Kara digested this. "So you kidnapped me to what, protect me?"

Conor shook his head. "No. There were other ways we could've kept you safe. We took you because you're ours, and this was the only way we could have you."

"But we'd do anything to protect you," Luke interjected defensively.

This should've changed everything, and if Conor hadn't been honest, maybe it would've. But he had, and she was right back where she started, because instead of presenting the facts to her, they'd never given her the choice.

Micah spoke. "Even though you keep hurting us, even though all you want to do is tear us apart, prove to yourself you're better off alone, we'd do anything for you. Don't you see, Kara?" and for once, Micah sounded vulnerable. "We'd do anything for you, and you won't give us the same."

"You kidnapped me!"

"Yes."

"Took me from my life!"

"Also yes."

"Kept me in the dark! You're still keeping me in the dark."

Conor glared. "Why would we tell you everything? We can't trust you."

"Trust me?" She gaped in shock. "I'm not the one going around stealing people from their lives! Why the hell am I the one who is supposed to be earning your trust?"

"Because," Conor said, glaring. "We're the ones with the power."

"Boss," Luke interjected, the nickname a warning. To Kara, he explained, "So far everything we've told you, you've used against us. Why wouldn't this be one more weapon?"

The confession seemed to rip something from him. Micah nodded. Conor stared at the table.

And Luke wasn't done. His throat worked. "And we'd never, not once, do that to you. We don't judge you, Kara, and by your own admonition, you broke up a marriage." Kara started to protest, and Luke put up a hand. "No, he took advantage of you, sweetheart. We know that. But we'd never hold it against you, even if you hold it against yourself. And you've done actual harmful things. You hurt us, and you hurt yourself. You've been reckless and scared, running from your life and avoiding connection or feeling anything. And sure, maybe that's not flat out murdering someone, but you could kill everyone in the world, and we'd still want you. We want you, flaws and all. We're asking for the same thing. That's all."

Kara was silent, her mind spinning. *That's all.* Like forgiving kidnappers and murderers, wanting to be with them because they took care of her was *nothing*. When Kara moved to Chicago, she had promised herself that from now on, she'd do no harm. And although Luke was right, because she'd hurt them and herself...

Was she really not living?

...had been reckless and scared...

Was she avoiding feeling anything? Connection? Was her life that empty?

...although Luke was right, he was creating a false equivalency.

"These aren't at all comparable."

Luke nodded.

Micah interjected. "We know what we're asking you isn't easy. But if anyone can do it, it's you. It's why we took you, because your broken pieces and ours fit together perfectly. And on some level, you know that, baby."

Kara wanted to accuse them of being horny psychopaths and storm back into the house, but where did that get her? Just more arguing.

"You expect me to rise above what you've done to me." She tried the words on.

"Yes." Conor, now.

"And you really expect me to what, wave the white flag and—"

That was it.

That was the answer. Fighting them wasn't getting her anywhere, Kara realized as they watched her, resolute and focused. The more she tried to draw a wedge between them, the more she bound them together—all of them. The harder she battled them, the deeper their claws would sink into her. The tighter they'd hold on, the less likely they'd let go. But if she stopped fighting, if she acted like she cared, like she wanted to be here with them? Maybe, just maybe, they'd relax their guards enough to give her a chance to escape. She didn't know how: There was no way she was shimmying over that monstrosity of a fence. But she knew in her gut this was her only opportunity.

Surrender.

Shouldn't be too hard, that voice in her head taunted. *You're already halfway there.*

"Do you know how much you're asking of me?" she cried. "To bend that far, for you all? What will I lose of myself in the process?"

The last person she'd bent so far for was Chris. Evil family conglomerate he might be a part of aside, he'd pushed her and pushed her until she'd twisted up into someone she didn't even recognize—someone who would destroy a marriage for her own pleasure and ego. She'd lost pieces of herself along the way, and only by running away had she managed to find them again. What would happen if she bent too far and lost herself now? There was no running away this time, no finding herself somewhere else. If she tried to put herself back together, who would she even be?

But this was her only choice, her only chance. If she had any agency, it was this.

Surrender.

"Remember the strawflower," Micah said. "The strongest ones bend, or they'll break. Be strong."

Kara inhaled.

You're making this choice, they aren't making you.

It was maybe a lie, but it was all she had.

She waved her hand back and forth half-heartedly.

"What are you doing?" Conor asked suspiciously.

"I don't actually have a white flag, sorry," she said sarcastically.

Micah chuckled with relief. After a moment, Conor joined him.

"Oh, sweetheart," Luke said, standing from his spot and crossing to her in two steps, wrapping one arm around her waist and the other in her hair, yanking her head back.

His eyes had gone gold-green with... what, happiness? He should be able to see through her, but maybe she was giving him what he wanted so he was willing to overlook any obvious flaws in this logic. She let him position her head where he wanted it, let him kiss her. And it was easy, so easy, to get lost in him, his mouth hot on hers as he coaxed her into a world-shifting kiss, a kiss so overwhelming, she briefly forgot this was all an act. Greedily, she sucked up his heat and the sweet sharpness of his tug on her hair. She wanted this, wanted him. She could admit that much.

She just wanted her freedom more.

When he released her, she glanced around. Conor and Micah were watching her, Conor's face still a mask. And although there was triumph in Micah's gaze, it was matched with skepticism.

But how did she prove to them she'd surrendered? She flashbacked to the night before, when she'd been a little vulnerable, and in return, Micah had lowered his walls and she'd seen who he truly was.

That was how she manipulated them. It wasn't enough, to try to control the situation through sex and a few well-placed barbs. It had become obvious, through Conor's over-the-top commands, Micah's observations, Luke's need to be someone she could care about, and the constant prodding for her inner self, that they desperately wanted the keys to her most secret self and they wouldn't stop until they got them. So she had to give it to them. She needed to make herself vulnerable to them, open up, tell them what they wanted to hear, know, learn about her. Not only would it make them start believing she trusted them, but it might make at least Luke feel guilty he'd stolen her from her life.

Her chest went tight, her hands clammy and cold, like she was on the edge of another panic attack. She willed it away, watching Luke in front of her and using him as a way to ground herself. Because she had to. This was a risk. Disarming them meant disarming herself, and vulnerability could lead to feelings. But big risks meant the biggest reward: freedom.

She only needed to keep her heart out of it.

"Okay," she said. "But can someone get me a blanket or a shirt or something? The breeze is a little chilly."

"I can tell," Micah murmured, looking at her hard nipples.

She snapped her fingers. "Eyes up here, Tech Geek."

He laughed, glancing back up, warmth in his eyes. "Fair enough."

Luke disappeared for a few minutes, returning with a huge t-shirt. When he handed it over, Kara put it to her face before she could stop herself. It smelled like Conor.

Conor raised an eyebrow at that, and embarassed, she

slipped it over her head, taking it as an opportunity to hide. When she reemerged, calm again, or as calm as she could be, they'd all taken seats at the picnic table: Micah playing with his beard that had continued to grow, Luke running a hand through his hair, Conor sitting with his arms crossed.

Kara took a deep breath and started to speak, forcing herself to remain standing.

"My parents are both college professors—philosophy and anthropology. They never intended to have children, but something went wrong with their birth control, as my mother often told me, and they got 'stuck' with me. Neither of them have great staying power, even though they love each other. The first time they got divorced, I was five."

"The first time?" Luke muttered.

Micah raised a hand to shut him up.

"The first time they remarried, I was seven. They proceeded to do that, three, four more times?" She shrugged, aware of their eyes on her. "I don't know, I lost track at some point. They traveled a lot—went on sabbaticals, taught at other universities, spent summers away, you know. But they never brought me with them. Instead, I stayed with put-upon relatives or well-paid nannies."

Kara paused, letting the breeze wash over her, looking off in the distance to stare at the mountains and gather herself.

"Sweetheart, I'm sorry, they never should have abandoned you like that," Luke said.

She shook her head. "It doesn't matter anymore."

But it did. She'd never really belonged anywhere, and so she'd made it a point to be tetherless, rewriting the narrative so her lack of attachments, home, wasn't loneliness but freedom.

"When did the reckless behavior start?" Micah prompted.

She swallowed, wanting to defend herself, but knowing that wouldn't serve her goals. Plus, he was right.

"High school, probably. I don't remember anything specific, but that's when I started drinking and flirting with men who were much older than me, going to parties alone, drugs, sex, traveling to places a seventeen-year-old girl had no business going on her own. I escalated the behavior, expecting some sort of response from my parents, but when I didn't get one, I escalated it again, and again. Honestly, sometimes I'm not sure how I made it out alive."

At this, Conor choked, but before he could speak, Micah put his hand out again. Kara was grateful; she didn't think she could get this out if there were any more interruptions.

And now that she'd started talking, it was like she'd raised the floodgates. "I got kicked out of two boarding schools, and would've been kicked out of the third except I had a writing teacher—a woman—who told me I had talent and not to squander it. So I didn't.

"I decided I wanted to be a writer, and didn't see the point of college, but my mostly absent parents still insisted I go to college and pointed out that truly professional authors went to graduate school. So I did... I went to Columbia, where my favorite author was."

At this point, all three men were leaning in.

"Chris Johnathan," Conor said softly.

"Chris Johnathan," she agreed.

This part was hard. She'd done work to let go of the shame, the self-blame, but it still held on with desperate claws.

But this was what they wanted. Presenting her sullied soul to them was torture, but it was worth the reward. "Chris was talented, and took an interest in me and my writing right away. I thought I was in love. I knew–" she hesitated. "I knew he wasn't going to leave his wife, no matter what he said. New York's a small city, when it comes to major literary scandals. But that reckless part of me that needed attention didn't care. I still thought he was mine. I thought he saw me, and no one else had ever bothered before." She stared Micah down, satisfied when he briefly looked away. "I thought he cared about what he saw. And god, was I wrong." She scoffed at herself. "His wife made that very clear to me when she showed up at my apartment and called me a homewrecker. She divorced him, and she was pissed enough she told the head of my department, and not only did the story get around in like, five minutes, I became the one at fault, even though he was in the position of power. They kicked me out of the program. I could've fought it, but—" she shrugged again, avoiding their eyes now. "But by then everyone was shit-talking me, and for the first time, I realized the consequences of seeking attention. So I left. And I met you," she jerked her head toward Conor, "about a month later."

She stopped, exhausted. Reliving this was painful. She remembered the stares, the whispers, the pain on Molly's face as she stood in Kara's tiny studio apartment and asked her if she was sleeping with her husband. The way the program director had smirked at her as he let her know her fellowship was being "discontinued" and Columbia was no longer a good home for her or her writing. It was too much: Her heart was racing and her arm felt numb, the panic attack symptoms returning, this time stronger. Her legs wobbled.

"Sweetheart, you aren't breathing," Luke told her, his voice sharp with concern.

Micah was already rising to his feet, but Conor beat him to it. He gently tugged Kara by her wrist and once she complied, stumbling toward him, he picked her up and deposited her in his lap. Wrapping her up tight in his arms, he murmured into her hair, "You're okay. Nothing and no one is going to hurt you, okay, sweet girl? Just breathe with us. You don't have to do anything right now but inhale and exhale."

All three men began to breathe, slowly and synchronized, and if Kara had been in a calmer state, she would've laughed. In lieu of that, she followed their suit, taking deep breaths with them and closing her eyes, allowing herself—just for a minute—to lean back against Conor and accept the warmth and safety he was offering her, even if it was a lie.

They brought her back inside. Ran her a bath, keeping watch over her the whole time. No one turned it sexual, and Kara was too tired from the almost-episode to get turned on by their eyes on her naked body. Save for some splashing water, the bathroom cocooned the four of them in comfortable silence.

After she'd become sufficiently pruney, Micah lifted her out of the tub, holding her steady in his arms as the others dried her and dressed her in a *Scrubs* hoodie. It must have been Luke's—he'd made her watch the sitcom with him back in Denver, and admitted he'd seen the whole show multiple times. Conor lifted her and carried her into bed.

Woozy, warm, and disoriented, Kara asked, "Can you be the one who stays?"

After a moment's hesitation, he climbed into the bed next to her and pulled her into his arms. It was still daylight outside, and as tired as Kara was, she couldn't manage to fall asleep.

Instead, she just drifted, only semi-conscious when Conor began to sing "Hallelujah" in a soft tenor.

She must have slept, because the next time she opened her eyes it was dark, moonlight pouring in through the window. She was trapped once again between Micah and Luke, Conor nowhere to be seen. Annoyed, she'd only just decided to sneak off the bed and go in search of him when the door to the bedroom opened, exposing a naked—and hard—Conor.

"Are you okay now? No more panic?"

"Yes," she confirmed softly.

"What do you need?" he asked.

She swallowed. "You."

He stared at her. "Are you just saying that because my dick's hard?"

How could she tell him that sex with them made her feel alive, and the control they had over her made her feel safe? She could barely even admit it to herself.

"Please, Conor."

He stared at her, as if checking his internal lie detector. Once she passed, he crossed the room, got on the bed, and prowled up her body. He must have kneed Luke in the groin, because with a groan the man next to her opened his eyes.

"Could you not, asshole? Some of us are busy sleeping."

"Some of us need our dicks sucked," Conor retorted. "Move out of the way."

"Who's doing the sucking?" Kara asked, amused, but also grateful that he wasn't making a thing out of her vulnerability.

"You know the answer to that," Conor said on a chuckle.

When he laughed, Kara always felt it everywhere, deep inside of her. Maybe because he laughed so rarely these days. She loved when he laughed. She shouldn't, but she did.

"Couldn't sleep, huh?" Micah said with a knowing, gravelly voice, also awake now. He and Luke moved over, leaving room for Conor to finish crawling his way up Kara's body until his cock was in front of her mouth.

"Open that mouth, brave girl," he told her, and with his endearment warming her chest, she did.

He entered her mouth slowly, taking small, smooth, shallow thrusts as she sucked around him. He'd never been gentle like this with her, not even when they'd first met, and while she appreciated the gesture, she wanted the real him. When he briefly pulled out, she glanced around. Luke and Micah were each on an elbow as they watched, hands on their cocks.

"I need more of you," she murmured in a husky voice.

"Anything you want," Conor promised, this time thrusting in deeper and faster. The only sound in the room was the wet suction of her mouth around his cock, and the whack-whack-whack as Luke's and Micah's hands worked their own cocks, in time, she imagined, with Conor's thrusts. As Conor pressed deeper and she began to choke—the way they both liked it, she admitted to herself—someone's hand teased between her legs and began to stroke her clit in tiny, perfect circles, until Kara was gasping and moaning around Conor's cock.

"That's it, brave girl, that's it," Conor crooned, and as Kara came, so did he, pushing deep one more time and releasing into her throat.

He left her mouth and Kara lay back, gasping, too tired to protest as Luke and Micah aimed their cocks toward her and came all over her breasts and stomach.

"Someone's going to have to be big spoon," Micah said, rubbing his come into her skin. "If Conor's staying, I mean."

Silence.

"Do y'all need to play rock paper scissors?" Kara teased.

They had some silent conversation, then Micah rolled even further out of the way and Conor took his place. There was a brief tug of war—and Kara was the rope—between Luke and Conor before they settled her between them. Kara noted that the two were still tense with each other, and filed that away for further perusal.

Once everyone was settled, Kara asked a question that had been plaguing her.

"Conor, why didn't you ever text me back?"

He exhaled with a surprised *puh*. Everyone was silent for some time, breathing so quietly she wondered if Luke and Micah were asleep.

Finally, Micah said, "Tell her."

When Conor spoke, it was into her hair. "You texted me while we were away on our mission. And when we came back and I saw the text...I no longer was the kind of man who knew how to respond."

Kara inhaled sharply, trying not to let herself feel sympathy for him, even if he sounded so, so very broken.

"I guess it doesn't matter anymore, does it?" she asked.

No one answered her.

16

"Tell me about your life before," Kara said.

She was lying on Micah's chest as they both recovered from a rough and wild bout of fucking. Micah played with her hair as he considered answering her. He knew this wasn't only curiosity on her part; she was searching for vulnerabilities in his psyche, ways to get to him. But if they were going to strengthen this shaky foundation, he had to give her something—even if it meant risking her using what he gave her now as ammunition later.

"I grew up in an ultra-Orthodox home, did I ever tell you that? Like as frum as you can get. Went to yeshiva, my mother wore a wig, we only ate food that was Glatt Kosher... the whole nine yards. Not everyone in the frum community is conservative, or closed-minded, but unfortunately, my family is. So," he scratched the scar above his eyebrow, "when my father discovered a Playboy *and* a Playgirl magazine with naked pictures of men and women hidden in my copy of the Tanakh, he was outraged. They kicked me out of the house, out of their lives—sat shivah for me. I was seventeen and ostracized from my whole community, had nowhere to go. So after a few homeless, sleepless weeks—an experience I wouldn't wish on anyone—I turned eighteen, went to a Navy recruitment office, and signed right up. Met Conor and Luke during BUDS, became a SEAL, had a family again. And this time, it was one who wouldn't judge or abandon me, no matter what I did."

Kara was quiet, and Micah felt weightless as he imagined all the ways she could hurt him with this.

Finally: "I'm not a violent person, but I could fucking kill your parents. Your whole community, really. You deserve to have a family, and I'm glad you found one."

Micah floated slowly down to the ground, and the foundation felt more solid than it had since Conor had first proposed kidnapping Kara.

He tilted her chin up and kissed her, murmuring against her mouth, "Thank you, baby. And so do you."

He didn't need to point out she'd found hers with them, because it didn't need to be said.

Not anymore.

When Kara asked Luke to share about his past before the Navy, he was already prepared. Micah had told him and Conor about their conversation, and Luke was relieved that Kara had been sympathetic and supportive—like the woman he knew her to be. Kara knew Conor's backstory: she'd learned it during their two night stand in San Diego before everything had gone belly up. It seemed counterintuitive that Luke had spent over a month with Kara back in Denver, but had never told her about his past. But then he'd been so busy keeping secrets from her, something antithetical to who he was as a man, he had to keep the box locked on all of them for fear the wrong stories would go tumbling out.

They were in the bath together, a slippery, sated Kara relaxed against his chest. Minutes earlier, he'd tied her down and spanked the shit out of her ass, tits, and cunt, first with his hand, then with his belt, then with the rough side of a hairbrush, before shoving deep inside her without warning and riding them both to quick, intense completion.

"Tell me about your family," she prompted.

His chest went tight. Yeah, it was hypocritical of him to expect her to open up when he hadn't and didn't want to, but the old wounds weren't buried deep enough and talking about his past would bring them back to the surface.

But she had opened up, and it seemed like things were progressing in a direction where their messy beginning could turn into something long and lasting, and he needed to do what he could to keep them moving toward that result.

Even if it meant baring himself to her.

"There's really not that much to tell. I was born in a trailer park. My mom died when I was really young—drug overdose—so I went to go live with my grandma in another trailer park. She did her best, but she was old and tired and we were poor, and there was barely enough food on the table for the two of us, much less time and energy for things like love and affection. When I say she did her best by me, I mean it. She attended all my football games and parent teacher conferences, and taught me that a good man never lies."

Kara craned her neck to look at him, eyes pensive. "So then why did you lie? To me and to Conor?"

Luke sighed. It was a question he'd asked himself multiple times, and had only been able to find one answer.

"Conor and Micah were all I had, for a long time. And loyalty was more important than lying to you, I guess."

"Then why did you lie to him?"

"Because…" he kissed her neck. "My loyalty was divided, and I wanted you for myself."

"And now?"

That was the question, wasn't it?

"And now," he said quietly, and the thought no longer felt like a lie. "I want you for all of us."

"I'll be honest, I'm impressed. I can't tell if she's faking it, or if she's actually decided to stop fighting us and is willing to stay. She's even got me stumped on what's real and what's manipulation," Micah said, perched on his desk, one arm crossed over his chest, the other scratching at his tattoo.

Conor rubbed a hand over his head. The three of them —him, Micah, and Luke—were sequestered in their office while Kara showered. They needed to connect on where things stood with Kara, and how to progress. Micah's indecision was concerning, because the hacker always knew where people's heads were at, even if they didn't know themselves.

And Conor, who had always prided himself on being a human lie detector, was too close to all of this, too twisted up inside by the beautiful, willful woman to get a good read on her. He didn't trust his gut, too afraid that his desire for her to choose to stay with them freely was overwhelming what was real.

"At moments, like when she's opening up to us, even during sex, she seems sincere," Micah said.

"Like she's ours and recognizes it and wants it," Conor said, wishing he sounded more sure. But how could he be? They'd stolen her from her life, were keeping her with them by force. Did they really believe she'd come around and fully surrendered to things as they were? Had she really given them her heart? Or—

"Or is she faking?" Luke posited, like he'd read Conor's mind. "And do we blame her, if she is?"

Conor bit back a growl and nodded.

"It's not that I blame her," Micah said, still rubbing his tattoo. "It's that I don't think we can trust her. But at the same time, we can't keep building on this foundation if we don't know if she chooses us."

Trust. It was a flimsy thing, wasn't it, Conor mused. He trusted the two men with him—even Luke, regardless of their recent issues. And even though he didn't have a heart, the empty space in his chest was theirs. Once upon a time, he'd wanted to give his heart to Kara, but he'd learned quickly in their two nights together that she was too much of a flight risk.

Luke rolled his neck.

"Need a backrub?" Micah asked.

"Badly."

Micah joined Luke at his desk and began working out the knots in his neck as Luke groaned gratefully.

"You're so good with your hands," Luke said, and Micah laughed.

Conor cleared his throat. "Here's what I trust. I trust that we need to keep her safe. I trust that I'm not willing to let her go. Not ever."

"None of us are," Luke agreed.

His lover and best friend's words warmed Conor's chest, especially as the taller man continued to speak.

"We started off on opposite sides of this. Maybe it was because I thought we needed to do the right thing by her, but if I'm honest—"

"I thought you were always honest," Conor teased.

Luke's lip quirked. He continued. "As an honest man, I'll admit that I was feeling territorial."

Micah chuckled. Conor glanced over at him. The broader, shorter man was rubbing Luke's arms, a small, approving smile playing on his lips. Because this was what Micah wanted, Luke and Conor at peace again, the three of them a team.

The four of them a team. But they weren't there yet. And that was the problem.

Healing things with Luke might be part of the solution.

Conor shrugged, also admitting, "I was feeling territorial as fuck. I'd never truly forgiven either of you for fucking her, being with her, when you were just supposed to be keeping an eye on her to make sure she was safe. This sharing thing is..."

"...fucking hard," Luke interrupted.

"It is." Conor laughed. "But it's the only way we can have her. I see that now. We all give her different things, we balance each other out, and she softens our edges. We're a family."

"We are," Luke said, glancing at Micah, who released him from his massage.

Luke rose to his feet, meeting Conor midway. They clasped hands, before Luke pulled Conor into a tight hug. Luke's smell, sexy and comforting, surrounded Conor, and Conor relaxed into the security of it.

"Good," Micah said simply from where he watched them. "Now we need to be sure she knows she's a part of this family."

They'd disappeared on her again.

They did that a lot these days—leave her alone, lock themselves in their office for hours, without telling her what they were up to. They'd also taken away her ability to eavesdrop by putting a white noise machine outside the office when they were in there. They were talking about her, she always assumed—or their secret mission, or the dirty hit jobs they took that paid for this cabin and all the land that surrounded it, all the cool high-tech gear, and the three swanked-up Jeeps she'd found in the oversized garage one day.

As Kara dried off in the bathroom, she stared at herself in the mirror, trying to catalogue what had changed. Her face was softer, jaw more relaxed, eyes less sad. But even with all of those arguably positive changes, something felt missing. Was it her ambition, her drive? Her spine? Probably her intelligence, she thought wryly, because she'd been behaving like a lovesick idiot for days now.

She froze, and forced herself to confront her reflection.

Love. Sick. Idiot.

She wasn't.

She wasn't.

She knew she wasn't, because love built you up, it didn't erode pieces of you until there was nothing left that you recognized. Who was Kara, without her independence, her spine, her recklessness, her will? Who was this woman, content to laze about a mountain cabin and get fucked all the time and snuggle with her fucking kidnappers? Who the hell was she? And what had happened to Kara Blum?

You're surviving, she told herself. *You're doing the best you can, given your circumstances, softening them so they lower their guards and you can escape. This was the risk you took when you allowed for emotional intimacy. It's scary, but you'll get yourself back. You'll be Independent, Bitchy, Reckless, Happy Kara again in no time.*

Well, maybe not the last. Kara wasn't sure if she'd ever been that last. She'd felt close to it, in the past few days…and that was the most terrifying part of all.

Ripping herself away from the mirror, she stalked into the bedroom. She was on a mission and didn't have time for self-recrimination or self-doubt. If anything, this proved she had to continue with what she was doing—it was her only way out of here.

The notebook—the one she had yet to touch—and the pen next to it beckoned at her from their new spot on the nightstand. The men had been leaving it for her with gentle nudges that this was the perfect time for her to "find her passion" again, annoying her with the condescending truth of it.

Maybe it was time.

Picking it up, she flipped to the first blank page, and wrote.

I don't know what I'm doing here anymore. Up is down, and down is up, and I've not only lost all sense of what is right, I've lost all sense of myself, my values, what matters to me. Before they took me, I thought I'd healed, and finally settled down into a good life, but what if they're right and I'm wrong? What if it wasn't a life at all?

What's even scarier is that the healing I've done in my heart, and my awareness that I'm not the destructive force I thought I was, makes it even easier to fall under their spell. They're promising me a life I could want, and I'm so drunk on lust and on…I'm so drunk on them I haven't been fully cognizant that I'm losing my agency, my will, myself more, day after day. I need to get home, wherever that may be, and learn how to grow on my own and build something without being forced to. I ran away for so long, and this, giving into them...what is it, but another form of running away?

I don't even recognize who I am in the mirror anymore. The woman I see...she looks happy, but she doesn't know it's a lie.

I do.

Kara, put down the pen. Something had released in her chest. She felt looser and freer than she had in weeks, even since before she'd been taken. Getting those words on the page was the catharsis she hadn't known she'd needed.

It also was a trap. If Micah saw it...

Picking back up the pen, she was careful to cover the words with black ink until they were illegible and there was no trace of her ambivalence and fear.

Dropping the notebook on the bed, she glanced around the room.

There was a sticky note on the door, Conor's handwriting, this time.

We're out on the patio. Nudity non-optional.

Swallowing, she left the unlocked bedroom and her redacted words behind, wandering down the stairs through the kitchen and outside.

It was a hot, dry day, the sun beating down, lighting the prairie grass in golds and yellows. Colors seemed more vibrant, the air clean and warm on her bare skin. Trees circled for miles, and Kara—still stuck on her confrontation with her mirror-self—considered for a moment, what would happen to her if she just...ran. Disappeared in the trees somewhere. Would they ever find her?

Of course they'd find her. If a bear didn't find her first.

She heard a whistle and walked toward the three men, who surrounded the picnic table.

"Good morning, fellas," she called, trying for light and breezy.

In response, they stared at her, gazes intense with something she couldn't read.

"Uh...did I miss something?" she asked. "Do y'all have to go on another job again, or something, because I promise I'll be fine this time..."

They still didn't speak, and their energy was so overwhelming, Kara began to back away.

Luke strode toward her, catching her up in his arms and turning her to face the other two men.

"Get on the table," Conor ordered.

An already shaky Kara wobbled in Luke's arms. "What?"

Micah was gathering up something from the ground— four lengths of rough rope, a blindfold, and...

...a spider gag. The kind that forced your mouth open so someone could thrust without the risk of being bitten, and you couldn't control the depth at all.

Kara shivered, even as her thighs clenched.

"On the table, submissive girl," Conor repeated. "You waved the white flag, got vulnerable with us. You're choosing to stay? Of your own volition? Now you're going to prove it. Prove that you're ours. You're going to let us do whatever we want to you, however we want to do it. Now."

As she obeyed, a thought ate at her:

Her fear had come true. She'd pretended to care about them, and even though her mind knew it was all fake, her heart had begun to believe the lie.

17

K ara climbed onto the table.

"Hands and knees," Conor commanded, and she obeyed.

He could see how aroused she was. The sun glinted off her wet upper thighs and even wetter pussy, and Conor had to resist diving in for a taste.

He told himself he had all the time in the world to eat her pussy. She'd given in, said yes to being theirs, and now her body was his to use whenever, wherever, however, wasn't it? As she fidgeted against the ropes, he could smell her bee balm scent, and the smell made him yearn for more than her body and her submission. But Conor didn't yearn. That version of himself had died in a flat in Frankfurt, staring into the eyes of two orphaned boys. The Conor that existed now took, without remorse or the longing for more.

But what if he didn't have all the time in the world? What if something went wrong?

The thought made him feel desperate, and his desperation made him angry. She'd twisted them up so much inside, until he couldn't figure out which way was north anymore. She deserved the same from them, and if sex was how he did it, how he got to her, got *inside* her head, then sex it was.

He nodded to Micah and Luke, who divided up the rope and began tying her to the four corners of the picnic table, checked her wrists and ankles for circulation issues, and then tied her thighs to her calves.

"She looks like a Thanksgiving turkey," Luke remarked.

"Sexiest turkey I've ever seen," Micah replied.

For a moment, Conor wondered if they'd all do Thanksgiving together this year: If they'd argue with Kara over the best turkey preparation until Micah banished them all from the kitchen; if they'd sit around the unused dining room table like a family.

Or maybe she'd go after them with a carving knife.

He banished that thought by delivering a sound slap to Kara's inner thigh, and her surprised cry drowned out that long-dead part of him who wanted something he couldn't, didn't deserve, to have. No more. He was here to have sex. To own every part of her, without giving anything of himself. Anything else belonged to heroic princes in fairy tales, and nothing about Conor was heroic. He focused on her gasp when Luke tied the blindfold around her head and whispered something in her ear that made her whole body quake.

"What did you tell her?" Conor asked, curious.

"That we're going to take turns taking her in all three holes, and she can't do anything to stop us. She'll only know who's using what hole by our cocks alone." Luke winked.

Conor didn't have the heart to tell him that even that wink counted as a lie.

"You really think I know your dicks that well?" Kara smartmouthed at them, the brat.

"Baby, don't bullshit. We've been inside you so much, you've memorized the feel of us. But I'm happy to give you a reminder and shut up that bratty mouth," Micah said, discarding his sweats on the ground and moving to the front of the table, thick cock in hand.

Conor admired the way Micah's tight, big ass cheeks squeezed as he walked. He admired more the way Micah worked Kara's protesting mouth open, forced the spider gag around her lips and buckled it closed.

Time to stuff her full. Time to feel in control again. Finally. And for as long as he could.

Damn, she looked good like this, Micah thought, cock in hand as he painted Kara's face with precum. He took immense satisfaction in the fact that she couldn't do anything about it, couldn't lick it off. It was what she deserved, rocking his foundation—and theirs. Having her there, tied and unable to see or move, settled something in him that had felt unmoored in his conversation earlier with Luke and Conor. She made him feel so helpless sometimes, and he needed her to feel the same way.

So her utter helplessness right now made Micah even harder. But then so did seeing his partners work together to reduce their captive—their woman—to a helpless, moaning mess.

Their woman. Theirs. She was theirs.

So then why did he have to keep repeating it to himself?

Luke stood next to him, stroking Kara's hair, and Micah forced himself to focus.

"Go find your own hole, Boy Scout," Micah told the taller man.

"Nah," Luke said. "I'm enjoying watching you defile her."

Conor joined them at the head of the table. Kara trembled, so overcome with fear and forced desire, Micah thought he could come right there. It would be fun, to come all over her face, but he wanted his dick in her hot, defenseless mouth too badly.

Another time.

They had all the time in the world.

The thought made his chest hurt.

"The least you two could do is give her tits some attention," he pointed out, satisfied when Luke and Conor went to work. Conor alternated between gently running his fingers in circles around her right nipple and pinching it so hard Kara jolted. Luke began slapping and spanking her left breast so hard, she began to wail, far back in her throat.

When they briefly paused, Micah gripped Kara's head, moving it into the perfect position, and lined his cock up with her forced open mouth.

"Focus on me, baby," he encouraged, and the moment he felt her attention shift, he thrust in—deep. No prep, no nothing, just bottomed out so Kara'd taken all of him, her lips and nose against his groin.

"Fuck," he groaned, pulling out and thrusting in again, holding Kara's head tight to control the depth. Her throat hugged him tight, squeezing his cock on entry and exit as he picked up his pace. Micah usually wasn't the zero to sixty type. He liked to work up to a rough fuck. It was a dance, manipulating his partner(s) into wanting it like that, especially Kara. But something about the conversation he'd just had, Kara's careful capitulation, and Micah's uncertainty, had unleashed the beast in him. And the beast wanted to face fuck her into submission, until he knew everything that had happened over the past week was real.

On that thought, he shoved deep in her throat—and stayed there. Kara tried to struggle against him, choking around his cock. His balls went tight, the feel of her around him so fucking good, but he forced himself not to come.

"Oh, sweetheart, is that hard for you? Is he taking your air?" Luke crooned, as he spanked Kara's breast so hard it turned red. "Is it scary, realizing how much you like it? Like us having that much control over you?"

Luke, who thus far had been the gentlest among them, was letting his inner sadist out. Micah leaned over the table, kissing his partner as a reward for finally joining in, and his movement pushed his cock even deeper in Kara's throat. She went rigid, and Micah reluctantly pulled out, letting her splutter as she inhaled.

"Breathe through your nose, baby," he said, before shoving back deep again and attaching his mouth to Luke's. As they kissed, Micah felt something in his chest loosen, because this was what he wanted, his family working together, taking their pleasure together.

Speaking of which.

He pulled back, out of Kara's mouth and away from Luke's lips with one last peck.

"I think some holes have been left out of the party," he said, and Luke slowly grinned, abandoning Kara's tit to make his way around to her pussy.

"Poor little fuck toy, you deserve to get attention everywhere, don't you?" he crooned again, pulling down his own pants. His cock, so long Micah knew from experience it was going to hurt her, was almost purple at the tip. It looked angry, and Micah watched as Luke followed his own lead and shoved straight into Kara's pussy without preamble.

Kara shrieked around the gag and Micah's cock.

"Fuck fuck fuck," Luke shouted, resting his head on her trembling back for a moment.

"That good, huh?" Conor said wryly, moving back down the table so he could rest a hand below Kara's pussy.

Kara moaned a protest.

"Oh, no, baby," Micah tsked. "You don't get to come until we all do. If we let you come at all."

It really was unbelievable that after having been inside her so many times, he could still want her this much, Luke mused. But as he moved inside Kara, shunting his hips and settling so deep he was sure she could feel him in her throat —the throat Micah had currently taken up residence in—he couldn't help but feel like this was his favorite place in the world, the place where he truly belonged.

The idea that he could lose it—lose her—was inconceivable.

"Total kryptonite pussy," he groaned out loud, spurred on by his partners' chuckles.

Kara spluttered protests—maybe at the nickname, but more likely at the orgasm denial announcement.

Conor spanked her pussy—hard enough that it delivered reverberations to Luke's own cock. The addition of her clenching around him in pleasure made Luke go harder. He wanted to hurt her, hurt her so much she needed to come with the pleasure-pain of it, a claim on her she'd feel for weeks, months, years.

Luke shoved faster, deeper, harder in her, knowing he wasn't going to last long and for once not caring.

"Hey, whoever comes in her first gets to be the one who finally gets her off," he called to Micah, visions of flogging her poor clit into a devastatingly painful orgasm filling his mind and bringing him that much closer to the edge. It was what she deserved, making him want her so much and question everything.

Making him lie.

"Do I even want to know what sadistic thing you're thinking?" Conor teased, as he stroked a hand over Kara.

"It's better if it's a surprise," Luke grunted. "Spank her clit again, I think one more clench and I'm done for."

"Not a fucking chance," Micah groaned, hammering his hips fast, then faster, until he was going at her mouth like a machine. "I've decided she's not coming at all this round."

With a shout, and a jerk of his hips, Micah released deep in Kara's throat. Luke imagined it coating her insides, making itself a home there, and her forced to just accept it, accept all of them, and that's all it took. His balls boiled before releasing in jet after jet. He came, long and hard, and as Micah stepped back from her mouth, Kara let out another long, unending cry. The sound released even more come inside Luke, and his satisfaction as he filled her, the thought of it taking root inside her, made his orgasm last forever.

Finally, he pulled out and slumped over her, his release dripping out of her and onto the ground.

"Oh, poor girl, he made a mess of you, didn't he," Conor tsked, reaching down for some of Luke's come and working it around Kara's clit. She shuddered, whining, but Conor stopped before she could tip over the edge.

She tried to moan something that Luke assumed meant "please." He kissed her spine, and she moaned again. The poor sweetheart clearly needed completion. And they weren't even close to done with her.

"My turn," Conor said, his voice dark with lust and something more.

Luke moved back to make room for him, but Conor shook his head. "Nah, I'm taking a turn everywhere. And our sweet girl is going to let me, aren't you?"

Kara had never needed to orgasm so badly in her life. They called her kryptonite pussy, but it was their cocks, their hands, their mouths, even their words—especially their words—that were truly deadly. The filth interwoven with sweet praise and the insistence that they knew her affected her everywhere, and not only sexually. Every whispered word impacted her in a way that terrified her.

The added desperation in the way they took her, like this was the last time, only made her feel *more.*

It didn't help that they wouldn't let her come. Her breasts and clit strained for completion, her pussy tightening and releasing as her body searched in vain for something to fill it. She'd never felt this needy in her life.

Conor chuckled. "Needy girl," he tsked, once again reading her mind. "I'd finish you off, but Micah's decided to be bossy and I'm going to let him dictate for once."

"For once," Luke laughed, sounding a little breathless. "He dictates all the time, he's just stealthy about it."

Conor ran a hand over her back as he paced back and forth next to the picnic table. "Here's my dilemma," he said, his voice oh so casual, Kara wanted to scream. "I'm hard enough that my cock could punch through a wall, so as much as I want to fuck your throat, desperate girl, I'm concerned I'll nut almost immediately, and I don't want to waste it in your throat today. Your sweet, sweet pussy is always an option, but I have a hunch you'll come at the first thrust, and we can't have that."

"She hasn't earned it yet," Micah called from somewhere. She couldn't see, but they were right, she knew their cocks by feel now.

"Have you taken her ass yet?" Luke asked.

Even blindfolded, Kara knew there was a wicked gleam in his green eyes.

"You know," Conor mused, as he made his way back down to the foot of the picnic table, delivering two hard slaps to her butt cheeks, one after the other, "I haven't had that pleasure. What do you say, needy girl, is it time to let me in your ass? Oh that's right, you can't actually say no, can you?"

She couldn't. What's more, she didn't *want* to. Because Micah had been right last night, all of them had been right this whole time: They knew what she wanted better than she did. Sexually, yes, but otherwise, too. She wanted to belong, to them, and it fucking terrified her.

Especially when Conor rimmed the last part of her he hadn't taken with his fingers and worked one in, then two. At some point, he must have added lube to them, because it was a cold, gentle glide, but an insistent one. If Kara could writhe or beg, she would. Her stomach bottomed out and everything went topsy turvy as he replaced his fingers with his huge cock and with an order to "bear down," began to slowly push inside her. She felt him everywhere, felt them everywhere, as Luke and Micah joined him at the foot of the table, Micah running gentle but rough fingers up and down her thigh, etching a pattern she was too overcome to discern; Luke delivering a litany of smacks to the inside of her other thigh.

She couldn't see. She couldn't think. She couldn't *breathe*. Conor bottomed out with a deep, satisfied sigh, his balls pressing up against her clit, so close to getting her there but not close enough.

She needed to come.

Please, she tried to beg, but all that came out was a scratchy moan, deep in her throat. Conor groaned in response, withdrawing and shoving back in, hard, setting up an exaggerated pace that delivered sweet pain to Kara's insides.

He thrust, again.

And again.

And again.

Kara lost track of time. In fact, time ceased. Her world became the rhythmic presence and absence of his cock inside her, the juxtaposition between gentle swirls and stinging slaps on her thighs, the filthy praise and promises of the men around her. Nothing had ever existed before, and nothing would ever exist again. And, trapped in this liminal moment, Kara felt shockingly safe and deliciously free, both tethered and released. Even her orgasm, dangling just out of reach, denied to her by the men in charge of her, felt right in this moment.

But then Conor picked up his pace, the table shaking underneath her, and time came rushing back. With a final groan, and a "oh, you precious, precious girl," he shoved deep inside her, so deep she couldn't breathe, and came, filling her up with the promise and truth of him.

Finally, he withdrew.

"Fuck. Our girl," he said, his voice satisfied, and, for the first time in a long time, soft with affection. And Kara, closed off Kara, independent Kara, self-sufficient Kara, lapped up that softness with something achingly close to need. She was sticky with sweat and filthy with them, and she still needed to orgasm or she felt like she'd die.

Someone removed the spider gag from her mouth, big soft lips drawing a kiss from her. Micah. Water dribbled into her mouth and she sucked it back greedily, until her biological thirst was sated even if her sexual thirst wasn't.

Hands stroked her, gentling her shaking body, or trying to. But her body pulsed with need, sensitive to the touch everywhere as if all she was, all she'd ever be, was her desperate clit and deprived pussy.

"Please," she heard herself beg. "Please please please please please pleasepleasepleaseplease…"

"If we make you come, sweet baby girl, then you never say no to us. Not about anything, not ever again."

"Yes!" she promised with a cry.

All it took was one featherlight touch on her clit, delivered by one of them but also by all of them, and the orgasm descended on her in a roaring wave, crashing over her and taking her with it.

Someone was still begging, and it sounded like her.

"Our greedy girl needs more, doesn't she," Conor crooned, and fingers thrust inside her and then circled her clit, over and over, and as she came, again, and again, and again, his declaration roaring through her head, time once again stood still.

Straps were unbuckled and loosened, hands rubbed feeling back into her extremities and checked for any strain or injury, and the blindfold was removed from her eyes. The sun was blinding, so when she was lifted by a strong pair of arms, she buried her head against his chest, too overwhelmed to recognize who it was.

Someone kissed her on the forehead, and carried her back into the house.

"Tired," she grumbled.

"Sleep, precious girl," Conor said, that same desperation in his voice. "Sleep and dream of us."

And Kara followed that last order and was out like a light.

This time when she woke up, it was night. Luke was on the bed next to her, head in his hands, lost in thought.

She sat up slowly, feeling satisfying twinges and aches from where they'd all fucked her earlier. She was bruised, sore, and sated—and not only sexually.

"How long was I out?" she asked, voice hoarse from all the gagged screaming and begging she'd done.

Luke raised his head to look at her. The tiny smile on his face didn't continue to his eyes, which were oddly anguished.

"A while. We must have tired you out, sweetheart."

"Yeah. Where are the others?"

"They got called out on another job. I told them I was staying in case you had another panic attack."

Kara remembered, not so long ago, when Conor had promised her "we'll never leave you alone again." Was this going to be her life now? Never alone, never allowed to go out on her own, do her own thing? Never free?

She welcomed the anger—she'd missed it. It kept her safe from them and their destabilizing softness. Because she'd been right to be wary that by opening up to them and sharing parts of herself, she'd get lost in them and forget why she'd begun sharing in the first place. They were growing closer, and as they did, not only did her goals begin to slip away—so did who Kara Blum was at her core.

Reckless. Willful. Strong. Independent. A survivor. Conor had said otherwise when they'd kidnapped her, that she was too reckless to be on her own. It felt so long ago now. But he'd been wrong. Her recklessness was a strength, it kept her going. She didn't need them, she needed to be free of them and hold onto her true self.

How could she, though, if she didn't leave?

The anger was good. It staved off the other emotions, the ones she didn't want to name.

Lust.

Which had turned to longing.

Which was becoming l—

No. Not that. Kara wasn't stupid enough to feel that.

"Sweetheart?" Luke asked, his voice so soft, almost bleak. "What's wrong?"

"I could ask you the same question," she purposely made her voice tender and curious.

He shifted around, gently stroking a piece of hair back behind her ear. He leaned in and placed his lips on her ear, and shivers wracked her body when he said, "Kara. Tell me about your life back in Chicago. Tell me why you love it."

I don't.

It was her immediate thought, and the two words made it hard to breathe.

She wasn't sure what she'd expected him to say—something sexy, or some other vulnerable confession, but not this question. Not once had these men seemed interested in what her life was like, or even acknowledged that there were things she'd loved about it. And what's worse, she wasn't sure how to answer. What did she love about her life in

Chicago? Everything was potential, not reality: A job she might like, one day. A dog she might get, one day. A dream home and community she could build for herself, one day. All she had was Lola, and she loved Lola, but was that a life? Was she content with her life, with the freedom and the potential it presented? Or had she been yearning for something, someone—someones?

And wasn't that a fucking terrifying question.

She reminded herself that even if she didn't love her life yet, she could, and that was the important thing. Potential was a good thing, after all. She had an opportunity to make it joyous and fulfilling, and they'd taken that agency, that choice, from her. That what she needed was freedom. That was her life, freedom.

She'd been tiptoeing around this realization for days, and it exploded in her mind. Because the immediate thought had been right. She *didn't* love her life now. She remembered the way she looked in the mirror. Happy. Was she happy? Had they given her more than they'd taken?

No. Because they'd taken away her choices, and her agency was what she needed most.

Still angry. Good.

So she answered him, and if she wasn't a hundred percent truthful, if she exaggerated slightly, well she wasn't the one who prided herself on strict honesty, was she?

"My best friend, Lola, means everything to me. We met in grad school and she was the only one of my friends in my cohort who stuck by me. I'm not...usually great at staying in touch with people,"—at that, Luke laughed, the sound wry and pained—"but with her it's easy. You probably already knew this, but I crashed on her couch for a while when I first moved to Chicago before I landed on my feet and could get my own place. We'd do anything for each other, and I know she's not going anywhere, even if I leave and go somewhere else, if that makes sense."

That much was true. She hadn't thought about Lola in a while, but her heart ached, thinking of her friend. Lola must be frantic with worry, she'd probably moved into the police station by now, demanding they find Kara.

"Yeah," he said. "I completely understand. That tie is there no matter if you're in the same place or separated by thousands of miles. I—" he started to say, but obviously changed his mind because he asked her, "What else?"

She took a deep breath. "I never thought I'd be someone with a corporate job—for a long time I only wanted to write full time, and I guess financially I could, thanks to my emotionally-stingy but money-generous parents. But I *like* my job." *That was a bit of a stretch.* "I like being part of a team, being a part of something bigger than me and my own ambitions. My apartment may not be huge or fancy, but it's mine, and after years of not being settled anywhere, it feels good to be settled. I like Chicago—I don't mind the cold, and the people are friendly without being in your face. And I like *who* I am...I can stand on my own two feet without feeling the need to take those feet and sprint away from what I've created. And I'm excited for the future. I think I want a dog—a basset hound—sometime soon, and I'm meeting more people—" *boring men* "—and building a community, one where I'm not this slutty, reckless, attention-seeking homewrecker, but someone worthwhile who people want to be around."

She wasn't exaggerating. Before she had, but this? This was true. This was real.

But she was lying by omission, because she didn't say the three words that would convey the whole truth: *I want more.*

As she spoke, Luke's jaw went tighter and tighter, until she could see veins protruding from his neck. Why did he seem so angry?

"Okay," he said, like he'd come to a decision.

"Okay..." she prompted.

He shut his eyes, throat working, then opened them. They were the wet, dark green of a rainforest.

"Okay. I'm getting you out of here."

Kara's heart roared in her ears. Could this be real? Had she finally done it, driven a wedge between the men and gotten through to them, by opening herself up and being vulnerable? Was she really about to go home? Escape this sexed-up, emotional rollercoaster of a madhouse?

She kneeled up on the bed, placing a hand on Luke's shoulder. "Do you mean it?"

He nodded, his green eyes dark with sadness and some other emotion she couldn't name. "That is, if you still want to go. Do you, sweetheart?"

Kara could feel her pulse in her throat, her chest tight as she hesitated.

She wanted her life back. All the things she'd shared with Luke—Lola, work, apartment, dog, community. But then why did it feel like she was giving up something as necessary as breathing?

Be angry, she reminded herself. A gilded cage is still a cage.

Except she couldn't feel angry when all she felt was a regretful kind of gratitude.

Leaning over, she placed a kiss on his cheek before pulling back. Luke's eyes had fluttered shut, his breathing shallow. "Thank you, sweetheart," she told him.

When he opened them, his eyes were so green. "Come

on. I have to get you out of here before Conor and Micah get back. They'll never forgive me for this."

He crawled under the bed, rifling around before he handed her jeans, a t-shirt, and a zip up hoodie—all her size. Shoes—also in her size, followed. Bemused and a little numb, she fumbled to put them on. They'd had clothes for her and had been hiding them this whole time?

Her hands trembled with the hiking boots, so Luke helped her tie them, placing little kisses on her calves that she imagined she could feel through the denim.

"I'm sorry," he murmured, and it lit her chest with dread. Was her escape going to break the link between the men forever? Guilt rose, but Kara shoved it away. She'd succeeded, and she was getting out. That was all that mattered.

She followed Luke out of the room and down the hallway, watching as he pressed a button on the wall and a hidden safe swung open. He loaded a gun before shoving it into his waistband and closing the safe.

Kara looked at him confused. "Why..."

"Just in case," he said simply, grabbing her hand and tugging her down the stairs with him. She stumbled behind him. They walked down the long hall, past the workout room where—it felt like ages ago—she'd walked in on Conor blowing Luke, and had her first face off with Micah.

"If you want to change your mind, now is the time," Luke muttered as he pressed his finger up against another sensor lock and with a beep the door opened into the huge garage.

One of the Jeeps was gone. The others were there. Luke located a set of keys in another hidden safe, and unlocked the forest green Jeep. Of course, his favorite color; he'd once teased her that it was his favorite color because it matched his eyes, and she'd teased him back that that made him a narcissist.

She wasn't going to miss him. She *wasn't.*

Opening the passenger side door, he boosted her up into the Jeep. He looked her deep in the eyes as he fastened her seatbelt, and she was suddenly reminded of the time, so long ago it felt like centuries, that Conor had fastened her seatbelt in his truck before taking her out for In-N-Out.

I always keep my promises, he'd told her then. He'd promised to protect her, and she was rewarding his commitment by leaving.

"Are you sure?" Luke asked again.

She had to be. Only a complete fool would stay.

She nodded.

He sighed. "I thought so," he said, before tilting her chin up and kissing her roughly, almost punishingly. Kara's heart raced. A discordant note sang in her mind. Did something feel off, or was it the adrenaline?

"Wait," she asked, "why not just give me the keys and let me leave?"

He shook his head. "Aside from trying to hike through the forest—and I'm not letting you do that, what with the bears and moose—the only way out is the main road, and there's a gate with another sensor lock on it. I need to go with you."

He closed her car door before she could protest or question him more, rounding the Jeep and jumping in on the driver's side. With a thrum and rattle, the garage door rose. Luke started the car up, backing out of the drive, doing an easy 180 turn. As he drove down the dark, long driveway, he was silent. All Kara could hear was their breathing, the quiet crunch of wheels on gravel, and her racing thoughts. She should be excited, elated, but she felt off, like the world had flipped upside down again and she was in freefall. Like she was back on that fucking rollercoaster and it was too late to get off.

Stop him.

Make him turn around.

Get out of the Jeep and make a run for it. You can handle some bears.

None of those thoughts made sense, so she concentrated on the dark road in front of her, surrounded by huge pine trees, a silent audience to her escape. The Tetons beckoned, dark, ominous shadows in the distance.

When Luke finally spoke, it was terse. "When you get out of the gate, make a right. Keep driving straight—it'll take you over the pass and into town. I've got some cash for you. You'll have to find your own way from there. The only thing I ask is you don't go to the police, at least not yet—give us a head start, because there are a lot of people looking for us."

"Okay," she said softly over her racing heart.

"You need to be careful from now on. We won't be watching over you anymore. I'll make sure of it."

Anxiety thrummed through Kara, but she forced herself to slow her breathing. Now was *not* the time to have a panic attack.

We'll never leave you alone again. You'll never have to brave these on your own again. Conor had said. Turned out he'd been wrong.

"Okay," she said again, her heart plummeting to her toes. "Luke, there's a reason I asked you all about the Johnathans the other day. I broke into your files and found things—redacted military documents, pictures of kids, pictures of me...and a list of names. You all told me some things, but there's more to it, I know there is. Am I in danger?"

In the darkness of the car, his throat worked, approaching a high-tech version of a ranch gate. Something still felt off. They had so many secrets from her, Luke included.

"Luke?" she asked again.

"Don't worry about it," he said sharply, pulling over and stopping the car. Hopping out—he'd never even bothered with a seat belt—he slammed the door and went to the gate, opening a box and fiddling around with the code.

Kara opened the glove compartment, rifling through it for any supplies that might come in handy. There was an energy bar, a bottle of water...and a case of bullets for the gun. Would she need extra?

She slid them into her pocket. *Just in case*, Luke had said, and Kara wanted to be safe, not sorry. If Micah and Conor followed her, she needed to be ready.

"Kara," he called.

She hopped out of the SUV, joining him on the pavement in front of the gate, where he was still fiddling with the sensor. Was his hand shaking?

"Luke."

He ran his hand over the sensor and with a click and a whir, the gate slowly swung open.

He turned to her, pulling her around to the trunk of the car, dragging her into his arms.

"I'm going to ask you one more time, sweetheart," he asked quietly, his face lit in the garish yellow beams of the Jeep, "are you sure you want to leave us? Leave this? I know it's been hard, but we can make it better for you, I promise. We'll give you more freedom. Take you hiking. We can go anywhere you want in the world, cheerlead you on as you write the book you used to talk about with me, remember? I'll get you that basset hound you want. You just have to want to stay on your own, and we'll give you *everything*, I promise."

There was so much desperation in his voice, and it struck another dissonant chord with her—this time in her heart. It had been such a short time with them, but she couldn't imagine leaving now. Not playing mind games with Micah as he made her tuna melts, or challenging Conor's authority only to submit to his every demand, or sleeping safely in Luke's arms. She ran her hands over his waist, memorizing the warmth of his body as her heart roared in her ears.

If you asked her later—and people certainly did—she couldn't explain why she did what she did next.

But with one trembling hand, she carefully pulled the gun out of Luke's jeans with one hand and clicked off the safety. Just like he'd taught her.

"I'm sure," she said breathlessly.

"Sweetheart?" he asked, surprise, shock, pain thickening his voice.

Kara should have been more surprised when she heard loud, sardonic clapping and a low whistle, as Micah and Conor came through the gate. But her instincts had been telling her something was wrong, hadn't they? That this was too easy? Betrayal settled the storm of emotions inside her. Her anger made her calm. She swung the gun around from one man to the next, proud of how steady her arm was, before settling back on Luke. He raised his hands to ward her off.

"What happened to never lying?" she asked him, her voice flat.

His voice echoed hers. "I told you, loyalty supersedes honesty."

"And what happened to loyalty to *me?* I fucking trusted you."

"Did you? Because if I'm not mistaken, you just stole my gun from me."

"You don't trust us, baby," Micah said. "If you did, you would stay." To Conor he said, "I hate that I was right."

"Time to go home, bad girl," Conor said, his voice chiding. "The gun isn't even loaded—and do you even know how to use it? Hand it over or your punishment will be worse, and you already aren't going to like it."

Rage, long banked, flared back to life. They'd played her again and she'd fallen for it. And they were treating it like a fucking joke.

She was going to kill them.

The fire in her chest grounded her as she pulled the extra ammunition from her pocket. It *was* time for her to go home—her home. She'd been so close, and they'd wrenched it away from her. It wasn't that she didn't trust them, it was that she'd been too trusting. She'd believed Luke had finally understood what she needed and was putting her needs above his own desires. And once again, a man had been selfish, putting himself first. Once again, trust had gotten her nothing but heartbreak and a ruined life.

No.

She could feel the panic coming on, and she fumbled the gun as she popped open the magazine and slid inside a round of bullets, almost dropping it.

Luke reached for her.

"Don't you fucking touch me!" Kara cried, closing the magazine and raising her arm again with a jerk, pointing the gun at him. She felt like she was going to have a heart attack, the open gate blurring in front of her eyes, the men in growing shadow, until they seemed to tower over her like monstrous giants.

Helpless. She was helpless.

"Kara, sweetheart, you need to breathe," Luke said sharply.

"Fuck this," Conor snapped at Luke, taking a step toward Kara. "She doesn't even know how to shoot that thing."

"She does," Micah said, dark humor in his voice. "Luke taught her."

The ground began to spin, and Kara felt faint.

No. Breathe, Kara. Just breathe. All you need to do right now is breathe. Her own voice, this time, strong and steady and sure.

"You know," she mused, "for a while I thought it was you all saving me from my panic attacks. But truthfully, I saved myself. You're the ones who cause them."

She aimed the gun at Conor, her hand steady again. "Stop. Don't move. Or I'll kill you."

"No you won't, bad girl," Conor chided, taking another step. Kara fought the impulse to back away from him, even as he moved closer, towering over her. Micah followed him.

"If you're going to shoot, then shoot," he said.

Air disappeared from her lungs again.

Luke strode closer, until he completed the triangle that surrounded her on all sides—except from the back, where the open gate beckoned.

"Give me the gun, sweetheart," Luke coaxed. She imagined she could smell his campfire smell, Conor's spicy musk, Micah's clean comforting smell. The mix was almost overwhelming.

"We know you, Kara. You aren't a killer," Micah called. "Give Luke the gun, baby, and we can all go home. We can talk about punishment later."

Kara took her time glaring at all three of them. No one spoke.

She finally nodded, slowly clicking the safety back on and lowering the gun to her side. Luke visibly relaxed.

"Good girl," Conor said gently.

Kara whipped the gun back up and re-released the safety.

"Kara," Conor said sharply.

"I'm not your good girl," she said to him, her voice steady and incandescent with rage, filling her with power. He backed up.

She turned to Micah, and he also took a step back, his eyes on the gun. "You don't know shit about me" she said.

She moved the gun toward Luke, one eye on his chest, unwilling to look him in the eyes. "And you? I thought you were a good man. But all you are? Is a fucking liar."

She moved the gun between them, watching with satisfaction as all three took another step back. For once—for the first time in what felt like forever—she was in control.

And she fucking loved it.

"You're all bad men, and you deserve everything coming to you," she told them.

And then she pulled the trigger.

Twice.

TO BE CONTINUED...
...in *Lose Me in the Shadows*.

ACKNOWLEDGMENTS

When I say it took a whole fucking village to write this book, I wish I were kidding.

First, to my editor, Jen Prokop. Jen, the very fact that you were willing to read and edit this book, even with a cliffhanger, means the world to me. That you told me you weren't sure the cliffhanger felt earned yet, and suggested how to make it earned, means even more—and I believe saved this story. I promise I will one day give you a stand-alone to edit.

Sue: Thank you for teaching me how to spell In-N-Out correctly and saving me from embarrassment.

Brittney: A girl couldn't have a better bestie, or better marketing manager. I truly don't know what I'd do without you, or how I survived so many years without you in my life. You're stuck with me now.

Lori: You keep me so organized! Where would I be without your help?

To my beta and ARC readers: It means so much to me that y'all took the time to read, offer feedback, and review my debut. THANK YOU!

Kenya, Sarah, Joanna, and Nisha, thank you for an ever-delightful group text, teaching me so much more about dark romance than I already knew, and putting up with my constant questions or nonsense TikTok sharing. You're the best dark romance mates a girl could have.

Also, Kenya, thank you for holding my hand through this whole publishing process.

To the Sisterhood of the Horizontal Writers: This book wasn't necessarily the kind of romance you usually read, but you stuck with me, anyway, and helped me figure out how to turn that initial 80-page-sex-scene-fever-dream into an actual story. Thank you both for your help and your friendship. I'm manifesting good things for all of us.

Julia, you may be the only person who has read every version of this book, and has never complained. Thank you for putting up with me.

Felicia, what the hell is there to say other than thank you? I may have thrown in the towel if you didn't keep reminding me how much you liked it.

To my critique partner and cheerleading squad of one, Sabrina: Thank goodness we found each other—there's no one else I can talk to about how much I love Carter Mahoney, and the nuances of power and consent in dark romance. This book wouldn't be what it is without your advice, support, and early morning DMs about plot points and character arcs you fell asleep thinking about. I'm so glad we're friends, and can't wait for our future dark romance podcast.

Shosh: What is there even to say? You've held my hand through so much over the past year, without a single complaint or judgment. (Well, some judgment, but then someone needs to keep me from going full chaos agent.) If it weren't for your edits and encouragement, this book wouldn't exist. More importantly, if it weren't for your support, I'm not sure I would've been able to keep my head above water. I love you.

And finally, to my readers: There are so many books out

there in the world, and the fact that you chose to take the time and read mine means the world to me. Without you, this would just be words on a page: You make it real. For that, thank you, always.

ABOUT THE AUTHOR

A lover of dogs, mountain adventures, and HGTV, Jo Brenner writes romances that are little bit twisted, a lotta bit sexy—and always have an HEA.

OTHER WORKS

Kara, Conor, Micah, and Luke will return in *Lose Me In The Shadows.*

Stay in touch and get the latest publishing updates, book teasers, and more by joining my readers' group, Jo Brenner's Bar, on Facebook, or subscribing to my newsletter. If you subscribe, you can get a sneak peek of *Lose Me In The Shadows*!